Brothers of Summer

Stan Morse

Published by Stan Morse

Copyright © 2013 by Stan Morse

ISBN-10: 098985132X

ISBN-13: 9780989851329

Thanks to the David Morgan Company of Bothell, Washington, and the manager Will Morgan, for providing me with the Akubra slouch hat which appears on the cover. "Akubra" is a trademark held by Akubra Hats Pty, LTD., Ian Dixon Pty, Limited.

Thanks to the rattlesnake that became a hatband. The poor fellow should have forsaken his buzz and slithered off to safety.

Thanks to graphic artist Tim Oldfield for the excellent book cover.

Thanks to my brother Ken Morse, and my childhood friend Clayton Belmont.
You guys know what for!

And finally, this book is dedicated to my friend Steve Milner, who taught me that friendship and forgiveness are two sides of the same coin.

OTHER BOOKS BY STAN MORSE
Circling the Earth in a Wheelchair
Goering's Gold (a novel, due out in the spring of 2014)

A boy on a bike swerved onto the road descending into town. As he sped through the shimmering heat you saw he was slim, with the build of a distance runner. As he came closer, you saw an intense concentration in his blue eyes that suggested there was some great purpose afoot, and not a second to spare.

Chapter 1

*B*illy Ward hunched forward on the banana seat of his chromed Schwinn Stingray as the pavement rushed beneath his knobby tires. His white knuckles gripped the ape-hanger handgrips and his brown hair lay slick against his forehead as he sped down Chelan's main street.

Without so much as a sideways glance he passed the Ruby Theatre where the marquee poster announced the latest John Wayne movie: *True Grit*. Next came Norm's Barbershop where Billy got his hair cut once a month whether he needed it or not. He flew past the Kier Drugstore and the newly opened Army recruiting office and the pink brick of the Vogue Beauty Salon and the Valley Hardware and Nutley's Jewelry and the Coffee Pot Café.

Billy braked and burned rubber and turned a hard right at the Chevron station on the corner. The right cuff of his blue jeans slapped against the chain guard as his Red Ball Jet tennis shoes pistoned the pedals at jackhammer speed, but his eyes never strayed as he arrowed straight through the residential neighborhood, past houses with shake and composite roofs and red brick chimneys and aluminum screen doors. Two little girls played Frisbee in one yard. A shirtless man mowed his grass. A gray-haired lady dug in her petunia bed alongside a driveway with a green Ford sedan that had a peeling landau roof and rust-spotted fenders.

Nearly there!

A stitch of pain lit up his ribcage as Billy doubled down, pedal to the metal. His lungs were on fire when he finally crossed the lawn of a white two-story house. He grazed the tire swing beneath the maple tree and slid to a stop, gouging a boomerang divot in the grass. Billy dumped the Stingray and scrambled up the steps, yanked wide the screen door, twisted the brass knob, and lunged into the cool of the living room, hands braced on his knees, fighting to catch his breath.

Colleen Ward was kneading bread in the kitchen when she heard the front door slam open. She waited to hear it shut. When this didn't happen, she calmly lifted the lump of bread from the wooden cutting board and placed it into a stoneware bowl, covered it with a linen cloth. She rinsed the flour and shortening from her hands and wiped them dry on one corner of her cotton apron and then walked through the hallway to the front room. She found her younger son panting and doubled over just inside the open door.

"Billy, you look as if you've just run a race."

Billy gulped down air. He glanced sideways at his mom, hands still braced on his knees. For a moment he wondered how she could be so calm. And then he realized she must not know the big news.

"I just came . . . from Dad's," was all he was able to manage in two great gasps before his burning lungs forced him to pause and re-catch his breath.

Hank ran the family's service station on the far side of town. If Billy had raced all that way in the late June heat—*And wouldn't that be just like him!*—no wonder he was winded.

"Would you like a lemonade?"

"No, Mom." Billy forced his breathing to slow, reigned in the last of the pain, and quickly added, "Thanks anyways." He finally managed to stand up, eyes pleading, face desperately eager. "Where's Mike?"

Colleen's interest took a big leap. As Mike had neared graduation from high school at the end of May, her two sons, after years of being nearly inseparable, had pretty much gone their separate ways. Mike was focused upon entering Central Washington's football program that fall on a full scholarship to play right tackle. Billy was deep into summer league baseball. *So why this sudden and dramatic interest?* She almost asked Billy if something important had happened. Almost. But not quite. Because Colleen knew that prying an explanation from a teenager, especially one who was in a hurry to do something, could easily take longer than her bread making would allow. So instead of asking Billy to explain, she simply said, "I expect he's upstairs in his room."

"Thanks, Mom!"

Billy bounded up the stairwell. Colleen watched him take the steps two at a time, marveling at his recovery.

The front door still stood wide open. Colleen gently pushed it closed. "Boys," she said softly. But as she walked back to the kitchen there came a mother's fleeting smile, full of pride and acceptance.

Billy reached the top of the steps and saw Mike's door was ajar. He paused, took one final deep breath, stepped forward, and poked his head across the threshold, leaning with one sweaty palm against the jamb, trying to sound calm while his heart pounded like a kettledrum.

"Mike?"

Sprawled comfortably atop a yellow-and-green-checked quilt on a twin bed, wearing blue jeans and a white crewneck T-shirt, his legs crossed at the ankles, head supported by a double-folded pillow, Mike didn't shift his eyes from the Spiderman comic he had been reading. "Yeah?" He mumbled.

Billy nudged the door with his shoulder and edged one cautious foot inside, his right hand clutching the doorframe.

"Dad says you're going backpacking with Stu."

Mike struggled to remain focused on his comic, hoping Billy would take the hint. No such luck. The Kid hung on the doorframe like a lizard. "So?" Mike finally grumbled.

"Can I go?"

Mike reluctantly closed the comic and deliberately rolled it up as if preparing to swat a fly. He swung his legs off the bed and his bare feet thumped onto the floor. Perched on the edge of the mattress and with his elbows wedged tight into his knees, Mike's hands worried the ends of the rolled comic. His eyes lasered pure disgust at his little brother.

"Nope."

"Aw, Mike. Dad said it'd be okay——"

"What part of *Nope* don't you understand?" Mike said, giving Billy an icy stare. "And since when did Dad saying something was okay make it *OKAY*?"

Mike's face was full of betrayal, confirming Billy's worst fear. Dad had done nothing to soften Mike up. It would be no easy task convincing his older brother to include him in the adventure. But Billy plunged ahead with the reasoning he'd been working on ever since Dad had let it slip that Mike and his buddy Stu Johnson were planning a weeklong backpacking trip along the Sawtooth Ridge.

"Please, Mike! I'm strong enough to carry all of my own gear. Coach Patterson will let me off from practice for a week, I'm sure of it. And I've even got enough money saved to buy all of my own food. I won't be a problem. I promise!" Billy would have belly-crawled across Highway 97 during holiday traffic to prove himself worthy. But Mike wasn't going to make it nearly that easy.

"When Stu and I talked," Mike began stolidly, losing patience with each word, his neck slowly flushing to scarlet, "it was just the *two* of us going."

A stony pause; Billy remained plastered to the doorframe. Mike's voice turned mean.

"This will be our last chance to do something *big* before I go off to college. And we're not going take a goofball like you and spoil the whole adventure."

So please just dry up and blow away!

But Billy couldn't go away, not yet, not on something this important. He pressed on.

"Could we maybe just ask Stu, please?"

"Oh, jeez!" Mike's elbows flew off his knees. He twisted the comic in his fists, nearly ripping it in half. He stood, towering six inches above his brother, but to Billy it seemed as if Mike's wrath descended from a mile high. "I can't go asking my best friend if my baby brother can tag along for a week up in the mountains!"

Billy looked down at the floor, fighting back tears. He wasn't a goofball and he wasn't a baby. He was fourteen years old and five-foot-six and he weighed 110 pounds. And why couldn't Mike ask Stu if he could come along? Didn't being someone's brother count for anything?

As these thoughts tumbled out Billy remembered how during the past few months he and Mike had done less and less together. Since school had let out Mike had practically treated him like a disease. But somehow Billy managed for the moment to bury the hurt beneath his hope for some kind of miracle. *Please a miracle!*

Mike was glaring at him. Silent. A rock.

And then an idea came. It was risky. Mike might come totally unglued. But Billy saw no other way. Besides, the worst he could suffer would be two months of complete hostility before Mike went off to college. Right?

No guts, no glory.

"Maybe we could just ask Stu? Please Mike? And if he says 'No' well, I'll accept it, and I won't ask Dad. Please?"

The threat of involving their father was extortion, pure and simple. And Mike nearly lost it right there. Billy saw the fury building. He cringed in anticipation of an explosion.

Mike was seriously considered reaching out and grabbing his little brother by the arm and pitching him straight out into the hall. But he began to realize that Billy's threat had teeth. Fangs, actually. Because Dad had apparently let news of the hike slip to Billy, and Dad must have developed some crazy hope that Mike would voluntarily agree to take Billy up into the mountains. But Dad hadn't openly asked Mike to take Billy along. *Not yet.* So there remained the possibility that Dad would remain neutral unless he was forced to openly take sides. And the last thing Mike wanted was Dad coming right out and telling him that he'd have to take Billy on the hike. That would present an impossible dilemma: angering his father, or crippling his and Stu's adventure by including Billy. Cripes! After you graduated from high school you weren't supposed to have to put up with this kind of crap!

And then Mike realized that in Billy's desperation he had made a big mistake. All Mike needed to do was to have Stu say "No" to Billy's face. End of dilemma! And there was an added bonus: it would lay the responsibility squarely upon Stu's shoulders. Dad couldn't put the same kind of pressure on Stu that he could on Mike.

It was perfect.

"Well, okay," Mike skirmished, faking uncertainty, straining not to smile. "But only if you swear not to ask Dad to force us to take you." Another squirm. "And remember *I told you so* if Stu says *No*." But Mike said it like Stu might actually say *Yes*.

Billy believed a *Yes* was possible because he *wanted* to believe it was possible.

"I swear! On a stack of bibles, I swear!" Billy backed toward the door. Hope was alive. *Barely.* But *barely alive* was better than *No Frickin Way!* "Thanks Mike!" Billy retreated out into the hallway. He never saw the smile of victory that burst across Mike's face.

Once inside his own room and with the door safely shut, Billy picked up his fielder's mitt and slipped it onto his left hand. The brown suede was warm against his skin, the cowhide pungent with bear grease. He began to punch his right fist into the pocket, knuckling the seams.

He looked at the framed picture that hung on the wall above his student desk, a close-in shot of he and Mike standing together behind home plate, Billy in his baseball uniform. It had been taken last summer, after Billy made first string and moved out to play left field. Mike's right arm was draped over Billy's shoulder. Billy's left arm was around Mike's waist. Both boys had huge grins. Billy remembered the moment like it was yesterday. His team had just won a game against Ritzville, seven to four, due mostly to a three-run bomb Billy had smacked over the center field fence in the sixth inning. Mike had wolf-whistled all the way as Billy rounded the bases. The stands were packed and everyone in the Chelan section cheered. The grass smelled sweet. The sky was pure blue. It had been a perfect day.

Billy pulled the fielder's glove from his hand and dropped it onto the floor. He clenched his jaw, and he bit his lip. But as hard as he tried there was just no way to keep the tears from streaming down his cheeks.

Chapter 2

*S*hirley Johnson awoke to the smells of frying bacon and percolating coffee. Her first thought was that Stu knew better than to disturb her this early in the morning. "I'll clobber you up-side the head if you *ever* wake me up before nine," she had warned in May when he had entered her bedroom at 8:30 AM with a tray full of breakfast. It hadn't mattered that it was Mother's Day. In fact, Shirley was especially angry because he'd interrupted her sleep on the very day he was supposed to treat her extra special. She had kicked the tray out of his hands, dumping eggs and hash browns and toast and coffee all over the floor. And then she had made him clean it up.

Shirley levered up on one elbow and squinted at the alarm clock on the wood dresser.

9:37

"Damn." She considered for a moment if there were any other possible reason to be angry at her son, found no convenient excuse, and reluctantly accepted the fact that she was now wide awake and there was nothing to be done about it.

She pushed back the covers with her feet and tried to ignore the stiffness in her joints. It was a full minute before she collected enough energy to finally stand and walk to the dresser. She retrieved a pair of elastic panties from the top drawer. It took a long and awkward moment to struggle them on. She reached down for the brown slacks heaped at the foot of the bed and wriggled them slowly up her unshaved legs and over her angular hips. She grabbed a pink sweatshirt and ran one hand through her lank peroxide-blonde hair, indifferent to the odor of cigarette smoke. A bra was too much effort to even begin to consider.

The bedroom door thumped open against the heel of her palm. Shirley plodded along the worn green runner toward the tiny kitchen. Her feet itched between her toes, and the approaching sound of sizzling bacon made her stomach gurgle up the odor of beer and pretzels. Shirley swallowed hard and the acid tang retreated back down her throat.

When Stu heard the *pop* and *slam* of his mom's bedroom door he quickly broke two eggs into sizzling bacon grease and punched two slices of Wonder Bread into the toaster.

Stu was basting the eggs with hot grease, using a thin metal spatula, as his mom entered the kitchen, bare feet slapping across the scored linoleum. Shirley sank into a green vinyl chair and propped her elbows on the black-with-gold-speckled Formica table, settling her chin upon her palms, watching out of the corners of her eyes as her son cooked her breakfast.

Stu kept working the eggs, watching the yellows turn cloudy as the hot grease dribbled off. He didn't look up but he felt his mother's eyes upon him the whole time. When the eggs were done Stu lifted them one by one with the spatula and gently slid them onto a plate, sopping off the extra grease with a square of paper towel.

Shirley lit up a cigarette, drawing the smoke deep into her lungs. She finally spoke.

"Stuie . . . do we have milk for my coffee?"

"Sure, Mom. I bought a quart last night at Thompson's Grocery."

Stu shifted the frying pan off the burner and reached for the handle to the fridge, pulled the door open with a soft sucking sound. A few drops of water spotted the linoleum. The freezer box at the top had shrunk to a frosty cave and Stu made a mental note to defrost it soon.

He grabbed the quart of Lucerne whole milk, kicked the fridge door shut, and snatched the aluminum percolator from the stove element with his free hand. He poured a cup of Maxwell's House into a mug and added a precise dollop of milk. It was only after he had slid the cup in front of his mom that he put the milk back in the fridge.

"Thanks," she said remotely, taking another drag on her cigarette and then a first sip of coffee.

Stu finally began to relax. He returned to the stove, took a fork and stabbed three strips of bacon from an aluminum pie plate set on the stove's back burner and laid them alongside the eggs. As he buttered two pieces of toast he gave silent thanks. It would be one of his mom's better mornings.

He lifted the plate, neatly arrayed with two eggs sunny-side up (dippable but not runny), buttered toast, a spoonful of grape jam, and the three strips of extra-crispy bacon. He set the plate in front of his mother with the same practiced skill as a seasoned waitress at the Apple Cup Cafe.

Shirley grimaced, wedged her smoldering cigarette into the glass ashtray, tentatively picked a toast triangle and cautiously poked at the center of one egg. She withdrew it slowly, examining the gooey yellow that clung to the bread.

Stu saw it was perfect.

Shirley took a tentative bite. She chewed briefly and downed it with a swig of coffee and settled more comfortably in her chair.

"Stuie?"

"Yes, Mom?"

"When you do your paper route today, don't forget to ask Mr. Radke if you can take over the Porter boy's route."

Gary Porter had caught mononucleosis during the last month of school. His route was up for grabs. The decision on who would get the extra work would fall to Charlie Radke, who brought the newspapers up from the press in Wenatchee to the deliverers in Chelan.

"Okay, Mom."

Shirley seemed not to believe Stu had understood the importance of her request.

"I *mean* it, Stuie. And don't be soft when you ask. You've worked for that newspaper for five years and you have every right to take over that boy's route."

Stu knew enough not to disagree.

"I promise, Mom. I'll ask."

"Good." The corners of Shirley's mouth struggled to form a smile, then quickly relaxed back to a half-scowl as she tried to figure the math in her head for how much extra weekly cash might go into to the glass jar on the upper shelf in the cabinet beside the fridge. As she struggled with the figures, she picked up the cigarette, put it to her lips, sucked hard; the ash glowed bright orange, consuming the last bit of tobacco right down to the brown filter. She exhaled a plume across the table, stubbed out the butt in the tray, and returned to picking at her eggs, gouging out the yokes but leaving the whites mostly intact. When her stomach could tolerate no more, she stood, stretched, and walked around the counter. She poured herself another cup of coffee, watching Stu as he worked on a sink full of dirty dishes.

"Stuie, I think I'll catch a few more zzzzz's." And with that pronouncement, Shirley headed back down the hallway, feet thumping in slow rhythm, coffee cup swaying in her hand.

When the bedroom door shut, Stu grinned. As soon as he cleaned up the kitchen and put out the garbage he was free to start his own day; his mom would be asleep for hours.

Nowadays, there was no reason for her not to sleep late, especially with the late nights—often early mornings as well—she had taken to spending at Dale's Tavern. She had no job and was on disability. The claim she had submitted to the state unemployment office was for a stomach ulcer, backed up by a doctor's note. Stu had no idea how she'd convinced Doc Franklin to write it. She had no prescription and wasn't even taking over-the-counter medicine.

Stu had long ago made peace with how his mom behaved. Life was a series of compromises. Life wasn't perfect. There were no guarantees. But she was his mom, and he figured that what he felt for her must be love.

When Stu arrived at the Safeway parking lot the blue delivery van with *Wenatchee World* stenciled on the side was already parked in the far corner. Charlie Radke was leaning against the truck's rear bumper, smoking an unfiltered Chesterfield. As Stu squeezed the caliper brakes on his ten-speed, Charlie smiled and rocked forward off the bumper.

"Hiya, Stu."

"Sorry I'm late, Charlie." Stu pulled off his NY Yankees cap and wiped the sweat from his brow before putting it back on.

Charlie glanced at the Timex on his left wrist. His shirtsleeves were rolled up, and the curly brown hair on his arm had bunched in the metal band. He tugged at the watchband, swearing as the hairs separated from the silvery expando band.

"A couple minutes ain't no big deal," Charlie shrugged, pinching the cigarette butt between thumb and index finger for one last drag before he dropped it onto the faded asphalt and ground it out with the heel of his boot. He pulled a cigarette pack from his breast pocket. "Want a cancer stick?" He chuckled at his own remorseless humor as he popped one up.

Stu glanced around the parking lot. "Nah, I better not."

"Suit yourself." Charlie pulled a cigarette with his lips direct from the cellophane-wrapped pack before stuffing the pack back into his shirt pocket. He rummaged in his pants pocket and pulled out a green Zippo, snapped up a flame, applied it to the cigarette's tip, drew deeply, and exhaled a cloud of smoke that drifted away slow as you please.

Charlie turned and reached into the canopied pickup bed and dragged out a thick bundle of newspapers, tightly bound with sisal twine. Stu helped Charlie drape the papers over the crotch-bar of his ten-speed. As they saddled the thick newsprint onto the tubular steel Charlie glanced around with sharp, conspiratorial eyes.

"Here," he said, pulling the cigarette pack out, holding it close so no one could see. "Take one for the road."

Stu accepted the cigarette, unwilling to deny Charlie, even though he had decided against taking up the habit. But where to hide it? His white crewneck had no pocket, and in his jeans pocket it would be crushed. He wanted to slide it behind his ear, like he'd once seen a carpenter do, but that would be too easy to spot. So he finally took off his battered NY Yankees cap, slid it inside the sweat band, and carefully snugged the cap back on his head.

"Thanks, Charlie."

"No problem, Stu. You're old enough to have a *man's* vices."

Stu smiled.

Charlie had brought papers for the route ever since Stu was thirteen and had first begun work as a delivery kid. As their friendship had grown, the kid-treatment had faded. Other than Mike, Charlie was his closest friend. *Maybe your only other friend*, he would remind himself in the dark moments of the night when sleep seemed impossible. Charlie was the only adult who had ever treated Stu like he might matter some day.

Stu suddenly remembered his mom's admonition.

"Hey, Charlie?"

"Yeah?"

"Is Gary Porter going to take his route back?"

"I think so," Charlie replied. "We've got Beulah handling it until he's better."

"Oh." Stu conceded defeat with that single word.

Beulah Jones—'BJ' to everyone who knew her—was a single mom who drove a beat-up green Lark station wagon. She handled half the deliveries in the valley and was the only deliverer who wasn't a teenage boy. It was the way she supported her family, and once BJ had sunk her claws into a route it never came open again. Gary would be lucky to get his route back even if he recovered from his illness real quickly.

Charlie gave a hard look. "Stu, did your mom say something to you about asking for Gary's route?"

"We could sure use the money," Stu answered defensively, but his ears burned with embarrassment.

Charlie's face soured. "I'm sorry, Stu. The Porter kid's got another year of high school left, and he does a good job. I can't ditch him just because he's sick for a few weeks. Till then, BJ has first dibs. She's my main carrier. The circulation manager said I have to go with her. But if it weren't for BJ, you'd be my first choice."

"Thanks, Charlie." Stu's chin was down, and Charlie gave him an affectionate pat on the shoulder.

"Buck up, Kid. You've got grander things to do in life than to be chasing after another paper route."

Stu smiled but said nothing as he swung his right leg over his ten-speed and climbed on. Charlie couldn't have been more wrong about Stu having better things to do. But what was the use in disagreeing? Adults never saw things from a teenager's point of view. Stu began to pedal away, careful to maintain balance with the heavy load of papers.

"See you tomorrow!" Charlie shouted after him.

"Roger Dodger!" Stu hollered over his shoulder.

Stu's smile and enthusiasm returned as he pumped out of the parking lot and down the street toward his rendezvous with Mike. As soon as he was out of sight of the Safeway lot he took off his Yankees cap and dumped the cigarette onto the pavement.

The papers came with a supply of rubber bands. Before the papers could be taken on the route they had to be rolled and banded. This made them easier to carry in the canvas bag and to throw onto stoops or to stuff into curbside boxes.

The rolling and banding left greasy ink on your hands. Banding the papers was Stu's least favorite part and he was thankful for Mike's help, especially on sweltering days like today. Mike volunteered at least twice a week, and on those afternoons Stu truly looked forward to working the route.

His friendship with Mike was a still a mystery. Mike could have picked anyone to pal around with. He was top-of-the-heap at high school. A star lineman on the state championship football team, first-squad baseball, a basketball starter for the last three years. He'd been the only triple letterman announced at graduation. And Mike was also a B-plus student and had been in Honor Society even though he'd missed making the top ten percent of their graduating class.

Mike also had nice clothes and got cool presents on birthdays and at Christmas. Each year the Ward family took a vacation, usually to a neat place like Yellowstone or the Grand Canyon. Mike would attend Central Washington State College on a full football scholarship.

In contrast to Mike, Stu had barely pulled a "C" average by graduation and had never turned out for a sport, even one of the wussy ones like tennis or volleyball. Stu figured he wasn't nearly bright enough to make passing grades in college and that it was better to be realistic and look for some kind of blue collar job than it was to flunk out, thus proving to the entire world that he was a real loser. And there was the issue of money. Or more to the point: the lack of it.

But despite their differences, Stu and Mike had remained friends.

Their friendship had begun at the start of their junior year when both were struggling in biology. Mrs. Jensen (the kids called her "Old Bunsen" behind her back) had paired them up for frog dissection. As they peeled back the abdominal skin and stuck needles into the rubbery flesh, they started cracking jokes, comparing the frog to one of the girls who was working on the far side of the lab room. Old Bunsen marched over and warned them to take the frog more seriously. But this only brought snickers when they thought she couldn't hear. They shared notes, talked out difficult assignments, and Mike got a B-plus and Stu a solid C at the end of the quarter. Both had passed Old Bunson's class! *Wonder of wonders.*

Their friendship endured after fall quarter ended. *Even greater wonder of wonders!*

Stu found Mike sitting beside a ten-speed in the shade of a giant elm at one corner of the high school practice field. Stu glided to a stop and dumped the newspapers with a solid *thwump!* onto the grass.

"Hey, Mike. How's it hanging?"

"Finest kind. How 'bout you?"

"Ditto!"

They laughed and high-fived.

Stu pulled a wad of rubber bands from his jeans pocket, split it in half, and tossed one gob to Mike, who caught it left-handed and in one smooth motion put it to his nose as if it were a gigantic booger he was in the process of picking.

Stu gave Mike an *Oh please!* look as he tossed Mike an extra delivery bag, then pulled a jackknife from his pocket and sliced the sisal twine binding the papers. He neatly separated the evening edition in half, handed one bunch to Mike, and then sat down cross-legged on the grass to roll, band, and stuff his half into his own delivery bag.

Mike expected no money for helping Stu on the route, because he knew where most of the twenty bucks Stu made each week went. Stu had told him after Mike had suggested Stu buy a new ten-speed and Stu had confessed he didn't have the dough. Stu then explained to his best friend that half of the money he earned each week went into a jar in the kitchen cupboard and the cash came back out only when it was Shirley Johnson doing the reaching. Mike had felt mortally embarrassed at learning this secret. It was the opposite of how he was treated at home. If Mike needed money, Dad would shell out whatever it took, within reason. The service station cleared big bucks by small town standards—nearly forty grand a year. To Mike, it seemed truly ugly for a parent to ask their kid for any part of the modest spare change a paper route earned.

Knowing about Stu's home situation had strengthened their friendship. If Mike had been asked to explain why the two of them were solid buddies, he would have said that Stu needed his friendship a lot more than the other way around. Mike might not have seen as clearly that Stu's friendship made Mike feel important. He would have simply explained that it felt good to have someone you could tell anything to, someone who would listen, and someone who really wanted you to be his friend. And that was enough to cement the friendship for a lifetime as far as Mike was concerned.

After the papers were rolled, the two boys pedaled off on their bikes, delivery bags bulging, weaving down residential streets, stuffing papers into red plastic boxes at the curbs or tossing them onto front porches beyond the range of sprinklers.

As they pedaled along they talked about girls, swimming, and adventures that absolutely had to be added to a list that was by now so long both knew it was mostly imaginary. Only when the subject of the hike came up did the conversation take on an edge.

"So we're heading out in six days?" Stu asked as they turned off Trow Street and onto Allen Avenue.

"Yeah," Mike agreed slowly. "Only, there's a problem."

"What?" Stu jammed a paper into a box and swerved back toward Mike. He pulled into formation alongside, waiting for an explanation.

"It's *The Kid*."

Mike had recently taken to referring to Billy as *The Kid*. Not *Billy the Kid*. Just plain *The Kid*. Stu only vaguely understood why Mike had begun to consider Billy to be some sort of ambulatory wart. Stu figured it must have something to do with breaking away from home and growing up. He didn't necessarily agree; Billy seemed okay, even if he was only fourteen. But Mike was his best friend. And disagreeing with your best friend was as dumb as climbing into the back seat at the drive-in with Suzie "Social Disease" Kurtz. No one with live brain cells did something *that* stupid. So Stu had readily agreed not mention the hike to Billy until it was so close to happening that Billy couldn't possibly ask to go along.

"He found out?"

"Yeah."

"How?"

"Dad told him."

"Jeez."

"Yeah."

"So?"

"Well," Mike said angrily. "Now *The Kid* wants to go with us."

Stu considered the problem. The answer seemed simple.

"Why don't we just tell him he can't come?"

"It ain't that easy. The little ferret threatened to ask Dad to make us take him along."

"You're kidding!"

"Nope, I ain't kidding," Mike swerved toward another red delivery box and was about to shove a paper inside when Stu realized whose box it was.

"Mike! Stop!"

"What?" Mike banked away from the curb and orbited in a wide circle out in the middle of the street.

"That's Old Lady Parker's box and she's three weeks overdue. Check to see if there's a payment envelope before you put a paper in."

Mike vectored back toward the box. As he did so he glanced at the house, across a lawn so perfect it looked like indoor-outdoor carpet. There were heavy metal blinds behind the big picture window. Mike saw a flicker of movement. Someone was peeking through. The blinds suddenly parted several inches and there was Eloise Parker squinting against the brightness, her white hair done up in a beehive as perfect as the lawn. When she saw Mike's eyes upon her, the slats snapped shut. Mike squeezed the caliper brakes and he slowed to take a peek inside the red plastic box.

"Empty!" He hollered out loud enough for practically everyone in the neighborhood to hear.

"No paper!" Stu ordered in as loud a voice. And in a softer tone filled with regret, "Mom gave me a bucket of grief for letting her go this long."

Stu coasted on down the street. As Mike caught up, Stu returned to the topic of Billy.

"So what do we do about The Kid?"

"I thought I had it figured out. I told him if you said 'No' then he couldn't go. And he agreed if you said 'No' then he wouldn't ask Dad. But now I'm afraid that if you come straight out and tell him he can't go without giving some kind of good excuse, he'll go to Dad anyways."

"Darn."

"Yeah."

A devious look came to Stu's face. "Hey, I've got an idea. How about if we come up with some kind of test he has to go through to make sure he's strong enough to go on the hike. Only we make it so hard he's bound to fail!"

Mike's face brightened. "Jeez, Stu! You're a genius."

"Tell me something I don't already know!"

As they pedaled on the conversation returned to the safety of girls, what was the hottest car on the road (*Mustang, of course!*), and whether the afternoon temperature might again bust past one hundred degrees.

Billy sat beside his bedroom window, staring past dark brown curtains occasionally ruffled by a hot breeze, waiting to catch sight of Stu. Most afternoons, Stu came by after his paper route. There would be the crash of his bike and the *slap slap slap* of sneakers as Stu ran to the front door. Billy hoped to catch Stu before he talked to Mike. If Billy got in the first word, his chances of going on the hike might improve. Not that he and Stu were great friends. But Stu usually said 'Hi' even when they accidentally ran across each other in town or down at the beach. So there was at least some hope that Stu might listen to Billy's plea to be treated with more charity than Mike had shown.

Then Billy saw Mike and Stu come pedaling down the street together and he knew it was already too late. He fretted for a moment before making up his mind, working up the courage it was going to take to confront the older boys. His heart was racing as he plodded downstairs. Mike and Stu were waiting at the bottom of the steps.

From beneath the bill of his NY Yankees cap Stu flashed Billy a know-it-all grin.

"Hey, Kid. Mike says you wanna go on the hike." It wasn't a *yes* or a *no*, just a statement of fact. Stu was good at letting things settle out before he took a position. He'd had lots of practice with his mom.

Despite careful preparation and Billy's hope to act as cool as he could possibly manage, the words now seemed to literally shoot out of his mouth.

"I was hoping I could go. I wouldn't be a problem for you guys. I'd do whatever you told me to do. I really, really want to go. Please . . ."

This barrage remarkably seemed to have some impact, because Stu paused a long moment before he answered.

"Hey Billy, you gotta understand this ain't gonna be no Sunday picnic. You'll bust your butt going up and down some truly gnarly trail. One morning, we might climb four thousand feet on some ledge cut into the side of the mother of all mountains. Then in the afternoon we go down a couple miles of trail with loose rocks and dust up to your ankles. One slip and it's straight off a cliff and by the time you stop bouncing off the rock face there ain't gonna be nothing left but wet hamburger. We'll cover at least ten miles each day, maybe fifteen, with no stopping except for a swig of water and a mouthful of jerky. Do you think you could hack that?"

Mike stood silent, admiring Stu's set-up.

Billy studied every word for some clue. He was pretty certain that Stu had never been on a long hike, and certainly nothing like he was describing. He couldn't really know what it was going to be like. He must be exaggerating. *But why all this drama?* Pointing out that Stu was making it all up would have been terminally dumb. *Be cool*, he reminded himself. Still, it was hard to see where this wild estimate of the difficulties was leading. Billy had no option but to play along. *Be cool.*

"No problem, Stu."

"No problem, huh. How do you know?"

"Cause I know what I can handle."

"Hummmm." Stu glanced at Mike, who returned an improbable smile. Billy's gut twisted. *Something was up!* But what?

"Well, if you can't cut the mustard, it's us that's gonna to have to carry you out. And neither of us is excited about *that* prospect. So I think we need to do a little test. Are you up for it?"

Billy's gut twisted.

"What kind of test?"

"First, do you agree?"

"What am I agreeing to?"

"I ain't telling till you agree."

"That's not fair!"

"Life ain't fair, Kid."

Billy knew he'd been had. *Nailed* was the precise word that came to mind. But what were his options? He had none. "Okay," he relented. "I agree. What do I have to do?"

Stu winked at Mike. "You have to hike up the Butte with a full pack, in one hour, and if you make it all the way to the top then you can go."

The confident way Stu said it, Billy knew there was something he wasn't being told. Not that it mattered. Just hiking up the Butte in an hour *without* a pack was darned hard. He fought the panic. *There's no way you're going to get a fair set of rules. But at least there's a chance! Stay cool!*

"Sure," Billy countered. "No problem. When do you want to do it?"

Mike and Stu chuckled.

"No problem," Mike mimicked.

Billy fought to remain calm and he mostly succeeded. But his heart raced and the blood pounded in his temples and his ears were ringing.

"Tomorrow," Stu said, suddenly businesslike. "We'll load up your pack tonight. You hit the Butte Road at nine."

"Okay."

"Catch you in the morning then," Stu said. "Hey Mike. Let's go for a swim."

"Race!" Mike shouted, dashing for the front door. Within seconds their laughter echoed from the street. It gradually faded beyond the roar of a neighbor's gas lawnmower.

Load up? Those two simple words went round and round in his mind like angry hornets. Billy stood at the bottom of the stairs, staring down at the carpet, wondering what he'd gotten himself into.

Chapter 3

Hank Ward grabbed a blue rag to wipe the grease and oil from his hands. He surveyed the two bays of the Chevron garage, one empty, one with a huge green car up on the rack. Beneath this monstrosity of Detroit rolling steel, Tim and Frank were busy with a full-service job on the land yacht that was Eddy Carter's prized Lincoln Continental. The massive sedan rested five feet off the concrete, perched on the pneumatic lift. Tim, a slim man in his late twenties, held a spanner wrench to the oil pan plug and was patiently working the plug loose above a drain funnel that snaked down into a fifty gallon drum on casters.

Frank, who had recently turned forty-five and had begun to grumble about a retirement that no one really believed would happen for many years, was inspecting the brake pads on the right front axle with a caliper gauge. From a transistor radio on the metal workbench along the back wall came the tinny blare of *Windy* by *The Association* against a background of scratchy AM static. The temperature inside the garage was ninety. Outside on the street, heat was radiating in lazy waves from the asphalt.

"You boys okay?" Hank hollered over the music.

"Yeah," Tim confirmed.

Frank mumbled "Uh huh" as he moved from the right front wheel to the left front wheel.

Hank had opened at six that morning and the pace had been non-stop ever since. They had pumped over two thousand gallons of gas and run fourteen cars through the shop—three of them with major repairs, one that required yanking an eight cylinder block to ship to the rebuild factory in Kent. It was Frank's turn to close. *Thank the Fates!*

Hank tossed the oily rag into a square metal waste can, went over to the sink in the corner and sprinkled Boraxo on his palms, scrubbed and rinsed in the small steel sink. Colleen had cautioned him that she had enough to clean up around the house without having to scrub oil from the porcelain in their bathroom. He smiled as he remembered the upturned corners of her mouth, a betrayal of love no matter how serious she tried to be. They had been sweethearts since ninth grade. She was only woman he had ever felt giddy around. He stripped off his gray coveralls and dumped them into the laundry hamper.

I'm a lucky man, he reminded himself as he climbed into the cab of the Ford F100. He turned the key and goosed the engine to a smooth acceleration. He imagined a cold can of beer and a hot dinner with cross buns and corn on the cob. The pickup window was open and a warm breeze whistled through the cab, evaporating sweat on his chest and back. His tiredness faded toward contentment as he drove down the hill into town.

His enthusiasm faded when he pulled into the driveway and saw three bicycles—two ten-speeds, and Billy's Stingray—sprawled on the grass. He remembered telling Billy about Mike's hike, and suddenly the day's hard work seemed to again catch up with him.

He grabbed his black metal lunchbox from the bench seat and for a brief moment wished he'd had a reason to stay at the garage. The moment passed. It was best to face the situation and get it done with. With that realization he felt better. He pulled the screen door, pushed the door open, and carefully wiped his feet on the mat before going in. He heard the distant rattle of pans in the kitchen. Upstairs it was dead silent.

He found Colleen setting out a stack of plates and a handful of silverware. There were two golden-brown loaves of fresh-baked bread set out on wire cooling racks. She paused as he placed his lunch bucket on the counter beside the toaster.

"Hi, Honey." She gave him a peck on the cheek. "Busy day?"

"Yup." Hank eyed the fresh loaves.

Colleen said, "Don't even think it! You'll ruin your dinner!" But her warning was accompanied by that little smile turning up the corners of her mouth.

Hank sighed.

"Why don't you go watch Walter Cronkite on the TV? You can catch the end of the news. I'll bring you a beer."

Hank retreated to the living room. He pulled the button on the walnut console and watched the screen fuzz into focus while he settled into the brown leather La-Z-Boy recliner. Cronkite's face appeared behind the familiar desk. He was reporting on the upcoming moon launch. There was a shot of the massive Saturn V rocket standing atop the pad at Cape Canaveral. But Hank's mind wandered back to his boys.

Had Billy confronted Mike about the hike? He had torn out of the shop that morning after Hank's casual mention of the backpacking trip. And Hank had instantly known he'd handled it wrong. He should have had a talk with Mike first, rather than unleashing Billy. But Hank had been overwhelmed with the workload and it was hard to find any extra energy these days, even for the family. He and the two mechanics had worked six days a week since late spring, after losing Jim, the lead mechanic, to cancer in March. Hank was still searching for a replacement. And on Sundays, Hank gravitated toward the couch to sneak a nap after church.

Not that Mike stayed around to talk. Since the weather had turned warm, Mike and Stu Johnson were almost always off somewhere on their bikes.

If only I had Dad to talk to.

The memory of the recent loss of his father—*Gramps* they had called him, ever since Mike was in diapers—caught him hard. He resurfaced to find Colleen standing beside his recliner, looking down at him with mild concern. She held a can of beer, and a small plate with a dollop of strawberry jam spread on a slice of freshly buttered bread. She set the beer down on the coffee table.

"Where were you just now?" She handed him the plate with the slice of newly baked bread.

"Oh, just thinking of Dad." He took a bite of warm bread and chewed slowly, savoring the flavors. He picked up the beer from the coffee table, popped the tab, and took a swig.

"Are you okay?" Colleen asked.

Hank had been unsure how to honestly answer that question during the past few weeks. Lester Ward—*Gramps*—had passed away in his sleep on the third of February. He'd been 74 and had lived a full life, but Hank had been very close to his father and he had to work hard to hide the pain of the loss that still seemed fresh, and at times even brought tears, especially late at night when Hank couldn't quite fall asleep. Hank tried to make everything seem all right and to convince his family and close friends that he was recovered. That was how it was with men in the Ward family. You kept your chin up and bulled ahead. But Colleen still saw the shadow of grief in his eyes, especially when Hank didn't know she was watching. It was there now, a dark cloud.

"I'm fine, dear." As if to prove it he sniffed the air. "Pot roast?"

"With potatoes and carrots. And lemon meringue pie for dessert."

"Whipped cream?"

"Of course!"

"You spoil me."

"As long as you remember that, I don't mind in the least."

Hank smiled and that was all the reward she needed.

Hank remembered his sons. "Where are the boys?"

"Mike and Stu are up in Mike's room. I think Billy is in his own room, but he's been awfully quiet since morning."

There it is. Hank took a couple gulps from the can of beer. "Did he say why?"

"No. He just came tearing into the house around noon, asked where Mike was. And then he went upstairs, and since then—Dear . . . what's going on?"

"I told Billy about the hike."

"Oh." In their marital shorthand, that meant she fully understood.

"Do you think I should I bring it up at dinner?"

Colleen thought this over for a long moment before answering.

"No. Let it rest awhile. I expect the boys will open up if there's trouble. It will probably come from Billy. Mike's been so—"

"Distant?"

"I think he's worried about college."

Neither Hank nor Colleen had gone to college. But they had stressed the importance of an education to both sons from an early age. They wanted something better for their children than running a service station. Particularly for Billy, who had been an apt pupil from the start, as quick at algebra as he was

23

with English or history. But Billy's grades had slipped to a B-minus average for the last quarter of the school year. The school counselor called it an adjustment phase. But Hank and Colleen suspected it had to do with Mike. They had reluctantly decided to let it run its course and see if it would work itself out.

Hank looked both apologetic and worried with a single frown. "I messed up. I hope Mike hasn't dumped on Billy."

Colleen reached down and squeezed Hank's shoulder. "The boys have always found a way to work out their differences. It's part and parcel of growing up. I'm sure they'll be fine."

"I hope so." But Hank was unconvinced.

When the boys finally came downstairs for dinner—Stu had been invited to stay—they were far too quiet. Hank and Colleen exchanged glances, but held their silence. Everyone ate like they had just come from a funeral, and in a few minutes the two older boys excused themselves, far too politely, and took their plates and silverware out to the kitchen sink and went back upstairs. Billy followed as close on their heels as he could without risking a confrontation.

As Hank helped Colleen clear the remaining dishes and then wash them in the double sink, he said quietly, "There's going to be trouble."

"They're boys," Colleen assured him. "They'll survive. Boys always do."

But Hank didn't share her cheery assessment. He smiled a reassuring smile even as he considered how he might set things right between his two precious sons.

Chapter 4

*B*illy awoke shortly after dawn but lay in bed for a long while considering the day and the coming ordeal. Beyond the parted curtains of his bedroom window he saw not a single cloud in the sky. The green leaves on the maple hung fat and limp in the still air. As the sun rose higher, brilliant shafts began to cut through the maple's limbs. The small comfort of nighttime humidity had faded, and the early morning birds now fled the city trees for cooler places.

He lay on his side, left arm curled beneath the pillow under his head, right arm pressed against his chest where he could feel the gentle beating of his heart, and imagined the Butte and its narrow dirt road. Could he really climb to the top with a full pack in just one hour? Billy was used to hikes partway up the mountain that loomed above Chelan. Those explorations usually took him no further than the cave, the crystal rockslide, and the tumbled boards of the long-abandoned homestead. These were grouped together in a narrow ravine where there were also shade trees. Around the homestead you could find old bottles and rusted square nails and horseshoes. The cave was wet and stinky, but it was still a cave! And even though the slide wasn't made of crystal—the boys just called it that because once in a while you found rocks that held slivers of quartz—it was still a nifty place to explore, as long as you watched out for rattlesnakes. Over the years Billy had accumulated three shoeboxes full of crystalline treasure, now hidden in the back of his closet.

Now facing a one-hour climb, any fun he'd had on the Butte seemed ancient history.

He finally rolled out of bed and showered, pulled on a worn pair of jeans and a white T-shirt. He reached down to the floor of his closet and grabbed the new hiking boots he'd gotten for his fourteenth birthday, and then sat on the edge of his bed and cinched the stiff laces through the brass eyelets and tied double bowknots at the tops.

Billy stood and flexed his feet inside the leather before going back to the closet to reach on tiptoes to the top shelf to retrieve the genuine Australian Akubra hat that Gramps had given him on his thirteenth birthday.

Before he'd received the brown felt hat from Gramps, Billy had heard the story at least a hundred times, usually at family picnics or at Thanksgiving or Christmas dinners, at which times Gramps had worn it like a crown. It never failed to draw stares and then excited questions from the youngsters or guests who had never seen such a special hat, especially with its wide rattlesnake-skin band. Gramps' tale was always delivered just as fresh and energetic as if it had happened yesterday and the story was being told for the very first time. In a grandly important voice and with just a hint of mystery and danger Gramps would describe in precise detail how he had bargained and finally arranged the trade of a pair of German binoculars that he'd found near a blown-up German tank for the Akubra with an Australian soldier at the end of WWI. Then he would let any one of his spellbound audience—But only if they asked politely!— stroke the soft dark-brown-dyed rabbit-fur felt. But he would caution them not to pick at the two-inch-wide hatband made from the tanned skin of a diamond-back rattlesnake he had killed in the summer of '32.

As far as Billy was concerned, it was the most special possession he could ever hope to own. Given the choice between anything else, like a .22 rifle, a 90cc Honda trail bike, or a trip to Disneyland, the hat would win in a walk-over every time.

On the day Gramps had handed it to his grandson, he had sworn to Billy that the hat was lucky, and that nobody could come to harm while wearing it.

The hat had reached that magical point where it was so perfectly worn it seemed almost indestructible, which only added to its value. Billy stored it in the security of the narrow shelf high up in his closet. He wore it only on the most special occasions, or when extraordinary luck was required. As he now snugged it on his head he felt goose bumps rise on his arms and on the back of his neck.

"Hope you're watching over me today, Grandpa, 'cause I'm gonna need it," said Billy in a soft and reverent voice, almost as a prayer.

He stole downstairs to the kitchen and poured a bowl of cornflakes and heaped on three tablespoons of sugar, cut up a banana and spread the round slices on the yellow flakes, poured in the milk right up to the brim of the bowl. Before the cornflakes got soggy he spooned them down in huge crunchy mouthfuls. There remained a half-moon sandbar of wet sugar in the bottom of the bowl. He tipped the bowl to his lips and downed the sweetness in one long slurp.

As Billy was rinsing his bowl he heard Mike and Stu tromp in through the front door. He racked the bowl in the drainer and went out to the living room.

The older boys waited with guilty eyes and half smiles.

It had remained a big secret how they intended to load the pack. "Never you mind," his brother had scolded when Billy pleaded for details before bedtime. Billy grumbled, but relinquished the shiny aluminum frame and brown canvas bag after it became clear his questions would remain unanswered.

Now the moment had arrived. Billy would finally get his answer as to *What was up.* He wasn't sure he wanted the answer, but he put on his game face, no way was he going to let the older boys see his doubts. *Be cool* he reminded himself.

"The mighty hiker," Stu said cheerfully.

"You ready for this, Kid?" Mike's tone hinted that failure was the only possible outcome.

"I'm ready," Billy replied confidently.

"I'm ready," Mike mimicked.

"Say," Stu said. "That's some hat you got there." He took a step toward Billy for a closer look. "I've never seen you wear that before." His voice held curiosity and a hint of envy. But when he spoke again the positive tone was replaced by sarcasm. "Where'd you get it? The second hand store? Or did you swipe it off some bum?" Stu laughed.

"It was our grandfather's," Mike cut in, not giving Billy a chance to explain. "Billy got it just before he died. I got Gramps' Swiss Army knife."

Each brother had always maintained that he'd gotten *the best.* But both knew the hat was the real prize. You could buy another knife; the hat was a family heirloom.

27

"Hey, I've seen that knife," Stu said. "It's way cooler than some scruffy old hat."

Billy said in a cold voice that left no room for doubt, "I'd rather have the hat."

"Well it's a real killer," Stu said. "A bear would probably eat you and leave that old relic alone. Me, I'll stick with the Yankees." Stu touched the brim of his navy blue cap. He wore it everywhere.

The cap had come to Stu by accident. A tourist left it on a bench at the city park two summers back, and Stu found it while he and Mike were cruising for girls. Then almost new, it now looked as if Babe Ruth might have actually worn *this very cap* when he signed with the Bronx Bombers in 1920. Seeing Stu without the Yankees cap was like seeing an American flag without the right number of stripes.

"Yep," Stu continued. "The luck of the Yankees is gonna beat out some crusty old Australian cowboy hat any day of the week."

Billy bristled. He had nothing against Stu's cap. And if Stu was not being so arrogant, Billy would have readily agreed that the Yankees cap was indeed cool. But before he could think of something snappy to say, his older brother cut in again.

"We're wasting time. Your pack's up in my room."

They trooped up the stairs and down the hall. Once inside, Mike softly closed the door all the way shut.

Billy's pack, bulging at the seams, leaned against the foot of Mike's bed.

Billy walked over and put his hands on one strap, intending to hoist it onto his right shoulder and then saddle the other strap onto his left. He gave a tug. The pack didn't move. He looked in disbelief at Mike, then over to Stu.

"What'd you fill it with, rocks?"

Both older boys snickered. "Nope," Stu said. "Books."

"Books?"

Mike said, "Well, you didn't expect us to fill it with a bunch of camp gear for a measly test, did you?" He shook his head in disbelief.

Stu rolled his eyes.

Billy's voice shot up half an octave. "We aren't taking *books* on the hike. We're taking clothes and food and cooking gear. None of that stuff weighs this much. This isn't fair at all!"

Stu shrugged. "*We* aren't going on any hike unless *you* can make it up the Butte with that load in one hour." He looked at Mike, who nodded in confirmation. Stu continued. "And who cares what's in the pack, anyways? I don't remember anyone saying that you had a vote in this. Right Mike?"

"Right-O, Stu."

Neither Mike nor Stu had actually tried to pick up the backpack. They had just pulled armloads of hardbacks from the shelves in the living room and carried them upstairs and stuffed in as many as they could until the brown canvas was solid.

Billy's voice continued to rise.

"But it's not *fair!*"

Mike took a menacing step forward. "Look, you little wart!" His voice matched Billy's in volume, but the tone was a growl and it was relentless. "Either you hoist that pack and march your butt up the Butte, or you quit whining about what's fair and leave us alone."

Then there came a soft knock at the bedroom door. All three boys froze.

"Mike?" It was Hank. "Billy?" Heart-stopping seconds of silence stretched into what seemed like an eternity. "What's all the shouting about?"

"Aw, criminey," Mike whispered. He looked at Stu, who just stared back. And then Mike looked Billy straight in the face and threatened in a quiet voice that their father wouldn't hear, "You say anything or make even one tiny little gripe to Dad, and I'll pound you straight into the ground all the frickin' way to China."

Mike had never before threatened him like that. Billy shut up, in dumb shock, as Mike walked to the door and grasped the knob. He pulled it open and there stood Dad with a quizzical look on his face.

Instead of coming inside immediately, Hank stood in the doorway, taking stock. He saw the pregnant backpack with sharp angles pressing the canvas, and realized it was filled with books. Mike and Stu looked guilty as thieves. Billy was clearly angry, and more important to Hank he looked frightened.

"Mike?" Hank said, leaving the question hanging.

Mike looked down at his shoe tops. He knew he couldn't lie, even if Billy kept his mouth shut. Finally, he said in a low and measured voice, "Billy asked if he could go on the backpacking trip with us. And we figure he has to prove he can keep up. So we're having him go on a short hike, just an hour or so, with a full pack to see how he does."

Hank looked at Stu and then at Billy and saw no disagreement. He turned his attention to the backpack.

"Is that Billy's pack?"

Mike said, "Yeah."

"And are those your mother's books inside?"

Mike's voice cracked just a little as he said, "Yeah, a few."

Hank finally stepped into the room. He put one hand on the pack and rocked it away from the bed. But he didn't try to pick it up. Instead, he turned to Mike.

"Have either you or Stu carried this any distance, Mike?"

"No."

"Do you know how heavy it is?"

"No."

Hank now addressed all three of the boys, having decided how to handle the problem, hoping his reasoning would be persuasive, knowing that if he tried to force Mike into being reasonable he might rebel completely. His voice shifted from a questioning to an informative tone.

"I did a lot of hiking when I was a teenager. We always figured a pack should weigh no more than forty pounds. That was when sleeping bags were made of canvas and cotton, not the lightweight nylon bags you boys own. These days, I'd think thirty-five pounds would be about the right weight for a backpack on a weeklong hike. Does that sound about right, Mike?"

Mike saw where the logic was headed and knew he was trapped. Dad was right, of course. So he mumbled, "Yeah, I suppose so."

Hank looked at Stu.

"Stuart?"

"Yes, Sir." Stu was blind scared. If Hank Ward had hollered "BOO!" he would have wet his pants right there on the spot. But he was trying hard not to show how crazy frightened he actually was and he thought he was succeeding. If he had asked Hank he would have learned just how wrong he was.

Hank didn't bother to ask Billy. He guessed that Mike had pressured him to keep quiet. So instead, he said to Billy, "Son, why don't you go downstairs and get your mother's bathroom scales. Bring them up and we'll weigh this backpack and, if necessary, we can make a little adjustment in the weight. That is," and he now looked at Mike and Stu as if they might have actually filled the backpack with a fair weight of books, "if it needs any adjustment."

Mike and Stu returned grim smiles of agreement.

Billy dodged out the door. They heard his boots thud down the stairs, only to pound back up within seconds at full speed. When he came to the door he carried the flat, white metal bathroom scale. He laid it on the floor directly in front of the backpack, careful to avoid eye contact with either Mike or Stu.

Hank grabbed the pack firmly with both hands and lifted it with great effort onto the scale. The boys moved forward to watch the dial spin beneath the glass. The red line finally came to rest.

79

Despite his fear, Stu whistled low and soft.

Mike glared at Stu.

Hank ignored both.

Billy's heart was pounding. A little thrill of victory surged through his body.

Without a word, Hank undid the laces that cinched the cover flap and began to remove books one by one, piling them on Mike's bed. *A Tale of Two Cities, The Odyssey, The Big Rock Candy Mountain, Hawaii*. The dial crept down below seventy. *Ben Hur, Tropic of Cancer, Of Mice and Men*. Down through the sixties. As the weighty hardbacks were piled onto Mike's bed the scale creaked with relief. Eventually, when Hank removed a thick volume titled *The Plays of William Shakespeare* the needle settled dead center on 35. Hank set the last book on the considerable pile atop Mike's quilt and turned to the boys.

"There," he said in a carefully neutral voice. "That should do it." He considered asking where they intended to have Billy hike, but decided that was going too far. Mike's sullen acceptance of the weight reduction was as much as he could hope for. It was now up to Billy to prove himself. If he failed, at least he would do so on a fair footing, one that hopefully wouldn't do any permanent damage to the boys' relationship.

"Alright," Hank said, stepping toward the door. "Mike, I expect you to act your age in conducting this test." And with that grim pronouncement, he left.

The boys stood like posts until Hank's footfalls ended with the sound of the back door opening and then being shut.

"Wow!" Stu said. "I thought we were goners."

Mike turned on Stu. "Why'd you have to whistle like some dummy?"

Stu's face grew red.

Billy ignored them both. He shouldered the backpack, which now seemed almost to be filled with feathers, and turned for the door, thumping down the steps one at a time.

When he reached the front yard he turned and saw that Mike and Stu had followed. They lifted two old bicycles which were laid down on the grass. These bikes were like Billy's Stingray, with butterfly handlebars and long narrow seats and knobby tires; perfect for a steep dirt road. Billy felt a wave of resentment that Mike and Stu would ride while he walked but knew any protest was pointless.

He strode out into the growing heat of the day, got to the end of the block, turned right and headed toward the Butte road.

Mike and Stu watched Billy turn the corner before they swung onto the bikes with teenaged bravado. They easily caught up, and trailed Billy in large, lazy S-curves as he trudged down the street, his upper body slightly bent against the weight of the backpack.

The Butte was misnamed; it had no flat top. Instead, it was a rounded mountain that looked vaguely like an elephant lying on its side. It loomed twenty-seven hundred feet above the southern end of Lake Chelan, camel-brown with a summer coat of dry cheat grass, bitter brush and sagebrush. This canvas was dotted with a few scraggly ponderosa pines and an occasional elderberry bush. It was only during the short weeks of springtime that the rolling hills in the valley bloomed lush with balsamroot, buttercups, crocus, yellow bells, birds' beaks and violets. By the time full summer heat had arrived these glorious flowers had withered into the crusted topsoil.

The mountain shimmered like a mirage and the boys' throats felt dry in anticipation of the climb.

It took several minutes to walk to where the dirt road began. As Billy paced evenly along the paved highway, Mike and Stu spoke of girls and swimming and the new movie at the Ruby Theatre. Every couple of minutes the older boys would stop, straddle their bikes, and let Billy trek on ahead in silence. And then as if it were some game they would pedal hard, catch up, and break to a stop just short of Billy's boot heels. They would laugh, and that was what hurt Billy the most. But he did his best to ignore them until he came to the start of the Butte Road. Then he stopped to check his watch, and Mike and Stu checked their watches.

"Ten-fifteen," Mike pronounced.

Billy nodded with a confidence he did not feel.

Mike looked at Stu with a look of amused exasperation, and Stu gave a hopeless shrug in reply.

Billy turned away from the older boys and began the climb.

The road already wore a summer coat of talcum-fine dust, and in places the sole of a shoe left a print so sharp that the manufacturer's trademark was readable. On any other day and without a heavy pack Billy might have taken an experimental stomp to see how clear of a print he could make in the dust. But those thoughts were as far away as the summit he now hoped to reach in sixty fleeting minutes.

The Akubra, with its rattlesnake band, was firmly wedged on his head. A fine sheen of sweat began to soak the leather band that pressed against Billy's forehead. He trudged up the first grade of the road and the metal frame and brown canvas pack kept a nervous pendulum time with each step.

The older boys dismounted and began pushing against the butterfly handlebars of their bicycles. They soon had sweat soaking through their shirts; it trickled down their faces and fell in salty drops from their noses, spotting the road dust.

After a quarter of a mile, Billy came to the first big turn. The road switch-backed and cut across the hillside facing the lake. Billy could see up lake to the mountain peaks where (he kept trying to convince himself) he'd be hiking with the older boys in just a few days' time.

And now Billy began to feel an aching in the backs of his legs. He tried to distract himself from the pain by counting his steps, but this only made the effort seem harder. He tried to imagine Mike staked out on an anthill. But this dark fantasy was short-lived, overcome by the constant pain inflicted by the pack, which had begun to feel like a sack of bricks. He shifted all of his focus onto putting one foot in front of the other, conserving his energy in short strides. But the task of climbing the mountain began to seem hopeless. The top of the Butte seemed as far away as ever.

Mike and Stu remained several yards behind, pushing silently against their bike handlebars, occasionally looking at each other, knowing that whatever pain they were suffering, Billy's was greater.

When they finally came to a flat section of the road, the older boys again mounted their bikes, tracing arcs in the dust as they looped along behind Billy. At one point Mike saw a grasshopper and tried to run it over, but the bug scared from the road and buzzed into the safety of the sagebrush.

All three boys had previously hiked this road too many times to take much notice of the birds that tweeted from the cover of the brush, and the occasional *ca-coo-kah* of a hidden quail. What all three did hear and think about was the far off drone of a ski boat down on the lake, a vivid reminder of the swim they were missing.

Thinking about water and diving off the city dock made Billy's steps seem longer and his feet heavier. The insides of his new boots were now hot and his cotton socks were sweaty. He was glad his toes were just a bit loose; it let air circulate.

Billy began another uphill stretch and found himself straining to keep the pace. The pack straps bit and pulled at the flesh of his shoulders. There wasn't huge pain, but there would be . . . soon. *Hang in there*, he thought. *You're almost a third of the way up.* But it seemed more and more improbable that he could complete the climb in one hour. A quick glance at his watch showed twenty minutes had gone by.

At the bend near the ranch house, the road leveled off again for several hundred yards. Mike pedaled up alongside his brother. Billy kept his head forward, eyes on the road.

"How you doing, Billy?" There was no pity or sympathy in Mike's voice.

Billy didn't look up; he plodded along without reply. Mike tracked his bike close until he was crowding Billy. Several yards behind, Stu grinned beneath the glistening sweat on his forehead.

Mike kept riding slow, nearly brushing against Billy's left leg. Billy finally said in a dull flat tone, "I'm just fine."

"You aren't mad, are you?" Mike ached for a confession that Billy had bitten off a bigger chunk than he could hope to chew, much less swallow.

Billy fought back his anger and managed a very neutral, "Nope."

"You sure?" Mike egged.

Billy glanced at Mike and their eyes locked. Beneath the sweat and the concentration on Billy's face lay a hard determination. "I'm fine, and I'm not mad, Mike." *I'll show you what tough is!*

Mike played his trump card. "You want a drink of water?" He held out a green plastic canteen. *Just let him ask. See where it gets him!*

Billy studied his brother's face, glanced at the extended canteen, looked back down at the road to where his next few footsteps would fall. "Nope."

"Okay, suit yourself," Mike said, disappointed. Billy heard this and fought to keep a straight face.

"If you change your mind, just holler." Mike circled back to Stu and fell in alongside.

"How's our little champ?" Stu asked loudly. He pulled off his Yankees cap and wiped the sweat from his forehead with the front of his T-shirt.

Mike looked skyward. "Still thinks he's going to make it to the top in time."

"Huh," Stu grunted, replacing the sweat-soaked cap. "Well, he's making good progress, I guess." Stu sounded genuinely impressed.

Neither Stu nor Mike could see Billy's brief smile as he heard this.

"He's not at the hard part yet," Mike said. "We'll see how he does when he reaches that last steep stretch near the top. If . . . he even gets that far! Me, I'm ready for a break."

"Okay." Stu would never have suggested that they stop, but if Mike said so, well, he was ready for a breather and a long drink of water.

"Hey Billy," Mike called out. "We're gonna take five. Too bad you can't join us." This was his final ploy to get under Billy's skin. It angered Billy to hear the smug satisfaction in his big brother's voice. But he had the perfect reply.

"Have a nice rest," he said evenly.

Mike gave up. "Okay," he said. "Catch up with you in a few."

Billy listened to Mike and Stu dump their bikes and start talking about a new shotgun that had come in at the Western Auto. But he never looked back. He was soon out of sight and earshot, left with the sounds of birds and grasshoppers and his boots clumping solid time. He wished for a breeze, but the air was dead calm.

The road now alternately climbed and leveled through a series of humps that led up into the narrow ravine where the settlers' house and the crystal rockslide and the cave were located. The house was just a roof collapsed onto floorboards, but there were plenty of lizards and chipmunks to be found in the tumble of aging lumber. Nearby was an old well that was fun to shine a flashlight into and say you had seen a skeleton down in the darkness, but Billy had never trusted the rusted metal rungs enough to climb down and explore the bottom. *And who knew . . . maybe there really was a skeleton down there!*

The crystal cave dug beneath the rockslide had once been used as a root cellar by the early homesteaders. It held a few inches of water that smelled like rotten eggs. It was hidden from the road by a thicket of pines and vine maple. If it had been dry inside, the boys would have carried boards from the collapsed house and made benches to sit in the cool and the dark. But because of the sulfurous stink, that idea was short-lived.

Today, Billy didn't think much about the house or the cave, giving both only a quick glance as he passed by. He focused his attention on the gravel used to build this section of road and how it made footing treacherous. One wrong step and you could turn an ankle. When the boys came down this stretch on their bikes, they stood on their brakes and took it slow. It was scrapes and bruises if you crashed, maybe a broken arm or a busted nose.

He was just past the cave, breathing hard, straining against the weight of the pack, when he heard his brother and Stu trying to catch up. Their labored words drifted uphill. *I'll teach 'em,* he thought, increasing his pace and ignoring the bite of the straps and the heat and the sweat that streamed down his back and chest and fell in a constant drip from the tip of his nose.

He made the hairpin turn out of the ravine and glanced over his shoulder; they were 200 yards back, pushing hard; it was too steep for them to pedal and they were not gaining ground. He quickened his pace until his knees felt weak.

He had now reached the limit of his climbing speed. Any faster and there would be cramps. But he was determined not to let the older boys catch up. Billy pushed on.

They continued like that, Billy pegging as if the devil were on his heels, Mike and Stu grinding their tennis shoes on the scrabble in dead earnest pursuit. Every once in a while Billy heard a few words exchanged by the older boys but they were too far back to for him to make out the meaning. He figured they might be swearing at him and that was just fine. In fact, he hoped they were swearing! Let them cuss all they wanted. It wasn't going to do them a darned bit of good. He fought off the pain and he kept climbing at the brutal pace he had set. After a while the distant words stopped and Billy knew that Mike and Stu were hurting bad and that felt just great and gave Billy a little surge of energy.

Billy reached the top before they caught up. He stood, winded and amazed, staring at the look-out tower that loomed just a few yards away. Mike and Stu finally pushed their bikes up behind Billy. The rasp of their breathing was all the satisfaction Billy needed, except—a glance at his watch told Billy he'd made it with three minutes to spare!

Mike and Stu dumped their bikes and collapsed at the edge of the turn-around; shirts pitted out and pant legs floured with dirt. Billy waited until they were down on the ground, then dumped his pack, gave a big "Whew!" and sat down a few feet away.

"Hey Billy," Mike said. "You want some water now?" The taunting was gone. Billy knew this time the offer was real. His throat felt like grocery sack paper. But all that really mattered was that Mike's voice held a tiny edge of respect.

"Yeah," he said, taking the plastic canteen. He drank until his stomach ached. "Thanks." He handed it back toward his brother, who made no move to take it.

"Keep it," Mike said. "We won't be needing it. Stu and I are gonna ride back down."

What?

Mike saw Billy's look of disbelief and now his reply sounded defensive, almost hurt. "Don't throw a fit! You made it to the top in time." Mike looked at Stu. "He's in for the hike. Right Stu?"

"Yeah," Stu replied, still trying to fully catch his breath. "I guess."

It sounded too good to be true! Mike was agreeing to take him? Stu was now on Billy's side? Both older boys sounded way too agreeable all of a sudden. What was the catch?

Billy puzzled about this sudden reversal in attitudes as Mike and Stu mounted their bikes. They took off down the road with war-whoop hollers, and Billy turned for his pack.

The books!

He had completely forgotten them in his excitement. Mike and Stu had known! Billy now wished they had used rocks, like he'd first accused them of. Rocks, he could throw away. But these were Mom's prized hardbacks, and he'd catch trouble big-time if he didn't bring them home.

And they had known!

Stuck, angry, frustrated, Billy finally set off down the road, canteen in hand, Akubra tight on his head, filled with a new resentment but also with a sense of purpose and determination. He'd show them what he was made of! And who cared if it was getting hotter with each passing minute. The last thing Billy wanted was to make the return hike last a leisurely two hours. He wanted to go swimming. He wanted a glass of cold lemonade to celebrate his victory.

As he picked up speed, his boots began to skid on the gritty dirt. His toes began to cram up inside his boots. Before long his feet felt like they were on fire. Rather than stop, he kept going, not realizing the damage being done.

When he got home, he put the books back on the shelf and trudged upstairs. It now felt as if he were walking on hot coals.

In his room he pulled off his boots and peeled off his socks. He was horrified to discover large blisters had formed between his toes and on the balls of his feet. The possibility of a backpacking adventure vanished in that instant of terrible discovery.

If Hank Ward hadn't heard Billy crying, Billy would have backed out of the hike with some bogus explanation; he would have been too ashamed to admit to the blisters and that the reason was his own stubbornness on the return to Chelan. But Hank did hear his son sobbing behind the closed bedroom door, and he stopped and knocked gently.

"Billy?"

Billy cried that much harder upon being discovered. One quick look at Billy's feet, propped up on the bed, and Hank understood.

"Is this from your hiking test today?"

Billy choked out, "Yes."

At the foot of Billy's bed lay the new boots. Hank took one look at them, looked back to Billy's feet, and examined the blisters closely. He put a gentle hand on his son's shoulder. "Let's get you down to Doc Manley and have him take a look. Before you give up on that hike, maybe he'll have something that'll help."

Billy pulled a sniffle and wiped his eyes. "Do you think he might?"

"Let's go see. But you better not wear these." Hank reached down and picked up the new boots. "Put on a clean pair of socks and your tennis shoes."

When Billy was ready, Hank helped him hobble down the stairs. In his left hand Hank carried the boots, which he dropped at the bottom of the stairs near the coat rack.

They drove to the clinic and learned that Doc Manley would be able to work Billy in but it would be half an hour. So Hank and Billy sat in the waiting area, beside a mother whose two-year-old was sniffling and crying, and across from a man in grimy brown coveralls and muddy work boots whose left hand was wrapped in a bloodied handkerchief.

The man went in first, and came out fifteen minutes later with a freshly bandaged hand and looking relieved.

The mother and child took as long. But finally the nurse beckoned Hank and Billy.

They went back to a white-painted examination room with a long counter and shelves and an enameled instrument tray on a chrome stand. In the center of the room was an exam table with metal stirrups, upholstered in black vinyl and with a clean sheet of paper pulled from a roll at one end to cover the top.

Hank explained about the hike and what had happened to Billy's feet. Doc Manley asked Billy to go into the bathroom and wash his feet in the sink. When he returned, the doctor asked him to sit up on the table. Once Billy was seated, Doc Manley pulled out a footrest so that Billy's feet were propped comfortably in view. Billy was up on his elbows, watching.

Doc Manley's eyes crinkled kindly at the corners as he gently held Billy's toes apart and scrutinized each fluid-filled bubble.

He then walked over to the counter and reached up to a shelf and took down a dark brown bottle of rubbing alcohol. From a wide-mouthed glass jar on the counter he pulled a large wad of cotton. He pressed the cotton against the bottle mouth and turned the bottle upside down for a few seconds.

He came back to the exam table and used the alcohol-saturated cotton to wipe down the skin around the blisters. Billy's feet still burned and the cooling alcohol felt nice. Billy hoped that was all the treatment necessary, but Doc Manley now lifted the lid from the tray and Billy saw neatly arrayed instruments, including two scalpels with razor sharp blades. Doc Manley selected one of these and turned back to Billy, whose eyes were now wide with fear.

"This is going to hurt a little," Doc Manley said calmly, "You let me know if it hurts too much, and we can stop for a moment."

Billy closed his eyes in anticipation of the pain.

"It'll hurt less if you keep your eyes open," the doctor said. He gently grasped the heel of Billy's left foot and held the scalpel like a pencil with his other hand, positioning the blade over the one blister. "But you don't have to watch. Why don't you look up at the ceiling?"

Billy stared up at the plaster and began to count the hairline cracks that had yellowed with age. He felt a sting as the scalpel slid into the first, and then the second, and finally the last blister on his left foot. But he was determined not to make a sound. He bit his lip and took short breaths.

Then came a sharper pain, and an involuntary "Owww!" escaped Billy's mouth. He looked down and saw the doctor now held a cotton swab, the end of which was stained reddish brown. It was Mercurochrome, just like in the bottle mom kept in the medicine cabinet at home. The doctor was swabbing each of the deflated blisters.

"Sorry Billy," the doctor apologized. "But we don't want these to get infected. Do we?"

"No," Billy agreed solemnly, tears leaking from the corners of his eyes. But he was determined there would be no more crying out and held a determined silence.

The doctor taped small squares of gauze bandage over the incisions, and moved to the right foot. He lanced blisters on the big toe and the second toe, and then disinfected and bandaged them. Billy clenched his teeth and no sound escaped as the doctor finished up his work with the antiseptic.

When Doc Manley was done, he turned to Hank.

"Go to the drugstore and buy a box of Epsom salts. Have Billy soak his feet two times a day. He may lose some of his calluses but they'll come back quickly once the blisters have healed."

He turned to Billy.

"Your feet need time to heal, Billy. I know you want to go backpacking with your brother. But if you go before your feet are completely healed you'll have a much bigger problem. Give it a few weeks and you'll be right as rain."

Hank thanked the doctor and took Billy home. As they pulled into the driveway, Hank said, "I think we need a family meeting tonight. Mike and Stu got you into this fix, and they need to help get you out of it."

Billy nodded in agreement, but couldn't imagine what his brother and Stu could do about his feet.

Chapter 5

"THREE WEEKS!"

Mike erupted in disbelief as he stood in the middle of the living room, fists clenched, facing Hank.

Stu sat in a chair by the wall, wishing he were invisible. Billy sat on the sofa, feeling vindicated but also very much alone despite the fact that Mom sat beside him.

Colleen's great struggle was not to reach for Billy's hand to hold. But to reach for Billy's hand would have made him seem to still be her "little boy." Which as far as Colleen was concerned he was. And he always would be. But she knew Billy needed his dignity and pride. Holding his hand would only encourage the image of Billy as a child in Mike's eyes. So Colleen intertwined her fingers on her lap and looked straight ahead at the conflict unfolding between father and son, focusing her energy upon not breaking into tears.

Hank was slowly losing the battle to keep his patience.

"It's not that long to wait," Hank insisted.

"It's forever!" Mike shouted back.

Mike looked over to Stu for support, but Stu was frozen like a dove on a high voltage power line, his eyes wide and face stone sober. Mike eyes continued to plead for help, but Stu didn't move. Mike gave up and shifted his stare toward the books, which had been neatly replaced back on the shelves, transferring his anger to them for just a moment. He spoke without looking away from the books.

"We can't wait three weeks," he said, more to himself than to anyone else in the room.

"You can, and will, wait until your brother's feet are healed up, Mike. You and Stu dreamed up this stunt of hiking up the Butte. In one hour, for heaven's sake! Now you'll just have to live with the consequences." Hank glanced at Billy, then back to Mike. "Billy made it up the mountain in your one-hour time limit, didn't he? So under your set of rules, he earned the right to go, didn't he?"

"Well—"

"Well, nothing. Billy passed your ridiculous test. He hiked to the top of the Butte in less than an hour, right?"

"I guess." And with that admission the wind came out of Mike's sails.

"You didn't make it a part of your test that he hike back down the Butte, did you?"

Mike simmered in silence, knowing he was trapped.

Hank kept rolling.

"There's no good reason why you and Stu couldn't have helped him by carrying some of those books down, instead of making him walk all the way back by himself with a full load."

Mike stared straight at the miserable books, his face becoming a dull mask.

"So you'll just have to wait until Billy's feet are ready to going on the hike. That's my decision. And it's final."

Once Dad said a decision was final, you might as well try to move the Grand Coulee Dam with a crowbar.

Hank tried one last time to win Mike over.

"You can wait a few extra days, Mike, can't you? Summer won't disappear in the next three weeks."

"That's not the point!" Mike practically screamed. His face was growing red.

"Mike!" Hank cautioned. His patience had finally run out.

But Mike was beyond caring and he simply steamrolled on.

"If we have to wait three weeks, we might as well not go," he said. "I might as well get a job for the rest of the summer. Billy can go on the hike alone if he wants to."

With this final pronouncement, Mike turned to Stu. "C'mon," he said, turning for the front door.

Hank almost ordered him to stop. But he feared it might cause an even greater disaster and decided it was best to give Mike overnight to settle down. Tomorrow, Hank would try to patch things up.

Mike was halfway out the front door before Stu stood up, uncertain. He looked apologetically towards Hank.

"Go on," Hank said quietly. Stu was out the door in a dash, running to catch up with Mike.

Out on the street Mike stomped along for a full block before he stopped and turned on Stu who was pacing silently by his side.

"Well that's just great, isn't it?" Mike cleared his throat and spat onto the sidewalk.

"What a bummer," Stu agreed. Although a part of him disagreed. Billy *had* passed their test. And it *was* mean that they had forced him to walk back down the Butte carrying all of those books. But there was no way Stu was going to disagree with Mike. It would have threatened their friendship—something Stu couldn't even begin to contemplate. So he followed and he listened as Mike raged.

"We can't wait three weeks!" Mike shouted up into the warm night air, as if to confirm the decision he had already come to. "If we do that, it'll screw up the rest of the summer!"

Stu nodded and kept his mouth shut, even though he thought Mike's reasoning was off base. After another half a block, Mike continued the train of thought he'd been working out, but now in a more normal voice.

"I heard Old Man Kelly is hiring summer kids for his orchard crew. You up for that kind of work?"

This wasn't particularly the direction Stu had been expecting. He'd thought they would just keep swimming every day, do the paper route, and maybe find some tourist girls to take out to the movies or for a pizza, and then Mike would be off to college, and Stu would probably be in boot camp—a decision he hadn't yet shared with Mike. But he still wasn't ready to even mildly disagree with Mike about anything. "Sure," he said.

"Good. I'll give Mr. Kelly a call in the morning and find out if he's got two slots open on his crew." And for the very first time that evening Mike sounded satisfied, if not exactly happy.

Chapter 6

Ryan Kelly's orchard stretched across a hillside five miles up the north shore of Lake Chelan. His father had first planted Common Delicious trees in the late 1920's. By 1969, many of those old trees had grown to become giants.

July was thinning season. The behemoth trees required sixteen-foot ladders to reach the tops, and even then you had to stand on the second-to-last rung and stretch to reach the highest clusters of green shooter-marble-sized fruit.

Mr. Kelly had agreed to pick up Mike and Stu early on Monday morning, four days after the big fall-out in the living room, and take them out to the orchard to show them how to do the thinning. "Be ready at five," Ryan Kelly told Mike, who passed this starting time on to Stu as they began the mid-morning bike ride to deliver the Sunday papers. Stu had decided to keep his paper route, just in case the new job didn't pan out. And also partly because he could not imagine any situation that would be the "right" moment for telling his mom that he had decided to drop the route in favor of orchard work.

"Five in the morning?" Stu said in disbelief. "Are you sure he said five? You must have got it wrong. Even the frigging birds don't get up at five!"

"Yep," Mike confirmed. "He said five. I'm sure of it. He says that way you beat the afternoon heat because you get to knock off at two."

"Well that's just great, isn't it!" Stu said, wishing he had stood up to Mike at the first suggestion of orchard work. But now he was stuck.

So on Sunday evening, Stu went to bed with his wind-up alarm clock set for 4:45 AM.

When it jangled him awake he almost reached over and punched off the dinger and buried his head under his pillow. But the weary recognition that

Mike would keep pounding on the front door, and eventually dislodge his mother from what would at that point have only been two or three hours of sleep, kept his heavy eyelids open. The last thing Stu wanted was his mom on the rampage before sunrise.

So he rolled out of bed, went into the bathroom and washed his face, pulled on clean shorts and an old pair of Levis and black sneakers and a faded purple T-shirt, and finally his Yankees cap. He softly closed the front door, walked out to the curb, sat down and wrapped his arms around his knees for warmth against the early chill.

In five minutes Stu heard the whine of Mr. Kelly's Willy's Jeep. The ancient gray war-surplus Jeep swerved around the corner and screeched to a stop in the middle of the street.

Ryan Kelly sat ramrod straight in the driver's seat, both hands gripping the black steering wheel. He was a wizened man of fifty with a bulldog face leathered by outdoor work and a two-pack-a-day habit. A smoldering cigarette drooped from the corner of his mouth. He wore a faded Texaco bill cap and a green windbreaker. "C'mon, Son!" Kelly yelled. "The day's a-wasting!"

Stu glanced up at the Butte and noticed that the sun had just begun to brush the top yellow. *Wasting?* He reminded himself how blistering the afternoon would be as he grabbed the sack lunch he had made up the night before—two peanut butter sandwiches, two cans of Shasta orange pop, and a thick carrot he had discovered in the bottom of the vegetable crisper where it had somehow managed to stay halfway fresh. Mike was already sitting in the front seat of the jeep, so Stu climbed into the back.

As soon as Stu's jeans hit the cracked black vinyl Mr. Kelly jammed the shift lever forward and stomped on the transmission pedal with his left foot; his right foot floored the shiny metal gas pedal. There was a grinding of cogs and the Jeep lurched forward. When the speedometer hit twenty he pumped the clutch and speed-shifted and the Jeep jolted into third gear. They sped away through the dawn light with all the streetlamps still aglow.

By the time the Jeep swerved off the main road and onto the rutted dirt track that led up through the center of his orchard, both boys had white knuckle handfulls of vinyl seat cover.

The Jeep ground to a halt with a final wheeze from beneath the hood as the engine died. Both boys jumped out.

Mr. Kelly sat a moment longer, just long enough to light another cigarette from the dying butt in his mouth. He stepped out and pitched the butt into the wet orchard grass where it sizzled. "C'mon, boys," he said, leading the way to where several aluminum ladders were piled in the deep grass. He grabbed one ladder and hoisted it up with surprising ease.

Stu looked up at the top of the ladder as it towered beside a tree. The lower rungs still held a fine sheen of dew. At the base, it was nearly four feet wide. But the top was barely a foot across.

Mr. Kelly thrust the tongue between two tree branches until it was lodged alongside the trunk. He settled the posts into the soft earth.

"See how it forms a tripod?

Both boys said, "Uh huh."

"Always keep the base of the ladder downhill. It's more stable that way. I don't want either of you falling off. That's how someone gets their neck broke."

The boys agreed.

"Now come over here and I'll show you how to thin."

They walked to a low hanging branch. Mr. Kelly grasped the leafy limb and pointed to a cluster of fruit. Three small green apples sprouted from the same woody shoot.

"That's a triplet."

The boys nodded in agreement.

"Three is too many apples. If you let all three grow you aren't going to get big fruit, just three little buggers and some limb-rub and punctures. So you need to thin out the weak ones." He studied the triplet for a second and pointed to the smallest apple. "Here," he said, grasping the stem between his thumb and index finger. He flicked his thumb and the stem parted with a little *pop*. "You snap it off at the apple. Don't pull the stem from the shoot because you'll damage the other stems and you won't get any apples at all." Mr. Kelly then popped a second apple. "Doubles are no good either." Only the single largest apple remained. He turned to look at the boys. "You got it?"

"Yes Sir," Mike said.

"Yes Mr. Kelly," Stu agreed.

"Good."

He assigned them each a ladder and started them on separate rows. As he walked toward his jeep, he called back over his shoulder, almost as an afterthought. "I'll be back in a while to see how you're doing. And by the way, I pay an extra buck for each mouse you kill. Those little twerps can strip the young bark clean around a sapling. So if you see one, stomp the hell out of it!" He laughed, jumped into the jeep, revved up the tired engine, and spun twin rooster tails of mud as he made a tight turn and bounded off down the hill.

"Let's get started," Mike said with resignation, turning towards his ladder.

Stu wished he were still in bed. But the reality was settling in. "Okay," he agreed, trying to sound at least resolved, if not happy. At least he would be making good money, and that was something to look forward to.

Stu grabbed his ladder and discovered it was heavier than it looked, much heavier than Mr. Kelly had made it seem. And it was also hard to balance, especially in the thick grass that grabbed at your legs as you walked. Stu broke off two small branches as he thrust it up into his first tree.

As he climbed into the tree canopy, it seemed far more of a struggle than Mr. Kelly had made it sound, fighting through the curtain of leaves to find the clusters. Small branches kept brushing at his face but eventually Stu found a rough rhythm working from top to bottom.

A few minutes later Stu realized that his hands were coated with something sticky and white that had a chemical smell. He looked through the green canopy to where Mike was busy pulling and dropping tiny green bombs that disappeared into the lush grass.

"Hey Mike!"

Mike looked up. "Yeah?"

"What's this white crap on the apples?"

Mike thought a moment. "Spray, I guess."

"Is it poison?"

"I don't know. Maybe. I wouldn't go putting my fingers in my mouth if I were you."

Stu studied his hands again, sniffed at the mystery chemical. Through the branches and across the opening between the rows Mike was looking at him.

"You getting a reaction like a rash or something?"

Stu looked at his hands again; they seemed unaffected. "Naw," he hollered back.

"Okay," Mike said. And he returned to plucking the little green apples from the nearest branch.

So that was that.

Stu returned to his own branch and tried to ignore the chemical feel and the chemical smell.

It was now just after six and the sun began angling through the orchard and heating the air. Sprinklers had soaked the ground and the humidity was beginning to rise.

Stu finished thinning his first tree and climbed down the ladder, wiping his hands in the wet grass. He retrieved a can of soda and drank it straight down. He removed his cap and carefully used the back of his forearm to wipe the sweat from his brow, put his cap back on, and shifted his ladder to the next tree.

He was up near the top of the ladder, concentrating as much on not falling as on the thinning, when he heard Mike start to whoop and holler. He looked down and saw Mike between two rows, hopping and stomping wildly, as if he had a hot foot. Stu quick-stepped down his ladder and ran to Mike.

"What 'n the heck are you doing?"

In answer, Mike pointed at the ground. A small gray mouse was embedded in the center of a shoeprint.

"Great," Stu said. "You got yourself an extra buck."

"Yup," Mike said, clearly pleased. He reached down and plucked the mouse by the tip of its tail, dangling the flattened critter like a prize.

"What are you doing?"

"Just watch!"

Mike carried the mouse and laid it across a low limb. He reached down and picked a long thick strand of orchard grass, tied a small noose in one end, and held it for just a moment enjoying his handiwork. Then he slipped the noose around the mouse's neck, gently pulled it tight, and tied the other end of the strand to a branch. The mouse now hung, crushed and bloody, its glassy black eyes staring off into space.

"Cute," Stu said dourly. "I'm sure Kelly will love it." He walked back to his own tree.

Just after seven the boys heard the whine of the Jeep. By now they were several trees down their rows.

The jeep ground to a halt and Ryan Kelly jumped out. They caught glimpses of him as he examined the first tree in Stu's row. And then came a distant, "Oh no. Not like this."

Stu's gut twisted.

It was soon Mike's turn to be nervous, as Kelly shifted to the first tree in his row. And again, "Boy, oh boy, oh good Lord this won't do."

And then Kelly erupted into laughter.

He came striding between the rows to where the boys were up their ladders trying to look busy. Kelly had a broad smile. He looked up at Mike, then Stu.

"Who caught the little devil?"

Mike said, "Me."

"Good job, Mike. I'm giving you two extra bucks for creativity."

"Thanks, Mr. Kelly," Mike said proudly.

But as if a switch in his brain had suddenly flipped, Kelly sobered up. "I'm going to have to teach you boys a few more things about thinning. You're missing way too many apples."

Mike's grin vanished. Stu climbed down and so did Mike. Kelly led them back up the row. He pointed to the crown of Stu's first tree.

"See up there on that high limb?"

Stu nodded.

"You missed most of them."

Stu saw that Kelly was right. How has he missed an entire branch?

Kelly walked across to Mike's row. He chose a low branch and pointed. Mike saw it before Kelly said a word. There were doublets, several of them, and Mike was at a loss to figure how he had missed so many obvious clusters.

"Gotta get them off there, Mike. Otherwise I'm going to have a shitty crop come September."

"Yes Sir, Mr. Kelly," Mike said glumly.

Kelly hooked his thumbs in the pockets of his jeans and looked mildly disgusted. Finally he said, "I'll have a couple of my Mexicans come up here and work with you boys today. Go ahead and take a half-hour break. I'll send Pedro and Martin on the tractor. You do what they say. Those fellas are the best-darned help I have. I wish I had more of them." And with that pronouncement he marched back to his jeep and shot off down the hill.

"Aw, darn it," Mike said. "That's all we need is a couple of Mexicans ordering us around."

"I don't see what's wrong with that," Stu countered. "If Mr. Kelly says they know what to do, I guess they can show us just as well as anyone."

Mike eyed Stu for a moment. "I suppose," he said. "Let's have lunch while we wait. I'm starved." Mike searched around for where he had left his black metal lunch pail. He spotted it in the deep grass, went to retrieve it, and he and Stu found a dry spot in the shade of a big tree. The sun was now full up and the temperature had climbed into the 80's.

Just as the boys finished their sandwiches they heard the low growl of an engine. A John Deere tractor with cleated wheels came churning into view. Aboard were two men wearing wide-brimmed straw hats. They wore high-top leather boots and long-sleeved blue denim shirts with the cuffs rolled up to their elbows; their Levis were patched on the knees. The man gripping the steering wheel was whipcord thin, dark-skinned and with a pinched face. He looked to be in his early thirties. The other Mexican was fiftyish, with a beer gut and bandy legs. As the green-and-yellow tractor ground to a halt, the older man smiled broadly at the boys, revealing a silver tooth. He turned to his companion and there was a brief flurry of Spanish. Stu and Mike had each taken a year of Spanish in high school, but neither understood enough to make any sense of it.

The Mexicans came to a quick conclusion, fell silent, climbed off the tractor and posted up in front of Mike and Stu.

"I am Pedro," the thin one announced in a drill sergeant's voice. "This is Martin." He nodded to the man at his side. Then he pointed an accusatory finger at Mike. "Which one are you?"

"Mike."

"I will work with you. Which is your row?"

Mike pointed toward the nearest line of trees.

Pedro walked to the first tree, made an expert scan of the spreading branches, walked around to the other side for another quick inspection. He returned and said simply, "Come, I show what you do wrong."

Mike looked at Stu, but all he got in reply was a hopeless look: *Don't forget this job was your brilliant idea!*

Stu turned to face his Mexican partner, hoping to see a more forgiving attitude. But the easy smile had vanished. The round face stared back with cold satisfaction at the prospect of for once being the boss. "Come," Martin said briskly. He turned and grabbed Stu's ladder, slung it easily on his shoulder and strode the short distance back to the first tree in Stu's row. He pushed the ladder up and thrust it expertly between the branches so easily that no leaves fell. Stu watched with fascination and respect. Martin spun around. "Come! We work now."

Stu kicked in frustration at a clump of dirt with the toe of his tennis shoe as he walked to where Martin had already climbed to the fourth rung of the ladder, his deft hands beginning to flick effortlessly amongst the leafy branches as a near-continuous stream of small apples began to plop into the tall grass.

Chapter 7

By Saturday morning, Mike still hadn't spoke to Billy since the family meeting. Avoiding The Kid hadn't taken all that much effort. Mike was up before sunrise, worked in Kelly's orchard till mid-afternoon, and spent the balance of each day swimming or helping Stu with his paper route. So when he finally got home around 6 PM he was exhausted. Instead of joining the family for dinner, Mike would go into the kitchen, make himself a peanut-butter-and-jelly sandwich, scarf it down with a glass of milk, and head straight for his room. He might still have enough energy to read a little and listen to music on the radio, but soon he was under the sheets. Sleep was no problem.

Each evening after Billy finished dinner he would go upstairs to soak his feet in the warm Epsom Salt water. When he passed Mike's room he would often hear the quiet strains of music from KOZI radio coming from behind the closed door. Sensing his brother so close brought dark moments. But there was nothing he could do. He would catwalk past and ease shut his door. Once in his own room he could still hear the music, so he would try to bury his attention in a sci-fi paperback. Or read comics, or go through his baseball card collection. These diversions never worked. He cried a few times, pressing his face hard against his pillow so no one would hear.

On the second weekend following the Butte debacle the mood lightened a bit. That Saturday marked Billy's return to the world of a kid on summer vacation. The doctor had been correct about soaking his feet. The blistered skin had slaked off. Pink skin emerged from beneath the dead blisters, tender at first but quick to toughen. The doctor gave his okay for Billy to resume baseball.

The first Saturday in August was an early game against the Caribou League-leading team from Tonasket. The coach had called the previous evening to make sure Billy was ready to play. The team was short two players to summer colds and Billy was needed. Dad approved. Mom had ironed his pinstripe uniform and starched the collar.

He left on his bike shortly after 10 AM. A few clouds had gathered up over the mountains along the western horizon. The forecast was for a cool front with the possibility of heavy showers. But the sky overhead during the late morning was still pure blue. A light breeze ruffled the leaves; sprinklers were watering yellowing lawns; the mailman was making house-to-house deliveries.

There was another reason for Billy's excitement. *Butch Cassidy and the Sundance Kid* was showing at the Ruby Theatre. Billy planned to catch the seventy-five cent matinee performance. As Billy pedaled down Woodin Avenue, past the Ruby, sure enough, there was the poster. He slowed, confirmed that the matinee started at 1 PM.

The ball field was near the river, on the other side of town. Billy pedaled toward the field, his fielder's glove dangling from the handlebar and his black Louisville Slugger gripped in his left hand. He looked up and saw the mountain that had humbled him. The Butte loomed as a reminder that winning didn't always result in *winning*. Billy's mouth got a metallic taste and the bottoms of his feet began to itch.

"Get over it," Billy said with a cold determination. He began to whistle the theme from *The Great Escape*. How could you not feel better with the thought of Steve McQueen jumping fences on a motorcycle in open country? The darkness passed. He made it to the ball field without a single tear being shed. And in the bottom of the first inning he hammered a ball so hard over the left field fence that one of his teammates wondered aloud if it still had stitches and a cover.

Stu awoke late on the Saturday of Billy's baseball game. Every joint in his body protested as he rolled over, pushed down the blanket with his feet, and considered his options for the umpteenth time. The orchard work was getting to him; he had calluses on his hands; his face and arms were tanned so dark he was beginning to feel part Mexican. But for the umpteenth time, he realized there was nothing else for him to do; he had no plan in place, no excuse not to follow Mike's direction. And so he arrived at the same conclusion as he had for the past two weeks: he'd stick it out with Mike.

He knuckled the crusty sleepers from the corners of his eyes and plodded toward the bathroom wearing just a pair of gym shorts. His mom was snoring. She had been out till early that morning and had made it clear before she left the previous evening that she wasn't to be disturbed before noon.

In the bathroom Stu squeezed a gob of toothpaste onto his brush and glanced at the white plastic clock hung from a nail on the bathroom wall, saw it was half past nine.

As the mint flavor flooded his mouth and his joints began to limber up, Stu realized he had all of Saturday and Sunday to recover, with just his paper route to work. The luxury of so much time began to seem glorious. He started to consider the prospects for something fun.

After a quick breakfast of Cheerios, he went back to his room and grabbed his jeans, then remembered the check Mr. Kelly had given him. It was for two full weeks of work, $217.84 after taxes had been taken out. A small fortune when compared to the pay for his paper route.

Stu took the check and smoothed it out. He didn't think the supermarket would cash it on a Saturday, and wasn't sure when he'd have the opportunity to go to the Seafirst bank. So he pulled his student desk away from the wall and reached back under the drawer to where the wooden Roitan cigar box was hidden.

The Roitan box had been his secret for five years. Beginning with his first yard mowing jobs Stu had always managed to stash a little of what he earned in the box before his mom took her inevitable cut. When the coins and singles had accumulated he would go to the bank and exchange them for larger denomination bills.

Stu briefly admired the neatly rubber-banded stacks of tens and twenties. He peeked beneath one banded bunch of bills and counted the four hundred dollar bills just to make sure, before laying the check on top. Then he put the box back underneath the desk and carefully pushed the desk back against the wall.

It was just a short walk to Mike's house and Stu decided against taking his bike. So he strolled along the street on the sidewalk, carefully stepping over cracks in the white concrete. It took just three minutes to reach the Ward house.

Before the family meeting, Stu would have simply pushed open the front door and gone in and found Mike. That luxury was now lost. Stu had taken to knocking.

In a few seconds he heard footsteps and then the door swung open. "Hello, Stuart," Colleen said. She pushed at the screen door and the hinges squealed in tiny protest. Stu caught the handle and pulled it open. His best friend's mom looked at him for a long moment. It gave Stu the creeps. Finally he said, "Good morning, Mrs. Ward," and the tension eased with the warmth of her smile.

"Are you looking for Mike?"

"Yes, Ma'am."

"I think he's still asleep up in his room. Would you like me to wake him?"

Mike was likely as beat up as Stu from the week of work. Stu said, "No, Ma'am. I should let him sleep."

A thoughtful look shadowed Colleen's face. "You drink coffee, don't you Stuart?"

"Yes, Ma'am."

"I've got a fresh pot brewed up in the kitchen. Why don't you come in and have a cup with me. And in a few minutes I'll take a cup up to Mike. I'm sure he'll want to know you're here."

"That's okay——"

"No, I'm sure he'd want to know you've come over, Stuart." And she turned and walked into the hallway that led to the kitchen. There was no way for Stu to get out of it, so he followed her inside, trapped by the uncertainty of this unexpected offer.

As he entered the kitchen the first thing Stu saw was that no dishes littered the counter or the sink. You clean a few thousand plates and forks and spoons over a young lifetime and you come to appreciate something like that. He almost commented on how clean the kitchen was, and then remembered this was how Colleen Ward's kitchen always was: spotless. He watched her lift the Pyrex pot from the automatic coffee maker and pour a brownstone mug full.

"Sugar or milk?"

"No, Ma'am."

She handed Stu the mug, poured herself a cup, putting one neat teaspoon of sugar in and stirring it precisely. She took a sip and her eyes came up over the brim of the mug to find Stu standing like a stone.

Stu nervously took a sip, thought to make a comment about how good the coffee was, but was scared his voice might break.

Colleen finally got around to what was on her mind.

"Stuart . . . how's Mike doing? He's stopped talking to his father and me. And we're a little worried."

Stu had a brief thought that his own mom never talked to him so direct. It made Stu feel honored. And that in turn made him want to be honest. Only, he wasn't quite sure how to reply.

Finally, Stu said, "I think he's okay, Mrs. Ward. I mean he's bummed about the hike and all. And he's still mad at Billy. But I think he'll get over it. Probably before he goes off to college."

Colleen looked relieved.

"Thank you, Stuart. You're a good—" she almost said *kid*, but instead finished with, "—young man."

The cup in Stu's hands seemed to double in weight. Grownups didn't call him that. Except maybe for Charley. But when Charley said Stu was ready for a *man's habits* that was different. Stu wasn't sure why. But it was.

"I think I'll take Mike his coffee now," Colleen said, reaching for a clean mug.

As she left, Stu wondered what his life would have been like if he'd had a mom like Colleen Ward. But as quick as the thought came, it was overridden by a thought far more realistic: *Life ain't perfect.*

In a small town like Chelan people quickly notice anything new, and gossip about it at the post office and the barbershop and most certainly at Meg's Beauty Salon. The topics of interest are endless. A juicy affair, first-year-teachers, what the fruit sheds are paying on year-end pools, the latest model of Ford pickup or Town and Country station wagon, all of these bring out the gab fest.

The current speculation concerned a poster that had recently gone up in the window of the vacated Valley Realty office. It read: *Your flag, your future. Join the U.S. ARMY.* The semi-gloss poster featured a handsome soldier with a James Dean chin and John Wayne's eyes, wearing a helmet cocked at a stylish angle. The blue-and-stars of an American flag waived above his right shoulder.

The final element of *The Show* (as locals had begun to refer to the recruiting office) was a pretty young woman in a crisp uniform positioned directly in the middle of the reception area behind a small desk. Comments from both women and men centered on the young woman's long legs, amply revealed by her short Army skirt.

As Billy breezed down Woodin Avenue on his bike, he looked through the expanse of sheet glass in the old realty building and saw the young woman in her Army outfit. She caught his glance and flashed him a smile. *A sucker smile* thought Billy. The sharp uniform, a hot chick, a cool poster; all of it designed to get a kid fresh out of high school to enlist.

Billy looked away and continued up the street. When he reached the Ruby it was still half an hour before the show. There was a bike rack a ways down the sidewalk from the theater and Billy pushed the front wheel into one of its vertical-barred slots. He walked up the sidewalk to the ticket window at the front of the theatre and laid three quarters on the gray swirled marble ledge. Old Man Trask, his thinning black hair greased flat against his skull, shoved an orange ticket across. Billy grabbed the ticket and tucked it into the pocket of his jeans.

Billy walked back to his bike and pulled off the Wilson fielder's glove and grabbed his bat. He carried both further down the block to the Kier dime store. The Kier stood next door to Meg's Beauty Parlor. The red brick Kier had two wide plate glass windows and behind them in this particular week were spread a collection of stamped-metal toy tops and a red Bakelite dish set.

He pushed open the door and his nostrils were flooded with the scents of boxed-up penny candy that covered most of the broad wooden counter fronting the register. There were watermelon strips, sour twists, malted milk balls, flat-strip taffy, jaw breakers, red and black licorice whips, sour balls, Pez, baseball card bubblegum packs, and Bazooka bubblegum. And plenty of other hard candies and a row of candy bars at the back.

Beyond that front counter, the long aisles that ran the length of the store were topped by showcases divided into neat rectangles by thick glass plates. Inside these bins were the cheapo quarter-to-dollar toys, usually with MADE IN JAPAN stamped in tiny print in the tin or molded plastic. Wind-up cars, hand buzzers, pump-tops that threw sparks, cap guns, toy soldiers, knights, spacemen, harmonicas, Silly Putty in colored plastic eggs, a true menagerie where a kid might spend an hour before making a choice.

As Billy entered he saw Mollie Cruikshank, who was roughly seventy million years old, standing sentinel at the front counter. She wore a plain blue cotton dress that brushed the tops of her black loafers. Her white blouse had black buttons and her hair was pulled back in a librarian's bun.

Mollie was watching two boys—the Carmichael brothers, who were known troublemakers—on the overhead mirrors, when Billy walked in through the door.

"Billy Ward!" she exclaimed the instant she saw him, forgetting the Carmichaels.

Mollie's attention always bugged Billy, but less and less as he got older. Mollie was a church friend of his parents. She had no children, and so she tended to go a bit overboard with other people's kids—that is if she liked them. There was a good side to it. Billy had lost count of the number of times he'd discovered that Mollie had slipped in an extra jawbreaker or a bonus piece of sour apple bubble gum into his candy sack.

"Hi Mrs. Cruikshank," he answered politely. "I'm going to the matinee and I was wondering if you could watch my bat and glove." Billy would have preferred to take the bat and glove into the movie house. But last summer a kid had done just that and a fight had broken out and another kid had picked up the bat and busted up the bat-owner's head pretty bad. So Old Man Trask had forbid anything coming inside the Ruby that even remotely resembled a weapon. Why Trask thought a baseball glove was also a weapon was anyone's guess, but rules were rules.

"Of course, Billy," Mollie replied, eyes bright as her smile spread and deepened into the field of wrinkles that were her face. "I'll put them up behind the counter." She reached and took the bat and fielder's glove and laid them on a shelf directly underneath the register. "There," she said, "that will keep them safe and sound."

"Thanks, Mrs. Cruikshank."

Mollie beamed. And Billy knew that if he were any closer she might reach to tousle his hair or pat his cheek. Totally gross stuff coming from someone as old as the dinosaurs—and not the plastic ones that were on the back shelves—we're talking real live dinosaurs, Jurassic Period at the minimum.

"Such a nice boy."

"Thank you, Ma'am."

"What's playing at the theatre?"

"It's the Butch Cassidy movie."

"Oh really!"

Billy groaned inwardly. Why did she have to reduce everything to a drama? But he tried hard to remember what Mom said about times like this: *A boy can always be a little more charming.* So with a bit of self control Billy's face showed no hint of anything other than appreciation for her attention. He now remembered that the theatre charged way too much for soda, and he was still thirsty from the baseball game.

"Could I please have a bottle of Coke?"

"Of course." Mollie turned to the small refrigerator at the end of the counter and pulled the door, took out a green glass bottle, handed it to Billy. He handed her a dime and a nickel, and Mollie grabbed a bottle opener which hung on a nail beside the cold case.

"No thanks, Mrs. Cruikshank. I want to save it for inside the theatre."

"Don't forget to bring it back for a two-cent deposit refund."

"Yes, Ma'am." As if any fourteen-year-old would forget something that basic! Two cents was, after all, *two cents*. Or to put it in real terms, it was a grape Tootsie Pop. Or two pieces of coconut strip. Billy turned for the door.

"Would you like to try our new bubble gum?"

Billy paused, the previous moment's embarrassment entirely forgotten. He turned back to Mollie. "There's a new gum?"

"Hot cherry," Mollie said, her eyes mischievous and conspiratorial as she handing him a dark red gumball.

"Thank you." Billy popped it in his mouth and instantly discovered why it was called *hot* cherry. As he crunched down the liquid center burst across his tongue like molten lava. His lips felt like they might burn right off.

Mollie asked, "Is it too hot?" And for just a moment Billy wasn't sure whether she was genuinely concerned, or secretly enjoying his pain. He decided she couldn't possibly be that evil; not with all that smiling.

"No," Billy mumbled through lips on fire. "It's great." He backed towards the door, hoping his expression didn't betray the agony he was in.

Out on the street he found the first garbage can and looked back to make sure Mollie wasn't watching and then spat the gum out.

Now all he needed was a center seat in the third row. The town's pillar clock on the corner showed the movie started in two minutes. *Time to get inside!* But as he looked in the direction of the theatre a quarter-of-a-block up the sidewalk he saw the worst possible thing on the planet, maybe in the entire universe.

Mike and Stu were buying tickets at the window.

Billy froze. Neither Mike nor Stu appeared to see him. So Billy did an about-face and headed back toward the dime store. When he reached the Kier he glanced back up the sidewalk. Mike and Stu had disappeared inside the Ruby.

He reached into his pants pocket. His fingers curled around the ticket. Old Man Trask had a hard policy on tickets. Once bought, you either used it, or you lost it. There were no refunds. Each ticket was stamped with the date and the time of the show it had been purchased for.

Seventy-five cents.

With this thought came another—of Mike and Stu coming up behind him in the dark and dumping a cold soda down the back of his shirt. Or worse.

Billy crept cautiously back up the sidewalk until he was standing just far enough away from the theatre so he couldn't be seen from inside. The tease of freshly buttered popcorn wafted on the cool air flowing from inside, where

Missy Baker, sixteen years old and wearing a red and white striped blouse, was dumping a fresh load of white puffs from the roaster into the glassed case.

Billy's resentment grew. Why throw away a big chunk of his allowance on the off chance that the older boys might give him a hard time? And what could they do in a theatre full of people? Really?

Heat waves danced in the street. Inside the theatre it was cool. And dark.

Billy pictured the inside of the theatre—the crimson carpet, the green vinyl seats in curved rows, the narrow balconies. He knew where Mike and Stu would be. They always sat in the right balcony, in the two front seats. If he were to sit at the back, underneath the balcony overhang, there was no way they would ever see him. Not in the dark.

A plan formed. He would sneak in and go straight to the left at the very back. By the time Mike and Stu came out at the end of the movie Billy would be long gone up the sidewalk, out of sight.

Billy checked the clock across the street. It was already five minutes past three! The preview for next week's movie would have already run. Billy was missing the start of his movie! He edged toward the main door, where Trask sat behind the ticket window, his spectacles pinched down on his nose as he counted change.

Trask looked up and spied Billy. He leaned forward until his mouth was nearly pressed to the chromed grill in the thick glass. In the loudest voice possible the old buzzard shouted, "Hey Kid, better get inside! The movie's starting!"

Billy pushed on the door and fled past Trask, whose head was again bent back down to his counting. Billy entered the magical realm of popcorn and butter and the musky odor from the maroon carpet that had suffered countless spilled cokes. With relief he saw that the lobby was empty.

Billy pushed through the heavy green velvet curtains and saw people seated toward the front but no one in the last four rows. He slid into an empty seat along the back wall. Safe!

Onscreen a cool-looking dude, whom Billy assumed must be that new actor Robert Redford, was playing poker in a saloon with three tough hombres. After a few seconds the meanest of the three observed that Redford must one helluva poker player, because the hombre was a helluva poker player, and the only thing he couldn't figure out was how Redford was cheating. And then things got tense, real fast.

Billy forgot about Mike and Stu, who were likely no more than thirty feet above and to the right. He took out his Boy Scout knife and used the bottle opener to prong off the Coke's bottle cap. He took a long swig, burped, and settled in.

Later on there was a really terrific chase scene. After Butch and Sundance finally lost the super posse there was a gushy scene and then it was morning and Butch was riding Emma around on a bicycle to the tune of Burt Bacharach's *Raindrops Keep Falling on My Head*.

By now the Coke had run through him like mercury and Billy needed to pee. The gushy part was perfect for a break.

He got up and poked his head through the curtains, saw the lobby was empty, and stepped out and quickly climbed the stairs. Nearing the top he took a cautious peek around but no one was near the door to the men's room. Billy looked across the balcony and thought he saw the outlines of two heads, where Mike and Stu always sat. So he pushed through the door into the bathroom.

And there was Stu, standing at the urinal, doing his business.

Stu glanced to see who had come in and his eyes locked with Billy's for just a second before he returned his focus to the urinal, his face frozen in neutral.

Billy's first thought was to run, even though he now needed to pee worse than ever. He stood in the open doorway until Stu finally said, "Better close it before someone comes along and sees me." And then, "The stall's open."

There was a toilet stall in the corner made of white-painted plywood, with a black metal pull handle and a hook latch on the inside.

Not fully understanding why he didn't just cut and run, Billy let the door close behind him. He brushed past Stu and pushed the flimsy plywood door and entered the stall. Billy slid the latch into the eye screw. He unbuckled his belt, cleared his drawers, and sat down. And discovered that no matter how hard he tried, his bladder refused to do the business. So he just sat there, feeling incredibly stupid, listening as Stu finished his business, zipped up, and washed briefly in the sink. There were no towels in the Ruby's bathrooms and Billy heard Stu wiping his hands on his jeans. And then the restroom door opened and thumped shut.

Billy was about to get up and head for the theatre exit when his bladder suddenly decided to cooperate. And once started, it proved impossible to stop. Billy sat on the stool feeling helpless, expecting Mike and Stu to burst back into the bathroom at any second. It would only take a few seconds for Stu to walk back to the front of the balcony. And it took Billy nearly a full minute until he was done. But in all of that time, no one came into the bathroom.

They're waiting for me outside.

Billy pulled up his pants and buckled his belt and went out and washed in the sink, carefully wiped his hands on his jeans, and stood undecided. Surely Stu and Mike waited in the darkness. But after two minutes Billy decided he had to leave; he couldn't stay in the bathroom all night. Eventually, Stu and Mike would come to look for him. And he probably stood a better chance outside of the bathroom's small confines.

Billy pushed the door slowly and looked through the widening crack. Nothing. Neither of the older boys stood outside. His eyes were dilated from the bathroom light and he couldn't make out if anyone was still seated at the end of the far balcony.

They're downstairs. Or waiting for me out on the sidewalk.

If Mike and Stu were outside then he could come back inside. And if Mike and Stu hung around following the movie, he could ask Old Man Trask if he could wait inside a little while longer, maybe even call Dad on the phone. Or, he could break and run for the Kier and Mollie's protection. But when Billy finally worked up the courage to push the exit door onto main street and step out onto the hot sidewalk neither Mike nor Stu were in sight.

Relieved, but disappointed about missing the rest of what had been a really great flick, Billy retrieved his bike from the rack and pushed it slowly down the sidewalk towards the Kier Drug to pick up his bat and glove.

Chapter 8

Stu awoke on Sunday morning to the rolling thud of thunder. He bent his legs and frog-kicked the single sheet from his body and rolled out of bed. Standing in his jockey shorts in front of the thin blue curtain facing his bedroom window he was momentarily blinded by lightning. His shadow limed against the faded blue of the wall behind. A massive boom rattled the window-panes and shook the walls.

"Cool," Stu whispered. He grabbed his jeans heaped at the foot of his bed and yanked them on.

In the hallway he passed his mother's bedroom and pressed his ear against the dark mahogany door. A reassuring snore came from within. He continued down the hallway as the flush of excitement grew.

Outside on the porch he stood in his bare feet on the rough cement, a warm downdraft from the storm pressing against his face and chest. A massive thunderhead towered in the center of the valley. Fat raindrops splattered the lawn, and out in the street they spotted the faded blacktop.

Stu walked out into the yard and his nostrils flared as he smelled the ozone tang in the air. He raised his arms and turned in a slow pirouette, face up to the heavens. To someone who might have happened to come driving down the street at that moment Stu would have looked like one of the pilgrims at the summer Baptist tent revival on the Mills homestead near the edge of town. But Stu's worship was not religious, it was purely elemental, a reverie of nature. He closed his eyes as the freshening rain beat down against his skin.

The sky grew dark and the street lamps began to come on, as if the town were awakening at the beckoning of the storm.

The rain began to pelt down with increasing intensity and soaked his hair; rivulets ran down his bare shoulders and arms and back. Stu connected to earth and wind and sky in a ritual as ancient as mankind.

Super cool!

A great lightning bolt fractured the face of the thunderhead and sizzled tendrils through the scalloped underside. The red afterimage painted a spider web on Stu's retinas as the rip of raw electricity tore through the air.

Stu spun faster.

The ozone was now overlaid by scents of sage and grass. A freight-train thunderclap tumbled across the valley. Stu twirled faster, stepping off the lawn and out into the street. The rain had by now soaked his jeans, which clung against his thighs. His brown hair was plastered against his scalp in wet chunks.

The street gutters began to overflow. Tree branches bowed low under the weight of the water. Flowerbeds laid down as the sky burst like a rising tide.

A sudden cold downdraft shivered gooseflesh on Stu's bare skin. He felt the sting of an ice pellet. Within seconds the street became a crazy tango of ice marbles dancing across the asphalt.

A large hailstone struck his nose.

"Ouch!" Stu yelled. He turned for the safety of the porch, but as he ran he slipped on an oil patch where the neighbor's Chevy usually was parked. His feet shot out from under him and Stu went down. The back of his head struck the pavement with a solid thud and the world blurred for a few seconds.

A fresh bolt of lightning lit up the sky almost close enough to reach out and touch. It blinded him for a moment. As his vision returned Stu saw little stars and heard a ringing in his ears. His skin was alive with the tingle of electricity. He heard the boom of an exploding power transformer that took a direct hit on the lakeshore road. The thunder pressed his body with an invisible weight.

Stu rolled onto his knees and reached for the back of his head and felt a stickiness. A throbbing pain stitched up in his neck. He pulled his hand away to see how much he was bleeding but the rain mingled with ice pelted away the blood. He put the tips of his fingers to his lips and tasted iron and salt.

The front porch was barely visible through a white curtain of hail. And for the first time Stu felt fear.

Another bolt crashed and the main fork zigzagged and struck an oak half a block up the street. Chunks of burning wood exploded in all directions. A great branch split away from the trunk and crashed onto a parked Buick and totally smashed the hood. The perfume of hardwood smoke came swirling on the wind.

Stu struggled to his feet. That last lightning bolt had been scary close. The next strike might find him and *shish kebab* would be all she wrote for the late great Stuart Johnson.

With his head down and his arms up to shield against the hail barrage Stu stumbled across the street and the yard and finally made it to the safety of the porch. He pushed open the front door and his feet slipped once more, this time on the linoleum. This fall was easier than in the street. He only bruised his elbows as he thumped onto his butt.

"Yowwww!"

Stu took account of this new argument lost to gravity, discovered he was more-or-less okay, and then, he began to giggle. It was suddenly just so . . . funny. The giggle burst into laughter. It drove deep from his gut and seemed to make everything that had happened okay.

When the laughter finally passed Stu got slowly onto his knees and stood with mild agony from his new bruises and walked down the hallway, past his mother's still-closed bedroom door, and into the bathroom, where he peeled off his jeans and shorts and climbed into a hot shower that never felt so good in all his life.

Billy watched the storm out his bedroom window and followed its progress until the strikes ended and the massive thunderhead drifted up lake towards Stormy Mountain and Slide Ridge. There wasn't much else to do but watch the storm. Television reception was crummy during storms. Chelan was served by a series of reflectors arrayed around the valley, and when the lightning came it royally messed up the three Spokane channels, crowding the screen with snow so thick you could barely see the faces. It being summer break, there wasn't even homework to escape to. But the storm was entertainment enough.

Billy remembered reading somewhere, maybe it was the *Scientific American*, or more probably *Reader's Digest*, that at any one moment there were thousands of lighting bolts pummeling the Earth. Their power was greater than all of the electricity mankind created with its dams and coal plants and even the nuclear power stations.

He had also read that the Earth was a giant motor, with the North and South Poles forming the armature and the Van Allen Radiation Belts and the Aurora Borealis and the lightning storms and all kinds of other nifty effects just part of the package. But it was hard to make a comparison between the Earth as a motor and his nasty tangle with electricity from the football-sized motor he'd salvaged at the dump from a discarded washing machine, with its cast iron casing and bright copper wire wound tight around the leaves of the inner core.

Billy had made the mistake of hooking up the motor with a ratty old extension cord he'd found in the shop. He learned a fast lesson about electricity when he held the motor steady with one hand and plugged the cord into a socket with the other. The shock had knocked him onto the floor and shorted the main fuse in the breaker box on the side of the house, which was fortunate because it cut off the power that might have gone on to electrocute him.

Dad later explained the concept of grounding, after he heard of the incident from Mom (who'd come running upstairs the minute every light in the house went out, cursing under her breath—it was quite unusual for Mom to curse at anything—because she'd seen Billy lugging the motor up the stairs and should have guessed what he intended to do).

"The electricity has to have somewhere to go, Billy," Dad patiently explained, examining the motor in Billy's room, whose armature windings had been fused and blackened. "If you don't complete the circuit with a wire that allows the current to reach the ground, the electricity searches for another pathway to travel. And that, Billy, was *through you*." Dad chuckled. Laughter was a signal that told Billy it was okay what he'd done. He would certainly ask Dad the next time he experimented with something that was maybe dangerous; there would be no punishment for his curiosity. Hank knew this too, as his own father had taught him in a similar way, except the example he remembered was how close you could stand to a mule without being in danger of getting kicked.

Not very close!

Dad examined the motor. "Fried," he concluded, fingering the fused copper. "When you find another, let me help you connect it up right."

Mom, who was standing nearby, frowned at this suggestion. But when it came to motors and electricity, or tools or anything mechanical, she knew the boss was the man who knelt beside Billy's bed, examining and explaining.

Billy's thoughts were pulled from this reverie by the sight of Stu pedaling fast up the street and turning into the front yard. The hail had already melted under the warm rain. A low cloudbank had swept in and settled against the hills; a thin drizzle now fell across the valley.

Stu's Yankee's cap was pulled down tight and the bill hooded off the fine rain. He dumped the ten-speed onto the wet grass and sprinted toward the front door. Billy heard the distant ring of the doorbell. The door to Mike's room thumped open.

"I'll get it!" Mike hollered. Billy listened as Mike's heavy footsteps descend into to the living room, the whoosh of the front door opening, the excited voices as the older boys climbed the stairs.

Billy's door was open just a crack. He reached and switched off his room light and eased the door open a little further, two inches, and stood back so he was out of sight. Mike and Stu tromped down the hall oblivious to Billy's presence. Stu was talking mile-a-minute. Mike interrupted and there was deep skepticism in his voice.

"Aw, come on! You're making this all up."

Billy moved closer to the narrow gap and held his breath.

"I'm telling you Mike, a bolt of lightning knocked me flat on my butt in the middle of the street!"

"So how come you're still alive?"

There was a longish pause before an answer came. Billy thought Stu must be exaggerating. He wanted to push open the door and see what Stu looked like. Was his hair burned? Did it stick out straight? Had the lightning given Stu an instant tan?

"Well, it didn't actually hit me. But it came so close it blew me right off my feet!" Stu regained his momentum. "It was like riding the tip of a bullwhip when it cracks! And then the air smelled like burning metal and next thing I know I'm looking straight up at the hail pounding down in my face, flat on my keester. Honest, Mike!"

Now it was Mike's turn to ponder. "Hmmmmm." He sounded like Mrs. Wise in Botany when she had discovered that John Fritch had inked his girl-friend's name onto the largest goldfish in the science room's fifty gallon tank.

Mike relented. "That's a nasty bump you got on your head."

"Yeah, but it's okay. It just bled a little at first."

Billy was dying to open his door. But he knew this would be foolishness and clenched and unclenched his fists in frustration.

The voices faded into Mike's room. Billy crept closer to his door, hoping to hear.

"You sure you don't want to go see a doctor?"

"Nah! I put iodine on it. And besides, the blood stopped flowing when I took a shower. It's alright."

"Why were you running around in the rain in the first place? Have you gone loony tunes?" But Mike's voice held a measure of admiration. Mike's door thumped shut and all Billy could now hear were muffled sounds from behind the wall that separated their rooms.

Billy had tried to eavesdrop through the wall once before, when Mike and Stu were talking about their senior prom dates. He had first pressed his ear to the wallpaper. That didn't work. So he had gone and gotten a glass from the kitchen and pressed it against the wall and put his ear to it, but the house was solidly built and it was impossible to understandable what they were saying.

Billy now lay back on his bed and tried to imagine the conversation. And he tried to puzzle out why Stu had been running around out in the street during the storm. Maybe Stu really was a little crazy. But as Billy mulled it over he finally decided that if Stu was crazy it was a *good* crazy and not a *bad* crazy. It was the kind of crazy that maybe caused Stu not to tell Mike that Billy was in the men's room at the Ruby. In which case, maybe it wasn't craziness at all. Billy finally settled upon another explanation for Stu's mad dash into the street in the midst of a thunderstorm, and also for his actions at the Ruby. No one told Stu what to think or do. If he wanted to run around in the middle of the street in a thunderstorm, doggone it he'd just do it!

The more he thought about it, the more he began to like Stu.

Stu left the Ward house to do his paper route at two that afternoon. A phone call had already come in from Mr. Kelly, relayed upstairs by Colleen; the forecast was for rain all day Monday. The boys wouldn't have to work in the orchard. They had finished thinning and had moved to cutting the sucker branches from two-year-old Granny Smith saplings. It was hands-and-knees back wrenching labor and Stu was happy they weren't going to also have to do it in the mud.

Mike begged off going on the route with Stu. "My body can only take so much," he complained.

Stu pedaled to the Safeway lot and picked up the papers from Charlie, lugged them over to his house to band and put into the plastic sleeves that Charlie gave him on rainy days.

As Stu heaved the papers over his shoulder and tromped inside the house he heard a voice from the kitchen.

"Stuie?"

His mom's voice was brittle. Stu's heart sank. This tone was reserved for disasters. Or fights. He remembered it first from when he was six and one of his mom's friends had died in an auto accident. Shirley Johnson used that occasion to explain to Stu about death and how unfairly it chooses the most deserving. The way she explained it implied that Stu might be next on the list if he didn't toe the line. She had promptly gone on a three-day Hearty Gallo wine binge, stumbling to the car to drive to the liquor store and buy another jug each time she ran out. Stu cowered in his bedroom.

One of the other times was when she had lost her job as a receptionist at the veterinarian's office and had told Stu he'd have to buckle down and earn more money to help pay for food.

And then there was the day that Stu's father had come into town and contacted her but never showed up at the house. That had been three years ago, and had resulted in a lecture that rambled across a landscape including the importance of responsibility and how most men were worthless pigs and how you had to take control of your own life—Shirley had called it "owing up." Because it was darned certain nobody was going to *owe up* for you. And then she disappeared for two days. The only reason Stu hadn't called the police was because a man had called the house the next morning and told him in a clipped voice, "Your mother slept at my place last night and she'll be back at your house later," then hung up with no further explanation. But Stu didn't need an explanation. By the age of 12 he knew his mother all too well. And he was smart enough not to poke his nose into *her business*, as Shirley called everything she felt even the slightest bit of guilt about.

Now Stu lowered his load of newspapers and laid them in the hallway and with dread stepped into the kitchen.

Shirley sat at the table, thoughtfully pulling a long drag from a cigarette. The ashtray was crammed with lipstick-smudged butts smoked to the quick and filters crumpled.

"Sit down, Stuie," Shirley said flatly. Her look was chiseled and unyielding, her eyes glassy and cold.

Stu's sank onto one of the vinyl chairs. The command to sit usually came with an anger that demanded a stationary target. Something awful must have happened.

He sat like a bird dog on point, awaiting direction from its master.

"I'm ending the lease on the house, Stuie."

The news was a shock. Shirley had cursed for years about getting out of what she called "this piss-ant dirt-bag town." But Stu had always thought she lacked the gumption. He had been wrong. The resolve was clear in her voice. But if they were moving, why was she acting so dramatic? The words bunched up in his throat. He waited.

"I'm moving to L.A. to stay with my sister for a while."

Stu's first thought was that he might like L.A. Kids wouldn't know about him or his mom, at least at first. With his background unknown, he might even have a chance to be a little bit popular. And then it registered what his mom had said.

I'm moving.

And there it was. The reason for the drama. She was going to get herself gone and Stu wasn't a part of that picture.

Shirley was staring at her son, dark brows arched, lips pressed thin, waiting. A response was required. Some acknowledgment that Stu understood that any protest would be futile.

The moment hung on forever.

"Okay," Stu finally said, the word creeping from his lips. He had been edged up to a cliff with no way to fight back. He sat feeling limp, drained, certain that if he stood up he would fall over on rubber legs.

With her arms folded, staring angrily, Shirley was unwilling to accept just that single word. She glared back with an all too common demanding look on her face. She might just haul off and smack him. Stu realized the danger and steeled himself.

"When?" Stu offered humbly, fighting back tears that threatened to cloud his vision. His body was trembling.

"The end of August," Shirley replied brightly, as if she deserved a fat gold star for her bigheartedness in giving any notice at all. Yessiree, three-plus weeks to reinvent a kid's life. Awfully generous indeed.

Stu desperately wanted tears. But not with his mother sitting there. That would bring retribution. And it might also cause a complete disintegration of whatever remained of their relationship. For in his heart Stu still had a small hard kernel of hope. He sat statute-like as Shirley's attitude shifted to *let's get this over and done with and don't give me any guff.* But she, too, was momentarily lost for words. The awkwardness of the confrontation ballooned. Shirley took a hurried puff from her cigarette, blew the smoke furiously over Stu's head.

"I can't be taking care of you forever. You let me know what you want to do." But even Shirley sensed how cold it sounded. She jammed the half-smoked cigarette into the corner of her mouth and planted her hands on the table, bent forward to confront Stu.

"If you need a place to stay, Sis might let you come down for a bit."

But Stu knew it wasn't a real offer. Shirley's sister Janet was as mean a bitch as ever pulled on a pair of high heels and fishnet stockings.

Two years ago Stu had met Janet Chadwick—her married name, by a man who died mysteriously and left her a tidy insurance sum on a policy taken out shortly after they were married and six months before his body washed up on the beach at Big Sur. Janet had driven up to visit Shirley in August of 1967. When Shirley had left the house to run errands Janet had told Stu that children were the biggest mistake a woman could make. She hadn't straight-out called Stu a mistake, but it didn't take a nuclear rocket scientist to do the math.

Shirley's meaningless offer played out on Stu's face.

Shirley huffed up and crossed her arms defensively. "You let me know when you get your act figured out." And then she got up and stomped out of the kitchen.

Stu heard the front door slam, the station wagon's engine struggle to life, a screech of angled tires as Shirley pulled away from the curb.

And finally it was safe to cry.

Chapter 9

*E*very teenager in Chelan knew about the Army recruiting office. It had been open for two weeks, smack dab in the middle of town, in the vacant space formerly occupied by a real estate office that had gone bust. The flashy poster taped to the glass said the Army wanted the best and the brightest young men who realized the Army was the path to a great future.

There had been an article in the *Chelan Mirror* describing how to enlist, plus a quarter-page ad encouraging young men to come down to the temporary recruitment office for a no-obligation interview. From the way the ad read you would have thought the Army was doing teenage boys a huge favor by allowing them to enlist for a tour in Vietnam. It described beautiful beaches, and friendly Vietnamese who loved the U S of A. It painted a picture of the North Vietnamese Army as a small bunch of Commie thugs stuck somewhere out in the jungle who were mostly pinned down by American jets and bombers and helicopter gunships that were rewriting how war was fought. And after your tour of duty, which was broken up by generous R&R leaves in exotic places like Thailand and Japan, you got a fat discharge bonus and an even fatter college scholarship package. That is, if you wanted to leave at all! Many chose to reenlist, and were given big resigning bonuses and then allowed to take on-the-job training in career fields like radar, meteorology, and diesel mechanics.

Stu hadn't read the newspaper article or the advertisement. But it was impossible not to hear bits and pieces of the gossip floating around town. Deep down Stu suspected that if the Army were all that great they probably wouldn't want someone like him. But this dark thought only overlaid a much stronger suspicion that all the hoopla about how great Army life was just so much horse poop.

The weather on Monday held to a steady rain, as predicted. In a brief telephone call, Stu and Mike agreed there wasn't much use in planning anything, what with the crappy weather. Mike was going to watch TV. He invited Stu over if the rain broke later on.

Stu sat in his room for most of the morning reading *City* by Clifford D. Simak. It was a cool story about a future when robots had taken over the world and dogs had developed intelligence. Science fiction was all Stu had read since discovering the city library had a big rack of dog-eared sci-fi paperbacks packed with action heroes who went around saving the galaxy and scoring with hot babes. Stu had formed a vague plan to someday write a science fiction novel of his own. It would be about this kid who was raised by a single mom and he went to college and invented an anti-gravity drive and then he built this spaceship in shop class and flew all over the solar system and was loved by everyone except for nasty government agents who wanted to steal his gravity-drive secret. He hadn't actually written down anything. But he knew his main character would be named "Lance Johnson" and he'd wear a NY Yankees cap instead of a space helmet.

The *City* novel he was now halfway through, lying on his back in bed in his small room, also helped keep his mind off whatever was going to be the next step with his mom. She had disappeared after dropping the bomb about leaving for California. Stu didn't really care. What was the point? They would just argue. And Stu knew who would win. That was a given.

Around noon the clouds finally backed up against the mountains and began to fall apart. Rays of sunlight began arrowing into the valley. The air warmed into the seventies.

Stu got tired of reading and folded a corner of the page he was on and slid the paperback under his pillow.

He went outside and shook off the water that still clung to his ten-speed, climbed aboard, and started to pedal toward the Ward house, shifting up through first and second and third gears and finally settling into fourth. Stu was in no hurry, but he did have a growing urge to tell Mike what had happened with his mom. If Stu kept Mike in the dark for very long he'd catch a load from Mike later. But as he got close to the Ward house he realized the hurt was still too fresh to lay it on Mike.

He wouldn't be able to hold back so big a secret. It would show on his face. No way was he ready. Stu hung a right at the next intersection and headed toward downtown Chelan with no specific plan except to put off the inevitable.

He turned onto the main street, moving at a smooth cruise, alert to any possibility. And then he saw the poster—the sharp-dressed soldier with John Wayne's eyes. And through the wide plate glass he saw the attractive young woman in a uniform sitting at a desk doing paperwork.

Almost as if she had been cued, the Army woman glanced up and for a moment their eyes met. She gave Stu a brief smile. Stu was so entranced he nearly rammed his bike into a car that was backing out from diagonal parking. He recovered, circled in the middle of the street, but when he looked again she had gone back to staring down at the work on her desk.

The Army? It actually seemed to make some sense.

Stu racked his bike near the Ruby Theatre and checked the reader board for films coming soon. At the Kier Drug he surveyed the gizmos and gadgets in the display windows. He watched people walking on the opposite side of the street. He looked up and down the street and saw no one he recognized. And finally he approached the window with the Army poster.

The woman looked up again and she was even prettier from just a few feet away. She smiled. Her eyebrows invited him toward the door. Stu felt a knot in his chest. Like iron filings drawn to a magnet he reached and pulled the door open, unaware that three people noticed him enter the recruiting office.

Amanda Bagwell, wife of Reginald Bagwell who owned one of the largest apple orchards in the valley, was coming out of the sewing store when she saw Stu reach for the door handle and pull it open. She shook her head. She'd lost a brother in WWII and she hated the Army with a passion so intense it was impossible for her even to talk about it without quickly dissolving into a rage.

Ernie Fouts was walking toward his car as he glanced up, from halfway down the block, and saw Stu enter. Ernie was in his early twenties and had considered enlisting. But then he read a piece in *Time Magazine* giving a brutal appraisal of the war in Southeast Asia. Ernie decided it wasn't for him. Ernie wouldn't have known who Stu was except that Ernie had a kid brother named Tommy who was Stu's age, and Tommy had talked about Stu, whom he admired because, as Tommy put it: "The kid's cool even if his mom is a skank." Ernie, who frequented Dale's Tavern, agreed with his kid brother's appraisal of Shirley Johnson. He had once overheard her talking about her son as if the kid were a wart in a bothersome place. A *barfly*. A *skanky ho barfly*. Ernie's thought upon seeing Stu enter the recruiting office was: *Maybe some time in the Army will at least give him a fair shot at life.*

The third person to notice Stu enter the recruiting office did so from behind one of the windows fronting the darkened interior of Dale's Tavern. Shirley Johnson saw her son pull the recruiter's door wide. She took a couple of gulps from her glass of beer. A smile twisted her mouth. She swiveled all the way around on her bar stool in celebration.

Sergeant James "Jimbo" Taglieri sat in the back office listening to the hum of the overhead fluorescent bulbs and the distant shuffling of paper by Corporal Anne Jones. He could have done some of his own paperwork. He could have read the new edition of *Stars and Stripes*. But his only real desire, one that had steadily increased since early morning, was to scratch the calf of his right leg. It had itched when Jimbo drank his first cup of coffee. The sergeant would have paid a month's salary to reach down and give it a good raking with his fingernails. Trouble was, from the knee joint down the leg was fiberglass and the itch was only present in some deep crevasse of Jimbo's memory of the leg that had been blown away by a Korean mine exploding underfoot as he and his squad charged Heartbreak Ridge on a sweltering afternoon in mid-September of 1951. Now the imaginary lower part of his leg was giving him holy hell. *Too much coffee*, Jimbo reminded himself. The caffeine always set it off. But Jimbo was as much addicted to coffee as he was to the military.

Phantom pain was what the doctors called it. But Jimbo Taglieri would tell you there was nothing "phantom" about it. It was as if his leg was still there and was coated with sand and stuck in a big bucket of warm tar. If you concentrated hard enough it seemed you could move it around down inside that big gooey black mass. But nothing real ever moved.

Nothing at all.

Jimbo stared down at what remained of his right leg, at the neat crease in his regulation trousers, at the spit-n-polished black shoe leather. He glanced over and his right leg appeared no different than his left. The prosthetics were good. Both legs looked perfectly normal. He glared at the right leg with resentment and anger.

Move!

But the shoe remained still-as-stone on the worn parquet floor. An ugly thought flooded in for a moment, about what he would do to the North Korean soldier who had planted that mine if he were here in the office right now.

Something else was on Jimbo's mind this particular morning. Business had been slow since he and the delectable Corporal Ann Jones had arrived ten days ago. (Their private joke was their name for their little team: Honey and The Bee.) So far, only two boys had come in to inquire about enlisting. Neither had signed up, and Jimbo doubted either would. If something didn't fall into his lap during the next two weeks Jimmy Taglieri wouldn't make his quota. And if he zeroed out too often, the Army might decide it wasn't such a great idea having a cripple work recruitment. Trouble was, there weren't all that many Army jobs someone with a missing leg could fill. And things didn't appear to be much rosier in the civilian world.

The prospects were made even gloomier by the fact that Honey and the Bee had arrived after the school year had ended, so there were no school counselors who might have helped to single out kids whose futures weren't set upon college.

Even worse, it was several months before the next draft lottery. The pressure was gone for kids with numbers high enough for exemption, and low-numbered kids had already entered basic training or obtained college deferments.

So when Jimbo heard the front door whoosh open he was at once hopeful and distracted from his imaginary itch. He heard a boy's voice, respectful but nervous.

Within a few seconds Corporal Jones knocked lightly on his door.

"Come." Jimbo sounded upbeat and happy.

In walked a teenage boy. He was a hand's width taller than the Corporal. Five foot ten. Short dark brown wavy hair. A wiry body, tanned skin and a slim nose.

This one should have no trouble finding girlfriends.

"Sergeant Taglieri," Corporal Jones announced. "This is Stuart Johnson. He has some questions about the Army." And Honey faded back to let Bee do what he did best.

Jimbo extended his hand without standing up. He'd learned that it scared kids when they saw right off that he had been injured. So he had invented a little show, leaning forward in his chair as if the informality was meant to make the interview as comfortable as possible.

"Sergeant James Taglieri," he said warmly as he shook Stu's hand. "My friends call me Jimmy. Do you mind if I call you Stu?" He gestured toward the single chair, across the desk, and the boy sat.

This wasn't what Stu had expected. This guy actually seemed, well, he seemed normal, a nice guy. "Sure, you can call me Stu," Stu said. "It's my name."

Taglieri chuckled.

Stu felt even more at ease. He looked at the small black plastic name badge, white lettering, pinned above the right pocket of the man's uniform. *Sgt. Taglieri.*

A handshake just right, not too firm. Friendly. Alright. Even cool. *Jeez, who woulda thought?*

"So you're thinking of joining the Army, Stu?"

"Kinda," Stu replied. "I'm not real sure about it." In fact, the reason Stu was now giving serious thought to joining the Army was the vast uncertainty of what his life would be like if he didn't do something to find a job before summer ended and Mike went off the college and Stu's mom exited for California and Stu didn't have a place to live or a way to support himself other than the contents of the Roi Tan box.

Jimbo continued his pitch with a practiced calm.

"No need to get up tight about being here. Most young men who come in through that door eventually decide the Army isn't right for them. I've sent more than a few away, if I thought they weren't a good match for us. Or, if I didn't think they would make the grade. I talk to dozens of boys just like you,

Stu, every month, and only a few are chosen." Stu appeared to relax just a little, and Jimbo motored on with the soft-pitch of a veteran bible salesman.

"You got a high number in the draft, right?" It was a safe bet. Otherwise, this kid would already be in boot camp.

To Stu it seemed like mind reading. He nodded in agreement.

"So there's no pressure, right?"

"No, I guess not." Stu began to feel downright comfortable. The Sergeant was right. He could walk out of here anytime he wanted, no obligations.

Taglieri made his pitch.

"You're what we call the *real deal*, Stu. Because young men like you, who have the choice to sign up, who aren't being forced by having been drafted, always wind up being our best soldiers." Taglieri's smile held uneven teeth that were yellowed by nicotine. But there was a real quality to the smile that Stu liked.

Jimbo continued softly. "You know what else, Stu?"

"What?"

"Guys like you get special consideration when it comes to training. Kids that get drafted get sent wherever they're needed. But the *real deals* . . . they get the choices. Most get high-end technical training. They become radar technicians, communications specialists; heck, some of them even make it into officers' training. The last time *real deals* fire a rifle is usually at the end of their basic training."

Jimbo watched Stu's face brighten. His breathing had slowed. His pupils had lost the dilation. *Time for another nail in the proverbial coffin. But don't hurry it!*

"Would you like a cup of coffee, Stu?"

"Yeah. Sure."

"Great." Another easy smile. Jimbo would have liked to put an arm around the kid, an act of brotherhood. But that would come later, after the kid had inked his name at the bottom of the form. First, there was one final hurdle to clear.

Jimbo stood up, carefully, and walked around the desk. And his limp was noticeable. Jimmy Taglieri had learned this most important lesson: at some point you have to let a kid see that there is something wrong with the leg. If you keep that secret until the very last, the trust you worked so hard to establish will vanish in an instant. So you wait for the precise moment when they feel most at ease, when they feel in control of the situation. Play it just right and a kid will believe practically anything. Because you are their friend, right? And they want to be generous, understanding, to behave like *The Big Man.*

So Jimbo stood and came around the desk. Stu saw the limp. And Taglieri didn't wait for the question.

"Korea," he said matter-of-factly as he followed Stu's eyes to the leg. "Bullitt ricocheted off a rock and nipped me pretty good." He smiled wide. "All healed now except for a little scar tissue that barely slows me down." A smile.

Jimbo watched carefully. Stu's expression remained calm, like it was no big deal, really no big deal at all. And Jimbo knew that Stu assumed there was still a real leg below the knee.

Because he wants to believe.

"Is there any pain?" Stu asked hesitantly. It was said out of polite curiosity. People always asked because they wanted to *believe* there was no pain.

"Nah," Taglieri replied, sounding a bit surprised. "It can get a bit stiff when the weather changes." He laughed and Stu smiled with relief. "When I'm back on the base at Tacoma I get massages from a Swedish masseuse at the rec center."

"Really?"

"Yes." Taglieri winked. "The Army has masseuses, Stu. One of our best kept secrets!" He walked to the door, careful to keep his gait even, careful not to bang the fiberglass prosthesis on the corner of the desk. He had done that once, after giving a kid the hocus pocus, and the kid had realized the enormity of the lie and had bolted from the office. That had been down in Ellensburg, and no one else had come through the doorway of the recruitment office for three full weeks.

Taglieri successfully negotiated the desk. He opened the door and called out, "Corporal, two coffees please." He glanced back at Stu. "Cream or sugar?"

"No thanks."

"Both black," Taglieri hollered. He left the door open and returned to his chair, sat down with apparent ease. It wasn't going to be such a bad day after all.

Near dinnertime Mike was lying on his bed, reading a biography of Babe Ruth. His window and door were open and a cool breeze teased at the curtains. The sound of the phone ringing drifted up from the living room. He paid it no attention. And then his mother's voice called out.

"Mike! It's for you!"

He rolled off the bed. When he got downstairs his mother's face was filled with joy and pride. "It's Coach Rollins." She handed him the phone and was still beaming as she walked back toward the kitchen.

Jim Rollins was the football coach at the University of Washington. He ran one of the hottest programs in the country. Mike had just barely missed a football scholarship at the U.W. and been told it was a long shot for him to make the team as a walk-on. So he had enrolled at Central Washington, which had offered him a full ride. He put the handset to his ear not knowing what to expect.

"Hello?"

"Mike?"

"Yes Sir?"

"This is Jim Rollins. I've got great news for you. One of our freshman recruits decided to opt out for Southern Cal, and it leaves a spot open on the roster. I'm calling to offer you a full athletic scholarship, if you still want to be a part of our team."

Mike practically dropped the handset. Every jock in high school fantasized about playing for the state's best football team. Even if it meant moving to Seattle and life in the big city, something that niggled just a tiny bit at the back of Mike's mind. Still, here it was: his chance for glory. His response, when it finally came, was a single soft syllable.

"Wow."

"I take it that means you want to come and play for me?"

Pure enthusiasm took over.

"Yes Sir. I mean, that would be great!"

"Good. I'll send the paperwork by express mail. Practice starts August fifteenth. Welcome to the team, Son." A click from the other end of the line.

Mike wanted to shout, to jump and slap the ceiling, to run out and tell everyone that he was going to be on Washington's football team. Maybe someday he'd even get a chance to play in the Rose Bowl! And then something the coach had said brought him back to reality.

August 15th.

"Jeez," Mike mumbled to himself. "That's just two weeks away." He hadn't planned on leaving Chelan until mid-September when Central's classes got underway. Now he'd be gone almost immediately.

And then enthusiasm took over again. Of course he'd be ready! And even better, he had a legit reason to quit the orchard job! But best of all, Mike couldn't wait to tell Stu. That was what best friends were for, wasn't it? They really cared when something great happened in your life!

Chapter 10

The clouds blew out during the night and by dawn on Tuesday the orchard showed every promise of turning into a sauna long before the sun reached its zenith. Mike could have cared less because he figured these were the last painful hours he'd have to endure anything to do with apples.

As soon as Mr. Kelly dropped the boys off in the orchard Mike turned to Stu and said, "Hey, Stu."

Stu, who wasn't looking forward to another hot and muggy day, mumbled back, "Yeah?"

"I've got something to tell you."

Stu looked over at Mike funny, having heard an unexpected intensity in Mike's voice. "What?"

"I got a call yesterday from the U.W. The football coach said they've got an opening on the team for me."

Stu's eyes grew wide with amazement. "Cool!" And then his face puzzled up as he kept looking at Mike. His friend's face looked less excited than it should be. Stu's excitement derailed. "What's wrong? Is there a catch?"

"Yeah," Mike replied. "Team practice starts up on August fifteenth."

Stu did the math and his smile faded. "You mean in thirteen days from now?"

"Yeah."

"In Seattle?"

"Yeah."

"So you've got to move over there by then?"

"Exactamundo."

"Oh."

Stu stood in the middle of the orchard, with his best friend of all time, whom he had just learned he was going to lose in less than two weeks. First his mom. Now Mike. The world had gone to shit in a hand basket. His face betrayed his shock.

"You okay?" Mike asked.

Stu wanted to explain about his mom's leaving, about his uncertain future. Maybe even the possibility of enlisting in the Army. But he couldn't find the courage. Maybe later. But not now. Not here in the orchard. He wasn't going to drop a loaf on Mike's big moment.

"Yeah, I'm fine," Stu finally replied. He tried to put some enthusiasm back into his voice. "Jeez, Mike. That's great!" And for the most part Stu succeeded.

"Yeah," Mike echoed in agreement. "But that doesn't leave much summer, does it?"

"Nah, I guess not."

They settled into uneasy silence. Overhead a single tiny white puffy cloud drifted westerly above Slide Ridge, limed by the rising sun. Stu watched as it sailed two thousand feet over the ridge top. He felt numb.

Mike saw Stu's reaction and realized just how big of a big bomb he had dropped. He had to make up for it. Somehow. Stu might have joined him at Central in a year or so, something Mike had hoped for. But the U.W. was beyond Stu's grades and what he could ever possibly afford.

"Know what?" Mike said.

"What?"

"We ought to do an adventure before I go. If we quit the orchard today we've still got plenty of time to do something *big*."

"Like what?" Stu was too mired in his dismal future to have any ideas or enthusiasm for an adventure.

"Let's go on the hike!"

Stu gave Mike a *get serious* look. "What about Billy?"

Mike said with amusement, "Well, we can't kill him!"

Stu gave a sour laugh.

"And Dad would never let me forget it if we just took off on our own."

Stu nodded in agreement, clueless to where this was headed.

Mike said offhandedly, "So I guess we'll just have to drag him along."

It would have been hard to tell which of the boys this surprised more. Stu, because Mike had been so insistent upon excluding Billy. Mike, because he hadn't really made the decision until the very instant he said it. It just popped out. But now that it had been said Mike wasn't the kind who went back on his decisions, even if they seemed somehow wrong. And the truth was Mike had already begun to reconsider his relationship with his little brother. An unexpected need had spiraled up. Mike found himself wanting his little brother to be proud of him. He'd made it onto the best football team in the state, heck, the best team in the Pacific Northwest. One of the top programs in the country. How many times had he and Billy played a game of catch with the pigskin? It seemed like a million. But not recently.

It was all Billy's fault of course. Had to be. Because otherwise, Mike would have to deal with the—

—guilt—

And that idea was troubling him at some mostly subconscious level.

So out of this growing confusion had come the spontaneous decision to take Billy along. Mike had declared that Billy would go. He already felt better about the decision, even generous.

And that was that.

Chapter 11

*S*av-Mart had everything imaginable crammed onto its shelves, piled in the aisles, and packed into the greenhouse which clung to the side of the rambling cinderblock building like a vast fiberglass blister. Rows of overhead flat-white fluorescent lights illuminated aisles filled with wrenches and refrigerators, mattresses and wheelbarrows, real ferns and plastic ferns and silk ferns, auto parts and fishing tackle, recliner chairs covered in green and brown Naugahyde and fuzzy orange and blue velour, sacks of fertilizer and sacks of birdseed. Baby toys and bicycles. Cuckoo clocks and sundials.

Mom had brought Billy and Mike to shop for the hiking trip. Billy roamed the aisles pushing a shopping cart with a bent right front wheel that wobbled and skidded on the dull yellow tile. He was still trying to figure out what had happened to change things so completely with his brother. Mike had shocked the entire family to silence at dinner when, between mouthfuls of corned beef, he nonchalantly said, "Stu and I decided we should go on the hike as soon as possible, and take Billy, of course." Hank and Colleen and Billy had exchanged looks every bit as stunned as if they'd just learned the President had been shot.

For the next few seconds the only sounds were the distant dryer turning over in the pantry, the tick-tock of the grandfather clock in the living room, and the *klink* of Mike's fork as he shoveled up another mouthful, acting as if his announcement was the obvious and natural course of things and who the heck should be surprised?

Hank Ward finally said, "Well, that's great, Son." But where in the world had this decision had come from?

They all stared at Mike.

Mike finally looked up. "What?" He asked innocently.

A nervous peace had fallen for the remainder of the meal.

Billy was so surprised that it took until the end of dinner before he dared speak a word. He kept expecting Mike to say that it was all a joke. *Hah Hah.* But it seemed more and more certain that Mike had really meant it. And then Billy's excitement began to build. As he swallowed a last bite of apple pie, in a voice both humble and uncertain he said, "Should we go shopping for stuff for the hike?"

Mom said with relief, "Good idea Billy. I'll take you and Mike and Stu down to Sav-Mart tomorrow afternoon and you can pick out what you need."

"Fine," Mike agreed. And then he excused himself with, "I've got some work to do checking the Forest Service trail map." And off he went, up the stairs, *whistling for criminey sake!* Seemingly oblivious to the impact of his announcement, although Billy knew darned well that Mike was thoroughly enjoying the moment. But that still didn't explain the complete about-face. What had changed?

Mom and Dad stared at each other. Mom looked at Billy and smiled and gave a nervous little laugh. "I guess he changed his mind."

Now, in the aisles of Sav-Mart, Billy was conflicted. He wanted to be excited. But Mike had said nothing in the car on the way down. He had given no clue about the sudden shift. Stu hadn't come shopping with them—Billy had no idea why—so he couldn't quiz Stu for details, or listen to the two older boys for telltale hints.

Billy wondered if Mike's sudden change of direction had something to do with being accepted to the UW football team. But he couldn't figure out why that had made such a difference, why it had suddenly made it okay for the older boys to take him along.

Billy turned the corner to a new aisle, fighting the wobbling front wheel as it resisted the turn, and there stood Mike. His older brother had found the hatchets. He was tossing up a black-rubber-handled chrome-plated model in shallow somersaults. Mike caught the hatchet neatly as it came down, looked up and saw Billy.

"Watch this," Mike said. He threw the hatchet toward the ceiling and it struck the acoustic tile nine feet overhead. The chrome blade glittered and spun in a wobbling blur and Billy saw the handle wouldn't be in position for a clean catch when it reached Mike's hand.

"Watch out!" Billy yelled.

Mike yanked back his hand at the last instant and the hatchet blade gouged into the tile floor, sending bits of tile skittering in all directions. Mike reached down to pick it up as the sound of a woman's shoes came clicking at high speed from the direction of the cash registers. Mike used his foot to brush the tile chips under the shelving and then moved his sneaker to cover the notch in the floor.

A chubby girl with heavy mascara, dark hair and black-rimmed glasses turned into their aisle and stopped, eyeing the brothers.

"Can I help you?" She asked in a voice that suggested something else entirely. She looked at the hatchet Mike held. Her lips pressed tight and her eyes narrowed.

Mike followed her gaze to the hatchet. "It's perfect," he said innocently. "I'll take it."

She raised one eyebrow in frustration and did an about-face and huffed back toward the front of the store.

"Whew!" Mike said. He broke into a grin. And then he turned and walked off as if Billy had never been there at all.

Billy stared at the fresh divot in the floor.

It was time to get practical. Billy went in search of the pharmacy. He found iodine and gauze and Band-Aids and a jar of Resinol and a spray can of Raid insect repellant and bee-sting salve and rolls of adhesive tape and a roll of Ace bandage. He found a snakebite kit and a book on camping injuries. Alka-Seltzer and Bayer Aspirin, antibiotic salve and Chap Stick. And three packages of Mole Skin in case his blisters reappeared.

The next stop was in the fabric department for a sewing kit. On to clothing, where he selected a nylon windbreaker, three pairs of wool socks and three pairs of cotton socks. A heavy cotton shirt and flannel boxer shorts in case it turned cold.

In the camping section he found a lightweight aluminum cook kit, a waterproof match container, wooden matches, a compass and a whistle that was advertised to scare away bears. He decided against the flare, but he bought a flexible mirror to signal search planes. There was a one-man plastic tube tent (the canvas and nylon ones were too large and heavy, and he doubted Mike or Stu would want to share a tent with him.) A three-ounce silvery space blanket. An air mattress.

On to food, where he pulled boxes of rice and raisins and pancake mix and dried syrup mix and instant soup.

Colleen Ward was on her own mission. When she had called Stuart that morning to ask if he would like to join them Stu had politely said that he needed to do something else. Colleen offered to buy what Stu needed and Stu said that wasn't necessary, he'd get his stuff later, but Colleen insisted and Stu had finally accepted and said "Thank you" three times before he hung up.

Colleen asked Hank for help, not having much of an idea what it was you took backpacking. She found him at the shop working on a carburetor at the back bench.

"Honey?" Colleen stood in the middle of the service bay. It was stifling hot and Hank had the bay doors fully open.

Sweat dappled his brow as he looked up. "Yes, Dear?"

"Stuart can't come shopping with us, so I thought I'd pick up the necessities for him. Could you please help me make a list?"

Hank laid down the Phillips screwdriver, grabbed a cloth and wiped the oil from his hands. "Sure."

Colleen held a notepad and a pencil. She waited.

"Better start with a lightweight aluminum pack frame and a canvas pack. Make sure there are plenty of side compartments and that the canvas is heavy duty." Hank thought for a second. "I remember Stu staying with us one night when they slept out on the lawn. He had a fairly good sleeping bag. But if he doesn't still have it, he can use mine. It's goose down and I wouldn't mind loaning it to him."

"What about food?"

"Dried soup mixes. Basic starches like rice and beans. They should be able to catch plenty of trout, and if they're lucky they'll find some huckleberries."

Colleen had something else on her mind. "Honey, do you think this is a good idea?"

"The hike?"

"Yes. I'm afraid Mike will punish Billy in some way."

Hank had already given this some thought, and had turned to his own childhood for insight. He had grown up with three brothers. Jimmy, four years older than Hank, had possessed the same stubbornness as Mike, and had been a tyrant at times. But he had never done anything purely mean or destructive. Hank didn't bother sharing this recollection with Colleen. But he shared his conclusions.

"It's a tough time for Mike. He's leaving home. Trying to break free from us, and to be his own man. I don't think Mike even begins to understand how big and important the process is that he's going through. But we've got to let him make his own mistakes or he'll never learn." That was the way Hank's parents had handled their boys. Hank could have recounted dozens of times when one of his brothers had done something that had seemed goofy or stupid or insensitive. But they had all grown up to be good people, all with families and stable marriages and good jobs.

Colleen remained unconvinced. "I just worry about Billy. What if Mike's carelessness gets Billy hurt?"

Hank got that funny soft look, the one that said he thought she was being too much of a mom, that she didn't really understand what boys were entirely about. But he knew better than to try and correct her. So he relented just a little.

"Would you feel better if I had a talk with Mike?"

"Do you think he'll listen?"

"He'll listen," Hank said gravely. "I'll also talk to Billy, to help him understand what his brother is going through."

"Thank you." She stepped forward and kissed Hank on the cheek, careful not to brush her blouse against his oily shop coveralls. And with this act she saw him melt. There were also a few things boys didn't understand about girls!

By the time Colleen met the boys at the checkout stand, Billy had a full cart. Mike saw Billy's collection of supplies and shook his head slowly. "We're only going to be gone five days."

Colleen also thought Billy had gone a bit overboard. "Billy," she said. "Are you going to be able to carry all of that?"

Mike added with a snort of disgust, "Maybe with a mule."

"Mike . . ." Colleen cautioned. Mike gave up on what would be a useless debate, and reviewed what he'd put in his own cart, though he was certain he had everything he needed.

Billy's hands grew warm against the push-bar of his loaded cart. "I guess maybe some of the stuff I could leave out."

"Well," Colleen said. "Let's not put anything back. I'm sure your father will help you do your packing. We can always return what you don't need."

Mike gave a snort of disgust but didn't meet Mom's reproachful look. He began to stack his purchases on the black counter.

The same clerk who had come running when Mike tossed the hatchet began to ring up Mike's selections and drop them into a large paper sack. She would occasionally glance suspiciously at the boys. Mike in particular. But she said nothing. Mike ignored her. When she finished there were five more bags and the pack frame sitting beside Mike's single large bag.

As soon as Colleen had paid the clerk, Mike grabbed his one bag and headed for the car. Billy started to say something, but Colleen stopped him with a look. "We'll take the rest out in a cart," was all she said.

Stu sat in his room, staring at the enlistment form. It had taken nearly the entire morning to work up the courage to start filling in the blanks. He had put it off at first by cleaning up his room, reorganizing his desk drawer contents, checking the cigar box beneath the desk and counting the money inside for the first time in two years. He was stunned to find the total came to $943.28.

He stared at the Roi-Tan box full of cash and coins for a while. It was reassuring; at least he wouldn't starve after his mom left. But he couldn't live on it for the rest of his life. He'd need a real job. So he finally returned to the enlistment form and began filling in the blanks.

It was noon when Stu carefully folded the completed and signed recruitment form, slipped it inside the stamped envelope, and put the unsealed envelope on top of the cash in the Roi-Tan box. He placed the box in its hiding place beneath his desk. He knew the Army would call as soon they received his application. There was no need to hurry and mail it immediately. After all, he had money to live on after his mom had gone to her sister's in California.

By the time Mike called that afternoon to ask if he wanted some help on the paper route Stu was feeling better.

That afternoon, before Hank had a chance to talk to either of his boys, he got sick with the flu. He drove home and spent ten minutes in the bathroom mostly on his knees in front of the toilet. When he finally staggered out his face was ashen white, his lips chapped, his throat raw, and he figured the worst of it was over. Maybe it hadn't been the flu after all? Maybe it was a mild case of food poisoning. But an hour later he was back in the bathroom, this time sitting on the porcelain throne. When he was finished, Colleen came at him with a thermometer.

"I must have gotten food poisoning," Hank said hopefully. It had to be the hamburger he'd snuck out for at the drive-in. They hadn't fully cooked the meat. When he'd bit into it he'd seen a ragged edge of pink. He liked the taste of raw hamburger at the center. But he'd known better than to eat it.

"Just the same, hold this under your tongue for a minute."

Hank let Colleen slide the glass thermometer under his tongue, into the soft channel where cheek joins jawbone.

When she finally pulled it out and read the mercury, she said, "One-oh-one-point-six. You don't get a fever from food poisoning."

Hank groaned. They were backed up at work, the yard needed mowing, and he was nearly finished with the carburetor he'd been tinkering with to find an extra couple of horsepower for the pickup. Food poisoning meant a quick recovery. But not a summer flu. Hank moaned in protest. "I can't be sick!"

"Of course you can, Sweetheart. And I'm going to take good care of you."

She hustled him into pajamas and set up a fan on a chair beside his bed. But he wasn't lying beneath its cooling breeze for very long. He was soon back in the bathroom where his digestive system purged itself again, this time from both ends. And when he collapsed back into bed Hank felt like a rusty nail that had been pulled from a weathered board; every joint in his body ached and his head was pounding.

He finally fell into a restless sleep and was snoring and sometimes talking a few words of nonsense from dreams. Colleen spent the night in the spare room, hoping Hank only had the 24-hour flu.

The following morning Hank couldn't keep food or liquids down. Colleen called Doc Manley.

"Keep him in bed. And if he can't keep water down by tonight you better bring him up to the hospital. We may have to start an IV to keep him hydrated."

The boys stayed away from Hank. Catching whatever he had would end the hike before it even got started.

Mike and Stu worked throughout the afternoon up in Mike's room, sorting through Mike's purchases. At one point they biked over to Safeway for Tang and powdered eggs and Bisquick to supplement the food from Sav-Mart.

Billy holed up in his bedroom and packed by himself. Mike had been right. He had bought way too much. Only half of his supplies would fit inside the pack. So he began to set aside things that didn't seem absolutely essential. The small flashlight. One pair of wool socks. The compass—they were, after all, going to on established trails, right? So what good was a compass!

Billy finally managed to cram all of what he figured to be the critical into his backpack and ended up with one extra empty side pocket. He knew just what he'd use it for on the morning of the hike. He had finally finished tying the last laces on the top flap when Colleen appeared in his doorway.

"Billy?"

"Hi Mom."

Colleen held her left hand behind her back. Obviously there was some surprise, but Billy hadn't a clue what it might be.

"How are you doing?"

"Fine. How's Dad?"

"He's pretty sick. But he's finally keeping water down, and even a little orange juice. Doc said he doesn't have to come into the hospital if he keeps improving."

Mom's hand was still behind her back and Billy's curiosity was growing by the second. What could she possibly be hiding?

"Are you all packed?"

"Yes." Billy pointed to his backpack with pride. It stood against the end of his bed, brushed aluminum frame and brown canvas buckled to thick padded straps, a canteen in a camouflage holder snapped into place, the pack's top neatly laced tight. "I left out a bunch of stuff." Billy pointed at the sizeable pile on his desk. "Mike was right. I'm sorry I bought all that extra stuff, Mom."

"That's okay, Billy. I saved the receipts so I can make returns to Sav-Mart."

Colleen finally pulled her hand from behind her back to show what she had been hiding. It was the boots Billy had worn on the Butte climb. Only they were now well-greased and there were creases in all the places where there had once been stiff new leather.

Billy hadn't even thought about the boots since Dad had taken them from his room weeks ago. He had an old pair of boots that he figured to wear on the hike. "How?" Billy said in surprise.

"You and Dad have the same shoe size. He wore them at work. And on his lunch hours he went walking. He also greased them up proper."

Colleen handed the boots to Billy. He took them and fingered the leather. It felt soft in all the right places; the creaky new-leather stiffness was completely gone.

"Your father planned to take you on a hike this fall, after Mike had gone off to school. It was going to be his surprise for you."

Billy held the boots, speechless. He wanted to run and tell Dad how much this meant. But he couldn't do that, not with Dad having the flu. Tears threatened to form in his eyes.

"Oh, Honey," Colleen said, moving to him and ruffling his hair. Billy didn't really think he liked Mom doing that. But as long as it wasn't where someone could see her doing it maybe it was okay. "Your father and I love you so much. You'll be careful, won't you?"

"I promise, Mom."

"And if Mike pushes too hard you just tell him to slow down."

"Okay, Mom." Billy doubted that would do any good. But Mom saying it somehow made him feel a little more secure.

"Remember, you can always come down and catch the ferry anywhere along the lake if the hike gets too rough."

The Lady of the Lake ferry made the round trip each day and stopped to pick up campers if they put out a signal flag at any one of the spots where trails ended along the lakeshore and where the ferry could pull up to the shoreline.

"I know, Mom. Don't worry. I'll take it easy." But Billy knew it would take a major disaster to force a split from Mike and Stu. This was a once in a lifetime event. He was no quitter.

Mom smiled and Billy saw that her eyes were now watery. She gave him a kiss on the forehead, something else Billy thought was way too gushy. But it didn't feel all that bad. Not really.

Next, Colleen checked in on Mike and Stu.

Mike had a USFS map spread wide on his bed. He and Stu were studying it when Colleen appeared in the open doorway.

"How are you boys doing?"

"Fine, Mom."

"Fine, Mrs. Ward."

Colleen saw both of their backpacks were full and propped against the wall. "Do you have everything you need?"

"Yeah," Mike said.

Stu nodded.

The boys waited patiently. Colleen knew what had to be said. Hank wasn't going to be in any kind of shape for a talk with Mike. It worried her deeply.

"Mike, I expect you to look after Billy."

"Aw, Mom——"

"I mean this, Michael!" The sharpness caught Mike by surprise. She hadn't called him by his full name since he was maybe ten or eleven. Mike felt a surge of embarrassment.

"I promise," Mike began slowly, "to look after Billy. I'm not mad at him anymore. I promise."

Colleen's grave look softened. Mike knew he'd mostly convinced her, even though he was a lot less certain than he had managed to sound. He had considered Billy's role in the hike in great detail. He hadn't shared his conclusions with Stu. Because he wasn't sure he could trust Stu, not while they were still in Chelan. Mike *was* still mad. Not nearly as mad as he had been. But mad just the same. And somehow, Billy was going to pay.

Colleen took a last look around Mike's room. "Okay," she said, seeming satisfied. She went out into the hallway. The boys listened until her footsteps were gone.

Stu looked skeptically at Mike. "You sure you're not mad at him?"

Mike dismissed the question with a shake of his head. "C'mon," Mike said. "Let's check the route one more time before we turn in."

Stu let it go. This was his best friend. Right? What more needed to be said!

Chapter 12

*I*n the morning, Hank's fever spiked at 103.1°. Colleen called Doc Manley and he told her to bring Hank in to the hospital.

For a moment it seemed that no one would be available to drive the boys to where they would start their hike, nearly ten miles up into the hills at the end of a primitive road. Then Colleen had a desperate inspiration. The odd thing was that the person she called was not only willing to help, she sounded positively excited about it.

The unlikely Shirley Johnson ended up taking the boys in her battered old station wagon. With their packs piled in the rear, the Ward boys sat in the back seat, and Stu sat in front. Shirley had a cigarette jammed in the corner of her mouth, and every time it got down to the butt she lit a new one from the smoldering stub.

The road the old station wagon traversed on that hot August morning had been built as a fire-fighting access road, but was also used by hunters to reach the high country. It was maintained by the US Forest Service. Maintenance mostly meant that each year as soon as the ground was free of melting snow and had dried out from the spring rains, the USFS crew would run a grader over it to knock down the middle ridge and to fill in the previous year's ruts. The road meandered through the foothills and made the Butte Road seem, by comparison, like a major highway.

As the boaty Town & Country gained altitude it spewed a blue haze of exhaust and drew a billowing dust cloud as it jounced and creaked ever upward toward the distant peaks. The air conditioner labored to keep the inside cool but with only modest success. Despite the windows being closed, dust filtered in and soon the interior was coated with a thickening grit, mingled with Shirley's tobacco smoke. On the outside the fake wood paneling and aging green paint were solidly caked-up and every crack and crevice was smoothed over brown.

The brakes and leaf springs began to squeal as the dust worked its way into every place where metal joined to metal. Shirley ran the wipers almost constantly to keep the windshield clear enough to see through. The dust rolled and rippled across the rear window and made it impossible to see anything out the back.

They were nearly halfway to their destination, the trail head for the Sawtooth Ridge trail, speeding along a stretch of road cut into the side of a hill, when the car hit a bump and the oil pan bottomed with a vicious scrape. It sounded to Billy like the underside of the car must have sheared clean off.

"Damn!" Shirley swore, but she kept barreling up the road and seemed to be pressing the wagon to go even faster. Shirley Johnson appeared, for some reason, to be in a great hurry. Miracle of miracles, the wagon kept going. Billy wanted to shout for her to slow down. But neither Mike nor Stu appeared to be concerned. So Billy hunkered down in the back seat and offered a prayer asking God to please get them there in one piece.

The oil pan incident wasn't to be their worst scare. For as they rounded a curve, the tires slewing dirt like a boat throws water, there suddenly loomed in the middle of the road a washtub-sized boulder that had rolled down from the bank above.

Billy saw it about the same time as Mike. Both yelled, "Look out!" Billy threw up his arms as he realized there was no way around. It seemed they must either crash into it, or leave the road and catapult over the steep bank on their left, since it was impossible to go up the nearly vertical bank on their right.

"Shit!" Shirley screamed. She stomped the brake pedal all the way to the floorboards. The cigarette flew from her mouth. The big wagon waffled and floated; its steel bones creaked and moaned. For a second the cruiser threatened to fishtail out of control. But the ruts in the road showed some value as the tires slotted into the deep tracks. The wagon arrowed on toward the boulder and a huge dust cloud enveloped them as the world disappeared. The balding tires finally bit though the loose dust and down to the hardpan dirt with a rasping like brick on cement and the wagon shuddered to a stop. When the air cleared, the bumper was two feet from the boulder.

"Stuie," Shirley said with a forced sweetness verging on obscenity. "Would you boys please get out and shove that *thing* off the road?" Her hands were gripping the steering wheel and her knuckles were white and the veins stood out on her arms. She relaxed her grip and reached down to pick up her cigarette which lay smoldering on the rubber floor mat.

The boys piled out of the car, squinting against the dust haze settling away into the surrounding brush. As they circled the boulder to find the best angle to push from, the driver's door squealed open. Shirley got out, slammed it shut, and began walking back down the road.

"Potty break," she called over her shoulder. "Be back in a sec."

Stu's head sagged forward.

"What's up with your mom?" Mike asked in bewilderment.

Billy sensed a wave of confusion from Stu. Something was out of place and it was more than this crazy dash up the road.

Stu shrugged. "I dunno." And what he meant was that he no longer cared. He just wanted to get to the trailhead and start the hike. Everything beyond the adventure along the Sawtooth Ridge seemed like a million years in the future. And Stu desperately wanted everything that had already happened up to that point in his life to now seem like it was a million years in the past. Stu turned away from Mike and bent over the boulder. It was roundish and roughly thirty inches in diameter. He began to single-handedly try to roll it toward the side of the road but with no success. Mike and Billy placed their hands to either side of Stu's and together all three began to push.

In a few seconds they had the boulder rolled over to the side of the road. Mike looked at Stu, smiled, and said, "Bombs away." One final shove from Mike's foot and the great rock nosed through the soft dirt at the edge of the bank. They watched with big grins as it pounded down the steep slope, smashing sagebrush and cheat grass. The visible path of destruction continued until it performed a small jump and vanished over a little rise. For a couple seconds they heard more crashing and smashing, and finally a massive *THUD!*

They walked back to the car with a feeling of satisfaction. The dust had settled, but inside the car was like an oven and the vinyl seats were molten hot. They rolled down the windows and stood by the front fender waiting for it to cool. Shirley Johnson walked back around the curve two minutes later.

The boys entered the car. Shirley was smiling as she got in, gunned the engine, and jammed the transmission into gear. But she now drove at a more cautious pace and Billy grew certain they would reach the trailhead intact.

Up into the mountains they went, and finally the scraggly sage and grease-wood gave way to firs and pines. A sharp granite peak loomed into view. In ten more minutes they arrived at a switchback with a half-moon turnaround. A wood sign just off the edge of the turnaround had cream-colored lettering proclaiming: *Boiling Lake -- 16 miles.* Beyond the sign a trail meandered into the sparse forest. Shirley pulled off the road and into the shade of a large pine. The boys scrambled out and shouldered their packs. Billy planted the Akubra firmly on his head. Stu pulled on his Yankees' cap. Mike put on a yellow felt hat, freshly embedded with a dozen dry flies he had purchased at Valley Hardware. They stood uneasily, anxious to be away, waiting for some pronouncement from Shirley.

She studied them like bruised apples at the supermarket, and finally said, "Don't get lost. I don't want to have to send someone out looking for you."

"Don't worry, we'll be okay," Stu replied evenly.

Billy didn't think Shirley Johnson was worried at all. She looked happy. The same thought was running through Mike's mind. There was something going on that he didn't know about. Mike finally decided she was simply glad Stu would be away for a few days. That had to be it.

Shirley seemed satisfied. She turned towards the car, looking pleased, but turned back with sudden concern.

"Stuie? You got someone to cover your paper route, didn't you?"

Billy saw Stu's face settle into a strange kind of satisfaction, almost as if Stu took comfort in being able to answer her accusation.

"Yeah, Mom. I got Jim Tyler."

"Jim Tyler." Shirley brightened. "The car dealer's son?"

"Yeah, that's him."

Shirley looked pleased. "He should be okay. We need that money, Stuie. I hope you showed him the route so he knows it."

"Yes I did, Mom." Stu now looked embarrassed. Billy wondered why. What was it Shirley had said? *We need that money.* What was that all about?

Shirley turned and walked to the car, jerked the door open, slammed it shut, turned the key and revved the engine and spun the rear tires backing up, then gunned a tight circle and shot off back down the road.

Billy's question tumbled out. "What did she mean, 'We need the money, Stu?'"

Stu turned without an answer and began to walk up the trail. Mike faced Billy with a look of total disgust.

"Why can't you just shut up and not be so incredibly stupid," Mike said. He sighed, closed his eyes as if to chase away a headache, opened them and stared at Billy. "Stu gives her half of what he makes on his route."

This was what Stu had told Mike. Stu had been too embarrassed to reveal that he gave his mom *most* of his paper route money, keeping only tips and the little bit she let him have for an allowance.

Stu heard Mike's angry words but kept walking up the trail, just wanting to get on with what was supposed to be the good part of the day.

Billy considered Mike's explanation. It hardly seemed right. Stu shouldn't have to help his mom out. Neither he nor Mike had ever been asked by their parents to "help out" with money from jobs they worked. And then it hit him that Stu must be mortified that a fourteen-year-old kid knew he had to turn half his wages over to his mom.

Stu was nearly out of sight. Billy tried to think of something to say, but was at a loss. Mike turned to follow Stu. Billy began to walk after the older boys, numbed by the stupidity of his words.

They trudged steadily upward toward the granite cliffs of the Sawtooth Range for what seemed like forever before there was talk again.

Shirley drove at a more leisurely pace down the road, quite pleased with her performance. On the trip up she had feared Stu would figure out something was going down before he got back. She had even sensed the Ward boys knew there was something going on. As hard as she tried there was no way to completely cover her pleasure, her excitement. So she had raced along the narrow dirt road at speeds that even scared her. But now she was safe.

That last little bit about the paper route had been a stroke of brilliance! She had seen the change come across Stu's face, going from uncertain to embarrassed, but also reassured.

When Stu had brought home the news that Mike had decided they would go on the hike, Shirley had waited for the first opportunity when Stu was out of the house to call her sister in California. Colleen had agreed to get on a Greyhound bus and come to Washington. She was due in the Wenatchee terminal tomorrow afternoon, where Shirley would pick her up. And together they would begin packing the contents of the house. By the time Stu arrived back in Chelan on the ferry in five days' time, Shirley and Colleen would have already held a yard sale, rented a U-haul to pull behind the station wagon, and left for California. Leaving Stu a note explaining that it was better this way. The rent was paid through the end of the month. He could sell his own furniture, or keep it, whatever he chose. And good luck kid. Now you'll find out what *being an adult* is really all about.

Joyful at the imminent prospect of her new life, Shirley turned up the radio volume full blast and chain-smoked all the way back to Chelan. At the top of Woodin Avenue she pulled into the Sudsy Buddy and pressure-washed the dirt from the Towne & Country, wiped down the interior with a wet cloth and vacuumed the floor mats. She drove across town to the liquor store and bought a fifth of Jack Daniels. It was a cut above what she was used to, but she had cause to celebrate!

Chapter 13

The boys trooped up the trail with Billy bringing up the rear. It took him a few minutes to catch up after Stu's head start. Even then, Billy held back several yards. He trudged along like an unwanted duckling.

The hike began at four thousand feet above sea level where the temperature was in the mid-seventies. The day was pleasant with an intermittent breeze that whispered in the surrounding evergreens and carried the twitter of songbirds from the forest and the clicking and buzzing of insects and the sharp smell of pitch with a hint of wildflowers. As they passed a gnarled pine that had been partially burnt in a forest fire a Steller's Jay scolded from a high branch, unhappy with the strangers tromping through *his* territory.

In the second mile the boys heard a sudden not-so-distant crashing from deep within a thicket of brush. They came to a nervous halt and turned toward the sound, expecting some large animal, probably a bear, to come charging out. Mike was fingering the hatchet sheathed at his belt. Billy was considering just how fast he could drop his pack and sprint back down the trail. But the sound stopped as abruptly as it had started. After a long minute Mike finally said, "I guess it's nothing."

"Yeah, I guess," Stu said with a nervous laugh.

Billy wondered if he could possibly say anything that wouldn't draw condemnation and realized he couldn't so he remained silent.

Mike and Stu began walking and Billy followed.

The granite peaks of the Sawtooth Range now towered above them, tearing a jagged line against the blue sky. Beneath this barrier the trail threaded through rockslides and around occasional massive boulders, twisting through the scree like a windblown string.

Like all of the other ranges along the western coast, these sharp mountains had been born from the geological upheaval of the colliding Pacific and North American Plates. When those great continental masses met, dozens of mountain ranges had sprung up, from the Olympics to the Rockies. The Cascades were later shaped by glaciers that carved deep gorges such as the Chelan.

Populating this wilderness of crags and defiles and meadows and ridges and rockslides were mountain goats, mule deer, brown and black bears, cougars, coyotes, raccoons, mink, badger, quail, ptarmigan, red-winged woodpeckers, marmots, snowshoe hares, bald eagles, golden eagles, hawks, beaver, elk, skunk, porcupine, grouse, rattlesnakes, garter snakes, toads, frogs, chipmunks, squirrels and a variety of mice, shrews and lizards. There had at one time been grizzly bears but they had been hunted out of existence. The lakes and streams ran ice cold and were filled with cutthroat and rainbow trout. But at the moment, Billy's awareness of the beauty that surrounded him was dulled by the guilt he felt about his bonehead question to Stu.

To distract himself Billy finally fell to watching his brother's yellow hat. Although the hat wasn't nearly as neat as the Akubra, it was still pretty cool. You could scoop it into a stream for water to douse away heat and sweat. And it was the perfect place to keep dry flies for fishing. If an errant cast caught a deadwood snag, or a big trout snapped the leader, Mike could easily reach up for a new fly and be back in business pronto.

Watching the way his brother walked, the confidence and power in his stride, Billy envied how much Mike had grown. Billy had practically worshiped Mike as he lettered three years straight as a defensive guard on the high school football team. Mike wasn't quick enough for offense, but he was a bulldog in the defensive trenches. No one got past Mike Ward without getting pounded. And if anyone ever tried to bully the younger brother, the older brother had always been there to set things right.

Nothing had diminished Billy's pride and admiration for his brother. Not even the recent unfair treatment. Sure, Mike had been a creep during the past few months, and an outright SOB the past few weeks. Billy wondered if it was natural that brothers grew apart when the first one became an adult. But also, could it somehow turn around when the younger brother reached eighteen?

Could Billy look forward to a renewed friendship with Mike when he, too entered college? He sure hoped so!

Billy tucked away that hopeful thought. For now, it was time to return to reality. All he could now hope for was to have everyone forget the drama of the Butte climb and its aftermath, and his stupid question to Stu. Mike hadn't said anything mean since the shock announcement at dinner. The only incidents had been the hatchet drop at Sav-Mart and Mike's comments about Billy's purchases. Otherwise, Mike had gone about his life as if nothing were troubling him. Maybe Mike really had decided to let bygones be bygones.

They crossed through a small field and into a grove of Ponderosa where the pine needles lay in a thick toasted carpet. As they moved through the woods they came upon a clearing just a few yards wide, with lush grass surrounding a dark patch where a spring had welled to the surface. The sun lanced down from its noontime height to illuminate the tiny meadow.

In the center of the meadow the black earth glistened, and upon this spot were gathered dozens of swallowtail butterflies, both the black-and-whites called Zebra Swallowtails and the yellow-and-blacks called Tiger Swallowtails. Dozens of smaller Lupine Blues also flitted amongst the larger butterflies. Where the butterflies had landed on the black soil they uncoiled their proboscises and sucked up moisture while their wings nervously folded and unfolded, ready for instant flight.

Billy wanted to stop and watch, maybe even try to catch one or two, wondering if they might make good bait for trout later on. But the older boys showed no interest. They tromped past the tiny meadow and into the trees beyond. Billy followed without a word. He gave one last regretful look at the butterfly gathering as they rounded a bend in the trail.

His thoughts returned to Mike. What it would be like when Mike went away to college? Would he miss Billy? Billy knew he would miss his brother a lot, even though he'd still see Mike from time to time. On Thanksgiving and Christmas breaks Mike would come home. But could it ever be the same? Mike would find a girlfriend. He'd get involved in college stuff.

Would Mike ever take him on another summer hike? It was hard to imagine. And it hurt to think this might be their last adventure together. Some adventure. Mike forced to drag him along. Stu humiliated right from the start. Billy the third wheel odd and out.

At that moment, Billy resolved that he and Mike would have to talk at some point during the hike. There would come a moment when Mike was relaxed, when he might listen. And then Billy would tell his brother that he understood he was a pain to have along. But just the same, he would always remember the hike. It would be the best thing he'd ever done. And he would always appreciate Mike for taking him along. Mike would probably laugh. He might say something rude. But years from now Mike would remember what Billy had said. And their friendship would have to improve. Wouldn't it? That thought made Billy happy, and his pack suddenly seemed lighter.

Two hours after they started Mike called out from his lead position, "Let's take five and have some lunch when we get to that log." He pointed to a deadfall trunk that lay alongside the trail.

"Gotcha," Stu agreed. Billy quietly accepted the decision. His feet weren't hurting, for which he was glad, but the rest of his body was sending little hints that he was in worse shape than he had thought. His calves were tight. His shoulders were sore. And his low back ached where the pack frame was strapped around his waist. For the past half hour the trail had been relatively easy, but up ahead it cut a sharp zigzag for several hundred yards up a rockslide before cresting a fractured granite ridgeline. He remembered Stu's warning about how tough the terrain would be. Maybe Stu had known more about this than Billy realized.

The three boys backed up to the log, crouching to unshoulder their pack straps. With an occasional swat at a deerfly, they dug into their packs for food.

Billy had no idea what Mike and Stu had brought for lunch. But he had used the empty side pocket in his own pack to bring what Mike would have called *school lunch food*. Two ham-and-cheese sandwiches, carrots, celery and a Snickers bar.

Mike and Stu now pulled packets containing strips of beef jerky and dried apricots and raisons from their packs. As Mike began to chew his jerky he took a long hard look at Billy's soft white-bread sandwiches and grumbled, "I suppose you've also got a thermos of cold milk."

Billy thought of something sarcastic to say, decided it unwise, and kept silent. He stared down at the ground where a line of ants was streaming from the end of the log and out into the forest. Billy took a crumb of bread and dropped it near the ant stream. Immediately a few of the ants broke from the line, seized the breadcrumb, and began to struggle it back toward their nest in the rotted-out end of the log.

Mike watched with disapproval and then looked at Stu. Stu shrugged. Billy bit into a carrot stick and Mike looked over and focused upon the Snickers bar that rested on Billy's knee. *I hope it's melted.* But the temperature was in the low seventies and Mike knew the candy was perfect and wonderful. Why hadn't he thought to bring a candy bar for the first lunch?

Mike tore off a ragged bite of jerky, and as he chewed he asked Stu, "How far do you think we've come?"

Stu reached inside his pack and pulled out the Forest Service map, opened it carefully so as not to tear the seams, and with his index finger traced the dotted line of the trail. "If those switchbacks are the same as these here on the map," he pointed towards the sharp rise in the trail that lay ahead, "I'd say we've come about four miles, give or take."

"We've come more than four miles," Billy blurted out. They'd come more like ten miles! Both older boys looked exasperated. Billy realized what he'd said was stupid. Even worse, he'd contradicted Stu. Stu might be starting to really hate him.

"Here," Stu said quietly, handing the map to Billy. "You figure it out."

He wanted to say, *No, I'm sorry. You must be right.* But he was stuck and there was nothing he could do but take the map. Stu returned to eating his jerky and dried fruit and ignored Billy, who now carefully studied the vertical and horizontal lines marked in one-inch squares, each representing a mile. On the map it did look as if they'd come just four miles.

"I guess—"

"Gimme that," Mike ordered, depriving him of even the small dignity of confirming Stu. Billy obediently handed Mike the map. Mike made his own brief calculation. "Yep," Mike concluded with authority. "Four miles."

Stu chewed on a dried apricot, took a swig of water from his canteen, silently wishing he'd been as smart as Billy to pack sandwiches and a candy bar.

Billy struggled to think of something positive to say. He finally asked, "How far do you figure we'll go today?"

Mike glanced at Billy and then swatted at a persistent deerfly that had landed on his arm. He gave the map a close look. When he spoke he talked only to Stu. "If it flattens out over that ridge, we can do five more miles. But if there's a lot more up and down, we'll play it by ear."

"Fine," Stu said, showing no particular concern for how far they would go that day. Stu looked at Billy. "How are your feet?" Billy couldn't tell if Stu was being critical, taking a shot at him, or if he was truly concerned. He finally decided it didn't matter. At least he could finally say something that wouldn't irritate Stu.

"Fine," Billy replied. And this was true. The rest of his body was a different story. But he would no more have confessed to these pains than he would have turned back for town. Billy folded the wax paper and the candy bar wrapper and stuffed them into the empty pocket in his pack. He would burn them in tonight's campfire.

Stu watched Billy and wondered, *Is he lying about his feet?* But The Kid seemed to be telling the truth. "Okeydoke," Stu finally said. "Then we better get going. I'll take the lead."

The boys shouldered their packs, and within minutes they had reached the zig-zag segment of the trail.

Halfway up the tight switchbacks, when all three boys were sweating and breathing hard, Stu glanced back over his shoulder. Mike was chugging along, and Billy was several yards back. "You holding up okay, Billy?"

"I'm okay," Billy struggled to make the two-word reply.

Stu pulled up, pretended to survey the trail ahead. He turned his head to look back the way they had come and Mike froze mid-stride with a *Whatza matter?* frown. Stu ignored Mike.

"Wanna take a few seconds?" Stu asked casually of Billy, a question aimed right around Mike. Mike gave Stu a second frown, this time his eyebrows coming up.

Billy didn't know what to say. Was Stu being sarcastic? Was he actually concerned? Billy realized it was a no-win situation. If he asked for a break, Mike would pile it on. Without a break he was going to suffer.

"No," Billy replied gamely. He would make it to the top no matter how much he suffered. *It's no worse than the Butte.* But then, the Butte had been pretty terrible. And the aftermath had been worse. Maybe turning down Stu's offer wasn't such a great idea. Billy saw a compromise. He added hopefully, "Maybe a little slower."

Mike groaned.

Stu said nothing as he turned back to the trail. But the pace he set was a little bit more comfortable.

Billy saw Mike's body language was now bordering on anger. Stu didn't have to look back to know. He had to do something to distract Mike. So at a point in the trail two hundred yards from where it crested the ridge, at the very stretch where it was the steepest, Stu began to sing.

"Hundred bottles of beer on the wall
Hundred bottles of beer
You take one down and pass it around
Ninety-nine bottles of beer on the wall . . ."

He sang in a chain-gang cadence that bordered on a funeral dirge.

Mike began to smile. At ninety-seven bottles he joined in. Billy waited and waited and finally decided that he'd better sing along. His tenor joined the baritones of Stu and Mike. They trudged on up the brutal trail with a chorus as strange as any ever heard in the wilderness.

Stu felt a little smug. Mike had been distracted.

They were well past three hundred bottles of imaginary beer before Stu reached the top and fell silent.

Mike and Billy caught up and looked out on what Stu had discovered.

"Crazy," Stu whispered reverently.

"Man-o-man," Mike echoed.

Billy was speechless.

They had been hiking through dry pine forest and fields of rocks and were totally unprepared for what lie on the other side of the ridge. Spread out before them was a half-mile-wide bowl meadow, blanketed knee-deep in grass and peppered with wild flowers in shades of red and yellow and blue. A narrow stream with grass-tufted banks meandered across the meadow in a sinuous ribbon. On the map it read *Horse Thief Basin*. But in reality it was simply paradise.

The trail traced through the middle of the bowl like a line drawn with a brown crayon. Billy wished it weren't there. It didn't belong. It hurt the pristine meadow. But then he realized they would never have gotten here if it weren't for the trail, and in that moment he found forgiveness for those who had built it.

The promise of cold clear water now beckoned, and the boys scrambled down the switchbacks, kicking up dust and sending dangerous little showers of sharp stones cascading across the steep slope. Once onto the smooth-packed dirt of the meadow trail they crossed the next hundred yards at nearly a trot and came to where the trail forded the stream. They dumped their packs and sank to their knees in the deep tufted grass along the stream bank and scooped handfuls of frigid snowmelt water to drink and splash their faces. Billy looked over at Mike and Stu as they drenched their heads and necks with icy water. For a moment they all wanted the same thing and there was no possibility of disagreement, no conflict in purpose. Billy felt hope for just a second, and then he looked away before either Mike or Stu could look up and spoil the moment with a negative word or sarcastic frown.

He stared back down into the crystal clear water, five inches deep, and studied a tiny bar of clean yellow sand edged by a run of smooth stones. There had to be something precious here, maybe gold, at least agates. Billy reached and scooped up a loose handful from the creek bed, and then a second and a third until his hands felt nearly frozen. Each time he let the sand and pebbles dribble between his chilled fingers, searching for a flash of color to betray treasure. But all he saw were ordinary rocks and plain sand. The best find was a rounded quartz pebble. But there were plenty of those on the park beach back home. After several more handfuls yielded no surprises, and with his hands numb from the icy water, he shifted his attention to where the stream deepened beyond the trail.

"Do you think there are any fish?" Billy asked, pointing to where the water was a foot deep downstream from the trail crossing. "Maybe we should cast a fly or two and see if we get a bite. Maybe we could even set up camp somewhere near here . . ."

Mike said, "I'll bet it freezes solid in the winter and there's no fish that can live in a block of ice." Billy felt the sting of his brother's words and knew he'd again said something Mike thought dumb. Mike continued in a low tone, "Besides, if there's fish, they'd be too small. You know the rule. Trout have to be at least six inches before you can keep them."

Billy fell silent. Couldn't he be right just once? After all, it was the first stream they had found, and the map didn't show another creek for a long ways— far beyond where they would be forced by darkness to stop and set up camp for the night. Billy desperately wanted to assemble his four-piece fly rod and drift a Black Gnat on the slow current—just to see if there were fish—and the size didn't matter. And what better place to camp than here? With clean water, and soft ground to roll out the sleeping bags, and plenty of places to explore while they still had some energy left and there was daylight to burn?

But Mike and Stu were already hoisting their packs and splashing across the creek bed, purposefully kicking clumps of dirt from the bank with the heavy toes of their boots to send lazy brown clouds downstream and probably, Billy thought with disgust, scaring off any fish. With resignation, he shouldered his own pack and slogged across the shallow water and followed Mike and Stu across the meadow.

In the new and now gently rolling terrain Stu picked up the pace. They were above five thousand feet and the temperature had settled into the sixties and the air was dry but comfortable with only an occasional breeze. For the rest of the afternoon they made just two brief stops to drink from their canteens.

Long shadows were already stretching to signal the onset of evening when they came to a small patch of dry meadow edged by a dribble of a stream. The only flowers here were a few clumps of faded orange Indian Paintbrush. The spring grasses had gone yellow and brown. At the field's upper end stood a small stand of ancient pine, scraggly survivors of avalanches that had rumbled down the steep rock slope in winter to crush most of the trees that had struggled to grow. A jam of bleached wood lay scattered across the base of the slide.

"How's this look for a campsite?" Stu asked.

Mike looked around and noticed that a few yards upslope someone had carried rocks and arranged a crude fire ring. Charred limb ends stuck out from the shallow pit and the center held a bed of ash studded with bits of charcoal.

"This will do," Mike agreed. "There's plenty of wood for a campfire up in those dead trees. There's water. Everything we need." He didn't bother to look to Billy for confirmation. Billy hadn't expected it. The sun had fallen against the western peaks and a chill was in the air. They couldn't have gone much further without being caught by darkness. Still, it would have been nice if Mike had at least looked to see if Billy might nod *Yes*. Tired and sore, he followed them up the slope to the old campsite.

Mike now took full command. "Stu, take Billy and get some firewood from the trees." There were no *maybes*. Just an order expected to be obeyed.

"Sure thing," Stu replied tiredly as he dumped his backpack near the fire ring. "C'mon Billy." He started towards the rockslide without waiting for a reply.

Without the weight of his pack Billy felt like he was walking on air. But the prospect of working close to Stu made Billy remember his dumb question from earlier in the day and he was trying to figure out what he might say as he followed Stu up the slope. They reached a large disintegrating pine log that lay like a broken dinosaur, limbs shattered, bark slaking off where rot had triumphed. The wood had already been picked over by earlier hikers, so they would have to break up large branches and scavenge for kindling.

"Time to do some serious damage," Stu said with a bit of mischief. With both hands and a straining back he lifted a massive six-foot limb section and laid one end against the log. He stepped up onto the log and jumped high. Both feet came squarely down onto the middle of the branch. It snapped with a satisfying *crunch*. But Stu lost his balance as the limb broke and he fell hard, skinning his left elbow as he went down.

"Damn!" Stu rolled onto his butt, experimentally flexed his elbow, and then reached down to feel his ankles.

Billy pictured the hike ending right there. They would have carry Stu, with sprained or broken ankles, back the way they had come. Billy moved to Stu. "Are you okay?"

Stu waved him off and finally stood up, brushing dirt and twigs from his pants and shirt. He rubbed the feeling back into his left arm and gingerly shifted weight onto his right foot and then his left until both seemed okay. He took an experimental step, then another, and sighed with relief.

"It's okay."

"Maybe that's not the best way to break up the wood."

Stu gave him a peculiar look and Billy thought he'd said yet another stupid thing. But Stu finally said, "Yeah. I've got a better idea." He grabbed one half of the thick limb he had just busted in half, and lifted it high above his head and then smashed it down on the log. It burst into several pieces and the crash echoed off the cliffs and across the rocky field.

"Your turn."

Billy picked up a smaller limb and swung it at the log. As it broke a shock wave radiated up his arms. "Ouch!" Billy yelled, shaking his hands.

Stu smiled. "No wussies allowed!" Billy returned the smile and felt a little better.

They began to stack the demolished wood into armload-sized piles. As they worked, Stu looked at Billy. After a moment he spoke, quietly so it wouldn't carry back to where Mike was making a clatter spreading out pots and supplies from their packs. "Hey, Billy. I'm sorry Mike's pissed at you. It'll work out. Don't worry." He added, "It might be best if you don't tell him I said this."

Billy couldn't have been more surprised. He shrugged. "He's just being a big brother."

Stu thought about this. "Yeah," he agreed. "I guess he is." Stu began to hunt for smaller sticks for kindling.

"But he sure can be a pain," Billy added to Stu's back as he walked a few yards away. Stu grunted his assent and kept gathering wood.

Billy thought the subject was finished, but Stu surprised him. He walked back and gave Billy a quick look before dumping a double handful of kindling onto the growing pile. "You're lucky to have a brother," Stu said quietly, as if he were speaking mostly to himself. "Sometimes, well, I wish I had a brother."

Billy's reply was off-the-cuff. "Stu, you'd make a great brother."

Stu was facing away from him, but upon hearing this he turned around and Billy saw a tear was rolling down Stu's cheek. Stu wiped away the tear with the sleeve of his flannel shirt.

Finally, Stu spoke. "Hey, don't tell Mike, okay?"

"Sure thing," Billy said, stunned. Stu returned to gathering on the far side of the log, and came back with a clutch of large pinecones. The momentary look of pain and sadness was gone, just like magic, and his easy grin had returned. "C'mon," Stu said. "Let's get this wood back and get a fire going."

They made three trips and gradually built a pyre in the ring of rocks, with twigs and pinecones for kindling at the center. Mike had doubled the number of stones in the ring and strung a wire between two stakes he had hacked into shape and then pounded into the hardpan earth with his hatchet.

Billy got the canister of wood matches from a side pocket of his pack and approached the fire with great anticipation.

"Give me those," Mike ordered.

Billy dutifully handed over the matches.

"I'm only going to need one," Mike declared confidently, pulling a single white-and-red-tipped wooden match out and then handing the plastic canister back to Billy, who carefully screwed the lid on and slid it into his pocket.

Mike struck the match and it burst to flame. He inserted it carefully into the heart of the wood and the wavering yellow tip caught at the dry pine needles and the small sticks and the fire crackled to life and sent pine smoke drifting in lazy tendrils as the flames spread rapidly through the center. Within two minutes a towering blaze forced the boys back. The sudden inferno crackled and popped and rocketed sparks and they were glad the campsite was barren of vegetation.

As the fire roared Billy waited on his brother for some acknowledgment of how successful his and Stu's fire making had been. But once the fire was going Mike turned businesslike to cooking. Billy and Stu left the dinner preparations to Mike's efforts and walked to their packs and dug out bug repellant for the mosquitoes that had begun to appear as dusk neared. They laid out ground pads and blew up their orange plastic Sav-Mart air mattresses and unrolled their sleeping bags.

Back at the fire Mike had filled the two-quart pot with water and set it on a flat rock alongside the fire so that flames licked near the metal. Billy and Stu returned to the warmth of the campfire, holding their hands out to catch the heat, watching the water come to a boil. Mike carefully dumped in three cups of macaroni elbows and dried vegetables, stirring with a long aluminum spoon to keep the pasta from sticking to the bottom.

He now looked up at Stu and Billy and uttered a single word, "Wieners."

For the first night they had brought a six-pack of hotdogs, frozen solid and double-wrapped in aluminum foil. Mike opened the package and laid them out beside the fire. During the day the wieners had thawed but they were still good. Mike had cut three long sticks and sharpened the ends and scraped off the loose bark.

Each boy now shoved two wieners onto his stick. They thrust them into the flames, growing hungrier with every second as the fire began to heat the pink meat. Soon the dogs were hissing and dripping grease onto the coals; black bubbles began to spot and crisp and wrinkle the skin and the smell was intoxicating for grumbling stomachs.

Mike handed his stick over to Stu after a minute and checked on the Bisquick he had dolloped into foil pockets and laid close to the fire. The biscuits had risen and pushed out the foil, and when Mike pulled the foil open the biscuit skins were golden brown.

Mike turned and ordered Billy, "Get some water from the stream and mix up some dry milk."

Grateful for something to contribute, Billy laid his roasted hotdogs on his tin mess kit plate and jumped up and grabbed the plastic jug and a packet of dry milk and trotted away from the flickering light thrown by the campfire. He knelt beside the tiny stream and pressed the mouth of the jug against the clear gravel and filled it nearly to the top. He dumped in the milk powder, screwed on the lid, and as he walked back toward the fire he shook the jug so the powder was thoroughly dissolved by the time he was standing before Mike, hoping for the smallest sign of approval.

"Hand me your mess plates," was all Mike had to say. Billy sat the jug of milk down next to Stu. Mike used a stick to lift the pot away from the fire and ladled each of them a portion of the thick soup.

"Chow time," Mike announced, as the boys divided the biscuits and fell to devouring every last morsel.

The meadow grew dark. Beyond the campfire the sparse grass and scattered rock lay in grays and shadows. One by one a chorus of crickets began to chirp, and an owl hooted from high up in the rockslide trees. Millions of stars spun overhead in the broad cottony band of the Milky Way that stretched from horizon to horizon across the jet-black sky.

The temperature fell to the point where sitting close to the fire became necessary. The campfire smoke also helped to drive away the mosquitoes which continued to grow in number and ferocity the colder it got.

The boys had eagerly anticipated the final part of dinner. Mike carefully doled out chocolate squares and graham crackers. As he handed Stu half a bar of Hershey chocolate, Stu gave him a look that begged for the other half. "We've got to make it last," Mike said pointedly. Mike wrapped the remainder of the bar back in its silvery foil and returned it to the Tupperware container that kept the chocolate from being squished in his pack.

Stu sighed as he skewered two marshmallows onto the end of his roasting stick.

Billy had already received his chocolate ration and now reached into the marshmallow sack. He removed two soft white puffs. Mike grabbed the sack and firmly tied a single knot in the plastic and stashed it with the chocolate. Stu gave a glance at Billy that said this wasn't where a battle should be fought.

They sat cross-legged around the fire and toasted their marshmallows, and when the white lumps started to flame they withdrew their sticks and blew out the flames and squeezed the marshmallows together with a square of chocolate between two graham crackers to form the greatest camp treat imaginable: Smores.

As Mike finished eating his own hot gooey Smore he yelled, "Little bugger!" and slapped at his neck. In the flickering light Billy saw that one of the persistent mosquitoes had left a smear of blood. He nearly offered congratulations to Mike on the kill, but reconsidered and kept quiet, figuring there was nothing he could say tonight that Mike wouldn't take wrong.

Billy gobbled down his Smore and licked the last trace of chocolate from his fingers. "I'm gonna hit the sack," he said.

"Yeah, I'm beat," Stu said.

"Okay," Mike agreed. "But you guys have to clean up before you turn in."

Billy made a trip to the brook to scour out his cook-gear with wet sand, and also to clean the soup pot. Finally, he brushed his teeth and washed his face and hands.

Mike stayed by the fire, storing utensils and putting food canisters back inside the packs where they would be safe from critters and insects.

When Billy had finished at the creek he walked back to the campsite and crawled into his sleeping bag. His body ached in ways he had never imagined possible and in places where he never thought he could hurt. The nylon bag felt wonderful against his skin. He heard Mike and Stu walk together down to the water, speak briefly about who should clean what, then work at cleaning the cookware, and finally walk back. They stripped off their dirty jeans and shirts and crawled into their own bags. Stu's bag was near Billy's; Mike's was on the opposite side of the fire.

Billy thought sleep would come easily. But as he stared up at the diamond band of stars he found it impossible to close his eyes to their beauty. He stared for ten minutes before he saw the first meteor.

"Wow! Did you guys see that?" The shooting star had traced halfway across the sky before it had burned out.

Mike, who had disappeared inside his bag and found a comfortable position, mumbled, "What?" But he made no move to poke his head out for a look.

"Shooting star," Stu said matter-of-factly.

"A big one," Billy echoed.

"Big deal," Mike grumbled. "Lemme get some sleep."

Billy continued to look up, mesmerized. This sky wasn't like at home. In town, where there were streetlights and porch lamps, the stars were fuzzy and only the brightest ones stood out clearly. Here, a mile high, and away from any light except the glowing embers of the campfire, the night sky was ablaze. Another meteor, then another, shot across the sky. The second left a faint red streak that glowed for several seconds before vanishing. Billy wanted to shout with delight. But he knew that would provoke Mike and he held his silence.

In a few minutes he heard Mike's breathing even out. His brother had fallen asleep. He whispered, "Stu, are you still awake?"

"Yeah."

"You watching the stars?"

"Yeah. Beautiful, aren't they?"

"Sure are," Billy said reverently. A thought had come to him, one he'd had before, but never so clearly as on this night when the stars seemed so close you could practically reach out and touch them. "Stu, do you think there's anything out there?"

Stu sounded puzzled. "Like what?"

"Oh, you know. Aliens. Life on other planets. Stuff like that."

"Oh." There was a long silence and Billy wondered if Stu had any opinion on the subject. But Stu finally replied, "Maybe."

"There's got to be something."

"Maybe there's just God and angels, like it says in the Bible."

"No way. Look at all those stars. What're all those for? There's got to be planets circling at least some of them. And there must be life on some of those planets." Billy paused, impressed by his own logic. "There's billions of stars up there, Stu. *Billions!*" Billy was suddenly scared he might have awoken Mike. But his brother's easy breathing continued and Billy relaxed in the security of his sleeping bag.

The idea of billions of stars, many of them with planets that might possibly support life, had Stu stumped. He'd never thought of it that way. And Billy was right, there had to be a billion stars. Or at least a million. Because the sky seemed to *dance* before his eyes with pinpricks of light. It was a long time before he spoke again.

"Maybe you're right," he finally said. "There's always a reason for things."

As he spoke, a brilliant meteor etched a long trail of light from the center of the sky, starting near the Big Dipper. The white line of the meteor's life zipped along until it disappeared behind the mountains. Both boys listened for an explosion from its impact, expecting it to be like an atom bomb going off, but nothing came and they realized the meteor's nearness had been an illusion.

What a shame.

The owl must have flown off in search of mice and shrews, for there was no more hooting from up in the trees. The diminishing sounds of crickets and mosquitoes were accompanied by an occasional *crack* or *pop* from embers in the fire.

Billy and Stu burrowed into the comfort of their bags without saying anything more.

The cold mountain night took over and the sound of the mosquitoes drifted away; the crickets fell out of chorus one by one as they sought shelter. The fire sank into warm gray ashes.

Finally, the only sounds left were the distant gurgle of the tiny stream and the measured breathing of three boys fast asleep.

Chapter 14

*D*uring the night Billy's air mattress was poked by a stick as he turned in his sleep. He awoke in darkness to a whistling sound and felt rocks gradually pressing into his ribs.

No matter how he shifted his hips or his shoulders or his legs or arms, some part of his body inevitably pressed against rocks. Even if he'd gotten up there was nowhere to move his bag that wasn't just as rocky. There was nothing to do but try to get back to sleep. He passed the few hours before dawn in a restless half-slumber.

Billy had bruises when he finally crawled out into the dawn light. The temperature had plunged close to freezing and it was too cold to stand around. Billy grabbed his jeans and made another discovery. The dew point had been reached and the clothes draped on the boy's packs were soaked. Billy dug into his pack for his only dry pair of pants and his other flannel shirt.

Stu and Billy built a fire and the boys hung their wet clothes near the flames, but it was midmorning before their damp pants and shirts were dry enough to stuff back into their packs.

Billy's final frustration was discovering that no one had thought to bring an air mattress patch kit. So after a breakfast of reconstituted scrambled eggs and flapjacks soggy with sugar syrup, Billy found a spot where the soil was loose and he scratched out a shallow grave for his now-useless air mattress. Mike didn't even give Billy a glance as he walked down to the tiny creek to fill his canteen. As Billy pressed the tightly folded orange plastic and covered it with dirt and stones, Stu walked over and quietly said, "Don't worry, we'll find campsites where you can gather up a bed of pine needles."

Billy was about to thank to Stu for the encouragement but saw Mike returning and he was giving Stu a suspicious look. Billy shifted his eyes back to the burial. Stu drifted away toward the fire while Billy finished covering the dead air mattress. Mike arrived at the fire ring, looked first toward Stu, then back at Billy, seemed about to make a comment, but instead walked over and began to roll up his sleeping bag.

They left their first campsite with almost nothing being said. Billy's soreness from the night's misadventure began to ease after a couple of miles. His spirits began to improve. They were at least making progress, skirting the jagged mountains, and his muscles were finally limbering up. Even his Akubra—which would have shrunk if he'd put it by the fire—was again dry. He was imagining how good a trout would taste for dinner when Mike, who was in the lead, abruptly held up his hand as a signal for the others to halt.

Billy and Stu froze in their steps, expecting to see a snake or a bear or at the very least a skunk or porcupine. But as Billy scanned the brushy slope to either side of the trail he saw nothing to cause concern.

Mike crouched, cautiously slipped his arm out of one pack strap, pulled the other arm free, and left his pack standing mid-trail.

Billy was ready to dump his pack and run if it was a bear that Mike had spotted. He watched his brother carefully dig a golf-ball-sized rock from the crusted soil alongside the trail. Mike stood very slowly and drew his arm back to throw. Billy looked in the direction Mike was aiming and finally saw what had drawn his brother's attention.

About twenty feet up the bank, perched atop a decaying log, a ptarmigan was snuggled down; it had frozen at the sound of the boys' approach; every feather of its brown summer plumage was motionless. Its eyes were unblinking.

Mike let loose with a major league fastball. It rocketed inches from the bird and buried itself in the soft dirt behind the log.

Billy saw the ptarmigan blink as the rock shot past its head, but the bird remained still as a granite statue. Mike slowly bent over to pick up another rock. Billy found himself silently rooting for the ptarmigan. *C'mon, stupid! Fly!*

It was as if the bird had read his thoughts. Or, maybe it had simply had enough of the deadly game of chicken. For just as Mike's arm whipped forward the bird leapt into the air, a flurry of feathers and wildly beating wings. The rock sailed through the exact space the ptarmigan had occupied a fraction of a second earlier, lightly clipped the log, and caromed off into the brush. By the time the rock came to rest the ptarmigan was sailing low and fast down-slope, far enough to make pursuit impossible.

"Damn!" Mike shouted. The curse echoed lightly from a small cliff face two hundreds to their right. "I had him!" He spun around to face Billy and Stu, face full of disappointment. "Did you see how close I came to nailing tonight's dinner!"

"You had him," Stu agreed. "One less second and that critter was barbecue."

"Jeez!" Mike continued. "Crap!" He flung his arms up in frustration. "The first chance at fresh meat and I blow it!"

Stu stood patiently watching Mike gyrate and swear. Billy felt the weight of his pack and wondered when Mike would let them resume the trek. At the same time he wondered what the meat would have tasted like if the bird had been carried, raw, all day long before being roasted over coals. Decidedly yucky, Billy thought, and maybe even dangerous. You could get salmonella poisoning from turkey that had been left out for too long. Why not also from wild bird meat?

"I'll bet we see more," Mike said hopefully. Still he made no move towards his pack. "I sure wish I'd brought my slingshot. I'd have had him dead to rights."

Stu waited patiently for Mike's tirade to subside. Then he said calmly, "We'll add slingshots to the list of things to bring next time." He twisted his head and looked back over his shoulder, at an angle where Mike wouldn't see the wink he gave to Billy. "And a patch kit," Stu added mischievously.

Mike seemed not to hear the second comment, or maybe he chose to ignore it. He said, "Right. Next time it's slingshots." He moved to re-shoulder his pack.

Billy suddenly felt like the luckiest fourteen-year-old in the world. He no longer cared about the night's misadventure with his air mattress. Or his soreness from the rocks or the aching muscles he would surely have at the end of the day. Because the hike had been miraculously transformed by a simple statement.

Both Stu and Mike had said *next time.*

They resumed hiking along the edge of the Sawtooth, skirting ravines and rockslides, bypassing stands of evergreens and dense brush thickets, looping around granite outcroppings. Mid-afternoon they came to a place where the trail split. The right fork was a lesser trail, the left fork clearly the main path.

"Hey Stu," Mike called back. "Get out the map."

Stu and Billy joined Mike and they dropped their packs and gathered round.

"Here's where we must be," Mike said, pointing to a "Y" in the dotted line; the right fork squiggled for a mile and a half before reaching a tiny irregular spot labeled *Boiling Lake*. The left branch of the Y went a couple miles until it reached a larger oval marked *Cub Lake*.

"How do we know this is the same Y in the trail?" Stu asked.

"Cause it's got to be. What else could it be?"

Billy offered tentatively, "Wouldn't the Forest Service have put up a trail marker?"

All three boys looked around. There was not even a rock cairn where a signpost might have been planted.

"Maybe this isn't it," Billy said, feeling empowered by the support Stu had shown him that morning.

"Yeah," Stu added melodramatically. "What if one of these is an abandoned trail that just leads off to nowhere? We could be lost for days. They probably won't find us for two or three years, except we'll just be bleached bones, gnawed on by coyotes and picked clean by ants."

Billy smiled. This sounded totally goofy, and he could tell it perturbed Mike, Stu being silly.

Mike leveled a glare at Stu. "Give me a break. This has to be it. The only question is: Do we go right, to Boiling Lake, which looks closest? Or do we go left to Cub?"

The idea of a short hike appealed to all three. But it was Billy who pointed out the obvious.

"What about the elevations?"

They looked at the elevation numbers written in beside each lake on the map and saw there was two thousand feet of difference between the two, with Cub Lake being the lower.

Billy said, "Maybe we should go to Cub. It's been kind of a long day, hasn't it?"

"Good point, Billy," Mike said derisively. "But only a wussy would choose the easy route. We go up, to Boiling."

"Now wait a minute," Stu countered. "I want a vote in this."

Mike turned on him. "Okay," he said in a slow drawl that signaled trouble. "Go ahead and vote if you want to."

Stu faltered. He'd heard the same anger in Mike's voice a few times during their friendship, always directed at someone else. And he knew he was stuck. He was tired and his feet hurt and he was getting hungry. But it was as certain as snow in January that if he said he wanted to go to Cub that Mike was going to take him to task for it. But if he now said Boiling Lake, Mike would surely find a way to rub it in. Stu got stubborn. He was ready to say Cub Lake and let the chips fall where they may when Billy interrupted.

"Boiling Lake is okay."

Mike turned on him. "I thought you wanted to take the easy way."

Stu's shoulders bunched. Billy heart raced. He had no idea how far his brother might go, but Mike was in no mood to play around. Billy said, "They're both lakes, right? So what's the big deal?" And he walked to where he'd set his pack down, shouldered it, and turned onto the trail to Boiling Lake.

Mike clenched his fists as Billy walked away up the trail. But what could he do? Billy had yielded. Was Mike now going to argue that they should instead turn off to Cub? Knowing that he'd won the argument but utterly lost the war, Mike moved to pick up his own pack. Within a minute he caught up to Billy and passed him, setting a furious pace. His fury continued to build for the next mile and a half of brutally steep trail. Mike barely noticed how difficult the climb was. He was too busy figuring ways to make his little brother pay for showing him up.

126

Chapter 15

$\mathcal{S}$hirley arrived at the Greyhound Bus depot at 4:15 PM. Twenty minutes later an aluminum-clad Super 7 Scenicruiser glided up the street in front of the terminal. At the corner it banked sharp left, rounded onto the side street, and circled half the block before it angled carefully into the cavernous parking shed. Its airbrakes shushed and the coach eased to a stop. The door hissed open and out stepped the driver in his gray uniform. He began to assist passengers at the door, holding firmly onto the arms of the elderly to keep them steady, counting off each person who climbed down the steps.

The passengers straggled across the asphalt tarmac, passed through the steel-and-glass doors, and trooped like ants across the smooth concrete toward a low steel counter where dollies began to roll in from the bus, stacked with luggage.

Standing off to one side of the concourse, nursing a Styrofoam cup of watery coffee, Shirley watched the faces. An old woman wearing a hand-knitted green shawl. A man in a brown polyester suit with a salesman's eye, scanning even in this unlikely place for an opportunity. A mother with her blonde hair in disarray holding a baby wrapped in a pink blanket. Two adolescent girls, arms protectively around each other, eyes wide. Three teen boys speaking what Shirley thought might be German. But no Janet.

When the last person had joined the group at the luggage pickup, Shirley tossed her cup into a waste bin and marched to the main counter. The agent had his head down and was checking off a list with a black marker pen.

"Excuse me," Shirley demanded.

The counterman's head came up. "Ma'am?" He had dark circles under his eyes and his skin was waxen. The collar of his white shirt was smudged with blue ink and the vague outline of an old grease stain spotted the fabric above his breast pocket.

Shirley hated being called *Ma'am*. But she needed help so she bit back mean words and instead said, "I was looking for my sister on that last bus but she wasn't there. Is there some way you can check to see if she missed a connection?"

The counterman's face assumed a bored look. He usually "lost" at least half-a-dozen people each day. Some were folks who had not even gotten on the bus—they had simply changed their minds and didn't bother to phone ahead. He had dealt with plenty of jilted boyfriends, upset parents, and ex-wives who were waiting with a (usually screaming) kid for daddy's first visit in months. And then there were the people who were too dense to remember that busses had schedules to keep. They went out back of the rest-stop restaurant for a quick smoke, or got entranced by a display of souvenirs at the gift counter, and were shocked when they heard the bus roar away (Did people not believe it when the driver said a *fifteen-minute* break?) The all-too-familiar litany now fell from his lips.

"Name?"

"Janet."

"*Last* name?"

"*Chadwick.*"

The counterman's eyes flashed up. *No need to get huffy about it. We'll find her.*

"Where was she coming from?"

"Pasadena."

The counterman scanned his schedules. "Pasadena, you said?"

"Yes."

He lifted another clipboard and scanned it. "Here she is," he confirmed. "That bus isn't due in until six-thirty. It's running an hour late."

"Oh, great. Just f—" Shirley froze. The counterman's face had turned hard. Truth be told, he didn't give a rat's ass about Janet not having arrived on this bus, and even if he had cared there wasn't anything he could do about it and his legs had varicose veins that hurt like hot nails. And if the woman standing in front of him cussed he would have to less-than-politely tell her to shut her big trap, there were kids around the terminal if she hadn't noticed. And what was he supposed to do? What *could* he do? The bus was going to be late *LADY*.

As Shirley lingered on the edge of mouthing an obscenity, she recalled a waitress job she'd had in '63. She and the other girls had been dished plenty of crap from customers, just like this guy had to put up with, only it was about food, not about busses running late. ("Ma'am, these eggs are *runny*." "Excuse me Miss, but I said *rare*, not *raw*." "Didn't you hear me say I wanted *half* an order of toast?") And there wasn't anything a waitress could do if she wanted to keep her job, except take the food back and argue with the cook that he hadn't read the ticket right. Although most of the time he *had* read the ticket right.

Shirley didn't want to make a scene. She softened her tone.

"When did you say it's due?"

The counterman appreciated this. His tone mellowed, even brightened a little. "Six-thirty." He looked her over again, really for the first time; saw that she wasn't such a bad looker. Suddenly he became mister helpful. "There's a little café a ways down the block. They've got a pretty good chicken fried steak." The smile looked sincere, at least.

"Thanks." Shirley tried to return the smile and fell short.

The counterman saw there was no prospect for later and gave her a quick smile and then dipped his head back down to his checklist.

Shirley found an unoccupied bench and sat down. The thought of greasy food made her stomach feel queasy. Little cafes near bus stations were all the same: a grill with a lump of lard to keep the frozen patty from sticking, a vat of molten grease with a stainless wire cage so you could quick-fry everything from potatoes to fish sticks. And if you were lucky, on the side you got canned peaches and cottage cheese on a wilted lettuce leaf. No thanks.

And then she had an idea.

Shirley walked over to the pop machine, pushed two dimes into the slot, pulled out a green glass bottle of Coca-Cola from the rack. She took the Coke outside to where the station wagon was parked, slid onto the front seat, unlatched the glove box and pulled out the bottle of Jack Daniels. With a bottle opener from the glove box she popped the Coke cap. There was nothing to pour off the extra Coke into so she drained half the bottle into the gutter. She carefully filled the Coke bottle back to the top with JD. It fizzed expectantly while she screwed the cap back onto the booze and laid it carefully back in the glove box, dropped in the bottle opener, slapped it shut. As Shirley walked back into the terminal she took a long hit from the bottle.

By the time Janet Chadwick's bus rolled in at half-past seven, Shirley was gloriously toasted and was entertaining herself by counting flies on the wall.

Chapter 16

Mike had pushed hard with every uphill step. Billy's pride required that he keep pace, even after his feet began to hurt. The soles of his feet were close to blistering. But he was determined not to give Mike one tiny shred of satisfaction.

Stu had been stuck in the middle between the two brothers while they made the fast-paced ascent. He had remained intent on keeping up with Mike and equally intent upon not slowing Billy off his older brother's pace. He was disgusted at Mike's meanness towards Billy but had said nothing and intended to say nothing. He found himself wishing he were still working in Mr. Kelly's orchard.

The boys crested the last ridge an hour before darkness. There was already a hint of temperatures colder than the previous night. They marched with a silent intensity into the bowl meadow that contained Boiling Lake. The trail split and circled a shallow patch of water so small you could nearly throw a rock clear across. A sparse pine forest edged three fourths of the encircling meadow. On the far side from where the boys entered there was a massive tumble of rocks that fell from a sharp peak to within fifty yards of the water.

As they approached the lake they now saw they were not alone. Across the shallow water just a hundred yards away and pushed up against the massive rockslide stood a worn canvas tent. It was an old-fashioned square frame with a center pole, large enough to sleep four. The brown canvas was stained by dirt and smoke and had been patched many times. A campfire blazed in front of the tent and two grizzled men wearing battered cowboy hats sat before the fire. Neither stood, but both gazed across the expanse of water to watch the boys. They shifted quietly and exchanged looks of suspicious interest.

"Huh," was all Mike said when he saw the strangers. He scanned the meadow and pointed toward a bare patch of ground on the near side of the lake. "There," he ordered, and walked on.

When they arrived at the spot Mike had determined was to be their camp Billy dumped his pack and eyed the lake. He felt the first enthusiasm he'd had for several hours. He pulled the aluminum tube containing his fly rod from his pack, unscrewed the cap, and carefully removed the four lengths of fiberglass pole.

Mike looked hard as Billy coupled two joints of the fly rod and twisted them tight.

"What do you think you're doing?"

Billy looked up and played dumb. "Putting my fishing pole together?"

Mike gazed at the peak on the opposite side of the lake to where the sun line was creeping up the granite.

"There's no time for fishing," Mike said. "Put that pole away and get down to the lake and fetch some water. Stu and I will get a fire started."

Billy made no move to take apart the two sections he had joined. He stared at Mike for several seconds. "Why can't I fish for a couple of minutes, Mike? What's wrong with that?"

Mike, in the cruel mimic of a little girl's voice, said, "Why can't I fish for a couple of minutes, Mike? Why can't I do what I want, Mike?" His voice plunged low and angry. "Because I say you go get water. And I give the orders on this trip. Or have you already forgotten?"

"I just wanted to—"

"What you *want* and what you *get* are completely different things."

Stu was losing patience as Mike laid into Billy. He finally cut in.

"Mike, I'll get the water. And I don't see any harm in letting Billy fish for a few minutes."

Mike spun to face Stu. "*You what?*"

Stu cringed. "I just thought if Billy wanted to do a little fishing, what's the harm?"

Mike's anger spiraled into a stunned look of betrayal. He threw up his hands in complete frustration and turned away and began to rip open his pack, throwing items both needed and unneeded onto the ground. "Fine," he shouted without looking back at Stu or Billy. "Go ahead and do whatever you want. No need to do any coordinating. What the heck, why don't we all just have our own campsite? We can all three go for water, build our own fires, cook our own dinners. I don't even know why I asked you guys to come along. I might as well be here all by myself."

Stu was hot with embarrassment. "Aw, Mike. I didn't mean it that way."

Mike looked up. "Well what way did you mean it, then? Huh! Just precisely what way did you mean it?"

Stu was lost.

And then Billy reached down and picked up his backpack and hoisted it back onto his shoulders.

Stu looked at Billy. "What are you doing?"

"Going somewhere I won't be yelled at," Billy replied evenly.

"Woah," Stu said.

"No, let him go," Mike ordered.

Billy glared at Mike for a moment before he turned and walked toward the left side of the lake.

Mike returned to unpacking, ignoring Billy. Stu stood dumbfounded, watching Billy track through the grass toward where the trees came near to the water, slowly circling around toward the men's campsite. A new thought now spooked Stu. How far was Billy prepared to go? And who were those guys? They sure weren't your average backpackers. Stu was ready to run after Billy and tell him to come back when Billy paused, looked around, and dropped his pack about fifty yards from where Mike was still throwing things around in disgust. Stu relaxed a bit. Billy was still closer to them than he was to the other camp-site. Stu turned on Mike, who had by now pulled absolutely everything out of his pack and was busy spreading his ground tarp.

"What's got you so pissed?"

Mike feigned puzzlement. "Nothing."

"Don't give me that crap." Stu's voice climbed. "You just dumped on your little brother and for the life of me I can't figure out why."

Mike stopped arranging his tarp. He walked slowly over to Stu and looked him eye to eye. "If you want to change sides, you're welcome to join The Kid."

And with that calm pronouncement he turned away and began to walk toward the nearby trees. Over his shoulder he added, "I'm going for firewood. If you want to stay with me then we'll need some water from the lake."

Stu wanted to scream, *Quit acting like a dipshit!* But then a sudden flood of memories came of things he and Mike had done together during the past three years. The paper route Mike had helped him with. Snorkeling for coins and room keys in front of hotel docks. Talks about Shirley and how Stu was trying to cope. And as much as Stu wanted to join Billy he knew he couldn't. Not now. Not without understanding more about what had gotten under Mike's skin. Not without trying to find some peaceful solution that would bring them all back together.

So Stu picked up the water jug and walked down to the lake. On the rocky shoreline he found a deep spot to fill the jug and then he wearily trudged back to where Mike was now laying firewood inside a ring of rocks.

By this time Billy had assembled his pole and he began walking to the lake. He stood intent for a moment and then began casting out onto the shallow water. Big looping arcs of green line sent the fly far out onto the mirrored surface. Stu was admiring Billy's clean sweeping casts when Mike erupted behind him.

"Oh, shit!"

Stu turned. "What?"

"Matches!" Mike howled. "The Kid's got the matches!"

Stu found this impossibly funny. He giggled.

Mike looked up, eyes full of hurt. And for a moment Stu wondered if Mike might actually cry. But Mike's face hardened. "We'll see how funny you think it is when you're chewing at a strip of beef jerky for dinner."

Stu realized there was no way he could explain away his laughter. So instead he said, "I'm sorry, Mike. I'll run over and borrow a match or two from Billy. I don't mind."

Mike was incredulous. "You'll what?"

Stu said patiently, "I'll go over and ask Billy for some matches." But even as he said it he realized the mistake.

"When hell freezes over," Mike replied crisply.

"But Mike—"

"You will not go and ask The Kid if you can have some matches." Mike looked around in frustration. "Maybe we can start a fire using my hatchet. Maybe there's some flint in these rocks. We can make sparks with steel and flint." Mike began kicking up dirt, prizing in the rocky soil with his fingers, searching out fragments of stone and then examining them and finally tossing them away when they didn't turn out to be anything remotely like flint.

Stu watched Mike's frantic effort with growing frustration. "You're being ridiculous," he finally said.

Mike looked up from his hands and knees, his face a wash of unsettled emotions. "Well it's better than what you suggested. If we go ask The Kid for matches, we'll never hear the end of it." He returned to his search for the elusive flint.

Stu doubted there was any flint. And even if there were he doubted Mike would be able to start a fire with sparks struck from a hatchet. Stu had come up with another idea.

"How about if I go over and ask those guys if we can have a couple matches?" He didn't tell Mike his other thought. Stu wanted to learn more about their neighbors. And whether they might be dangerous to Billy.

Mike paused in his fossicking for flint and looked up. "Are you nuts?"

"No," Stu replied evenly. "I am not nuts."

Mike mulled it over. Finally he said, "Okay, go ahead if you want."

"Okay," Stu said. And before he lost his nerve he started for the other side of the lake, taking the route opposite where Billy was camped so as not to further aggravate Mike.

The closer Stu got the less comfortable he became. From a distance they had just looked old. But from closer range Stu began to realize they weren't old. They were just . . . *rugged*. And even from twenty yards away they *smelled*. Of sweat, cooking grease, and something that seemed familiar but which Stu couldn't quite place. An *animal* smell.

The two men watched him all the way. And so did their dog, a splotched gray and white mutt with pointed ears and a wolfish body. As Stu came close the dog rose from where it lay by the fire. It began to take slow menacing steps toward Stu. A low growl issued from deep in its throat and its lips peeled back to reveal sharp teeth.

The man the dog has been lying nearest to gave a command that was as mean as the dog's growl.

"*Pete!*"

The dog's growl ceased. His eyes flicked between his master and Stu.

"*Heel.*"

The dog turned and slunk back to where it had been, laid down with its chin resting on its outstretched paws. And not once did the dog take its eyes off Stu.

The man who had ordered the dog now looked pleasantly at Stu. He had a scrawny body and wore a never-washed red plaid shirt and ancient army fatigues. His face broke into a wide grin that was missing two teeth. "Name's Burt," he said with mischief. His dark eyes settled momentarily on the other man. "This here's my partner, Tom."

The stockier man, with a salt-and-pepper beard, dipped his battered cowboy hat slightly but did not smile. "Howdy," he said, and fell quiet to watch Stu as intently as the dog.

"I'm Stuart . . . Stu," Stu replied nervously. "Sorry to bother you, but we—" And Stu suddenly realized he didn't want to tell these two men what had happened. Because as soon as they knew Billy had abandoned them, they might get ideas. Bad ideas. Stu struggled for an answer and found one that sounded somewhat believable.

"We got our matches wet. Fell in a stream earlier today and they got wet." *Don't repeat yourself! You sound like you're lying!*

"And we were hoping, maybe you could lend us some matches to get our campfire started."

Burt and Tom began to chuckle and they looked at each other and that just made it worse. They burst into laughter. Stu was about ready to turn and run. Burt calmed a little.

"Sure, Sonny. We can give you a few matches." There was an unpleasant twinkle in his eyes. "Tom, why don't you get Sonny Boy some matches from the tent. I don't think I should get up, what with Pete itching for some action." He looked at the dog, whose eyes blinked at the mention of its name but still remained riveted upon Stu.

"Sure thing," Tom replied, stretching his legs and then walking achingly slow toward the tent. He pulled back the flap and went inside. There were sounds of rummaging, a grunt of approval, and the tent flap pushed out and Tom emerged carrying a jar full of matches. He unscrewed the lid as he approached Stu and fingered several matches into his palm.

As Tom handed Stu the matches Stu caught the full impact of the mystery smell. As the odor swept over him he flinched. Tom glanced back at Burt. "He smells the sheep," he said.

Burt asked, "What's the matter, Sonny Boy? Never smelled sheep before?" The men laughed and the dog took this for encouragement and made a guttural sound. Burt's hand stretched out, almost lazily, and came down with a solid *Thwap!* square on the top of Pete's head. The dog yelped once but stayed down. And still the dog's eyes never left Stu.

Burt swore, "Damned Australian Kelpies. They're great sheep dogs. But you gotta keep 'em in line. Let 'em get out of line even once, they're likely to turn wild on you. Specially this one, seeing as how he's part coyote. Don't keep him in line you're likely to wake up one morning and old Pete's got half your throat dripping bloody from his mouth!"

Stu wasn't sure whether Burt was playing with him or if he was serious. But Stu wasn't interested in learning the truth. With the matches safely in hand Stu took a nervous step backwards. "Well, I guess I better be getting back so we can get the fire started. It's getting dark." Another step. "Thanks for the matches."

"Yep," Burt observed. "Sure is getting dark." His toothy smile was predatory. "Better run on back to camp, Sonny Boy. Skedaddle now."

Stu turned, relieved. And then he saw across the lake that Billy had started his own campfire. It shone like a beacon and branded a lie to everything Stu had said about the matches. He could feel their eyes on his back now. And their laughter had vanished as they too saw the fire.

Stu half-stumbled, and began walking quickly. And before he had gone many yards the men began to laugh again. But now it was a mean laughter of condemnation. It echoed out across the mountain bowl and it didn't stop for a long while.

Chapter 17

Colleen Ward had good excuses to put off thanking Shirley in person for taking the boys to start their hike. Hank continued to be quite ill. He hadn't required hospitalization but it had nearly come to that. And when she wasn't fussing over Hank, Colleen went to the service station to carry Hank's instructions and encouragement and to make certain the employees were keeping up with the workload, and at the end of each day she took the cash and checks for the bank deposit.

By the morning of the third day Hank finally began to keep down food like chicken broth and applesauce. His temperature returned to normal. On a sunny Wednesday morning Colleen found Hank comfortably planted in front of the TV watching *Jeopardy*.

"Honey, I think I'll go over to Shirley's and thank her for taking the boys up to the trailhead. Is there anything you need?"

Hank looked up from his recliner, wearing a fresh pair of paisley pajamas, eyes bright, but still looking like he'd been hit by a train. "I'll be fine, Sweetheart."

Colleen drove the few blocks to the Johnson house and parked on the street. As she walked to the front door she carried a pint of homemade strawberry jam and a loaf of homemade bread wrapped in cellophane. She knocked three times. In a moment she heard sounds and then the knob turned and the door pulled inwards.

Shirley was confronted by a stranger in her thirties with dishpan blond hair pulled back in a ponytail, gray-blue eyes hard as glass chips and a thin unsmiling mouth.

The woman asked in a calm voice, "Looking for Shirley?"

"Yes," Colleen replied, uncertain. "I'm Mike and Billy's mother, Colleen."

The woman returned a blank stare.

"Those are my sons. The boys Stuart went hiking with."

"Oh," the woman said with disinterest. "Shirley's in the bathroom. She'll be out in a moment. Would you like to come in?"

Colleen stepped across the black rubber doormat into the small living room. The woman pulled the door nearly shut but not all the way, leaving a suggestive crack at the edge of the frame.

Shirley was now confronted with another surprise.

There were boxes everywhere, filled with dishes, clothes, bedding, some still empty. The boxes all had liquor logos on the sides. The state liquor store was a popular place to get boxes for moving because the cardboard cartons were sturdy and small enough to easily lift and stack. The clerks piled them at the front of the store, as happy to be relieved of the job of crushing and putting them in the dumpster as were the people who needed them for moving.

Colleen tried not to fidget while she waited for the woman to say something . . . anything. The woman finally said, "I'm Janet, her sister."

"Oh."

More waiting.

Janet finally seemed to understand that Colleen didn't intend to leave no matter how long Shirley took to come out. She hesitantly asked, "Would you like some coffee?"

"Yes," Colleen replied politely. She really wanted to ask what was happening but doubted Janet would volunteer anything.

"Be back in a sec," Janet said as she walked off toward the kitchen.

In a few seconds Shirley appeared in the hallway. Her hair was wet and wrapped up in a towel and she wore a white terrycloth bathrobe with a stylized HC sewn in black thread on the left lapel. She looked unpleasantly surprised and sounded unhappy as she greeted her surprise visitor. "Hello Colleen. We weren't expecting company."

"I wanted to thank you for taking the boys up to the trail." Colleen held out the bread and the strawberry jam.

Shirley left wet footprints as she came and took the food. "Thanks." There was finality in the word. Shirley expected Colleen to leave.

But Colleen wasn't ready to leave, not until she had been told what the boxes meant. She looked around the living room at the general confusion. "Changing things around?" It sounded lame. Neither woman was fooling the other.

"I'm having a yard sale," Shirley replied curtly.

The question came tumbling out.

"Are you moving?"

Shirley's reply was set in concrete. "Yes, to California. My sister came to help pack."

Colleen's next words were practically an accusation. "Stuart's been over at the house a lot lately but he hasn't mentioned anything about moving."

Shirley clipped a curt reply. "It came up real sudden."

Janet hadn't reappeared with the promised coffee. It was now obvious that she wasn't going to reappear. Colleen wanted to know details, but she wasn't going to cause a scene. She finally turned for the door and pushed it with a hard palm so that it slammed open; she marched down the skinny concrete path and crossed the sidewalk to her car.

After Colleen had driven off, Janet came out from the kitchen where she had been listening. "Is this a problem?"

"No," Shirley replied firmly. "They were going to find out at some point. There's nothing they can do with the boy up in the mountains." She held up the bread and the strawberry jam. "Let's have breakfast."

Stu was bothered by a nightmare and felt exhausted when dawn broke. Mike had slept soundly but was reluctant to get up; dealing with Billy was going to be unpleasant and he hadn't yet decided how he wanted to play it out. So both boys remained burrowed in the safe warmth of their sleeping bags until well after the sun had risen.

When Stu eventually poked his head out of his bag he discovered that the dew had again fallen heavy during the night. In the meadow the wide-bladed grass was bent and clung to the ground in lumpy green waves. Their fire from the previous evening was long cold. The few chunks of half-burnt wood around the edge of the fire pit were as wet as the grass.

Stu finally worked up the energy to emerge from his bag. He dug out dry clothes from his backpack and stepped into a pair of jeans and then sat down on his sleeping bag and pulled on wool socks and laced up his boots. When he had finished the last button on the corduroy shirt he finally looked across to where Billy was camped.

Billy was gone.

Stu looked around the meadow. He looked across the lake at the campsite of the sheepherders. Their tent and trappings were still there but of the men there was no sign. Nor was there any sign of the dog. And their campfire had not been kindled for there was no wisp of smoke.

Mike's inert form lay inside his sleeping bag. Stu reached down and shook Mike's shoulder.

"Mike!"

"Uhhhh."

"Mike! Get up! Billy's gone!"

Another grumble. Then a word that was finally aware. "What?" Mike's head poked out from the end of his bag. "What did you say?"

"I said, Billy is gone."

Mike was bewildered for a moment. "When did he leave?"

"How should I know? For cripes sake, get your butt out of that bag. We've got to find him!"

Mike returned a glazed look of comprehension. "You mean you didn't see him go?"

"No! Now get out of that bag and help me find him!"

Mike reached to zip the bag open and then stood in his shorts and scanned the near side of the lake. "Maybe he's down behind some of the taller grass," Mike offered lamely.

"What about his pack? I don't see it anywhere. And with the grass laid flat there's no way you wouldn't see it. Mike, he's gone!"

Mike began digging out jeans from his backpack. He dressed quick and finally grabbed his felt hat. "Let's go check it out."

When they arrived where Billy had made camp they found the bed of charcoal was cold. The grass where Billy had laid out his sleeping bag was easy to spot, but there was no clue where he had disappeared to.

It was Stu who finally said what both were thinking. "What about those sheepherders?"

They turned to look at the square tent across the lake.

Stu said, "What if they got him?"

"What do you mean?"

"Jeez, Mike. Are you stupid? What if those two weirdoes came and took Billy during the night!"

"Why would they do something like that?"

"Are you joking?" Stu wondered if Mike were actually that dense. "What if they're the kind of men who like boys instead of women?"

"That's crazy." But Mike's denial was thin, his voice shaky.

"We'll maybe it's crazy and maybe it isn't. But where's Billy and where are those two creepy guys?"

Mike blurted, "Jeez, I don't know." And there was now an edge of fear in his voice.

"We have to find him!"

"Okay, then let's go and find him."

"Right."

"We start with the campsite. Maybe they're inside the tent. Maybe they're still asleep."

They began walking in the wet grass and then they started trotting and when they arrived Mike stood in front of the tent and yelled, "Hello!"

Nothing.

Mike took a step towards the tent flap.

"Watch out for the dog," Stu cautioned.

Mike glanced at Stu. "If that dog were inside it would have been out here by now." But Mike wasn't entirely certain of this. "Hello!" He yelled louder. Still no answer. Mike took another step, hesitated.

Several thoughts collided in Stu's brain. What if the sheepherders were inside and had guns? Maybe they were hiding nearby and watching. They'd be unhappy with kids poking around. But Billy might be inside. Tied up. Or unconscious. Or worse. Stu's heart began to pound as Mike grabbed the tent flap and pulled it back. After a long moment Stu stepped up behind him, breathing hard, and looked over Mike's shoulder and into the tent.

There were two wood frame cots covered with sheepskin blankets. A rawhide chest sat near the foot of one cot. On the floor was a battered blue Coleman kerosene stove. Pants and shirts were hung from a cord stretched between the center pole and a corner of the tent. The stench of sheep and sweat was overpowering.

But no Billy.

Mike let the flap go. "Whew! What a stink!"

"What next?" Stu demanded.

Mike looked confused. "I don't know."

Stu had had enough. "You fool!" He erupted.

"What?"

"This is all your fault and you're a damned fool!"

"Wait a minute——"

"No!" Stu faced off, shaking with rage. "You ran your *fourteen-year-old* brother out of our camp like he was some stranger. He's just a kid! Do you have any idea how lucky you are to even *have* a little brother?"

And there it was. He hadn't intended confronting Mike like this, but now there was no turning back.

"Cripes, Mike. I'd give just about anything to have a little brother like Billy. And you go and treat him like dirt. And I just don't get it. What in the world is wrong with you?"

Mike stood dumbfounded. Billy's disappearance meant trouble. And he felt the weight of responsibility to find him. But this thing Stu had said, the *brother* thing, especially about knowing *how* to treat a brother. Mike retreated to the safety of what needed to be done. But it sounded entirely lame when it came out.

"Getting mad isn't going to help."

Stu nearly punched his best friend in the face right then and there. His fist was clenched and ready. And he might have, except he saw that Mike was right.

First they had to find Billy. Then he and Mike could go at each other, if it came to that.

"Okay," Stu backed down. "Where do we start?"

Mike scanned the meadow and the cliffs where the trail wound up the rockslide towards the pass over into the Twisp Valley. Finally he looked where the meadow inclined gently into the forest.

"I'll bet they've got their sheep somewhere over there," Mike said. "Let's check that spot first."

"Right." Stu strode off through the thick grass without waiting. Mike followed.

When they reached the far edge of the meadow and still saw no sign of sheep or the men or Billy, they climbed the forested ridge and broke through the trees into another meadow that stretched across the flank of the hill. Honeybees were busy in the lupines and paintbrush. A redheaded woodpecker was drilling holes in a dead tree trunk. High above a hawk circled searching for prey in the grass below. The sharp peaks stood like dark sentinels marching towards the blue horizon. But there was no sign of sheep or the men or Billy.

"Shit," Mike said.

"What next?"

"Back to camp."

They scrambled over the ridge and around the lake to where their backpacks and sleeping bags lay. Mike stood looking up at the trail that led through a rocky defile to the other side of the Sawtooth.

Stu asked, "Do you think they took him through there?"

"I don't know." Mike's voice now held something Stu didn't want to hear. Defeat.

"What next?"

"Maybe he hiked down to Cub Lake." Mike looked at Stu hopefully and Stu felt panic return. Mike waited and when Stu said nothing Mike said, "What do you think?"

Stu thought for a second. "Could he have come that close and not woke us up?"

Mike studied the sea of still-wet grass that led to where Billy had camped. There was no sign that Billy had broken a fresh path earlier that morning, but it was hard to tell with the grass all laid down. "Maybe," Mike offered. "I was really conked out last night."

"I wasn't," Stu countered. "I think I'd have heard him."

"Maybe not," Mike said hopefully. "Maybe he came through here real quiet. He probably sneaked right past us without making a sound." It was more like an accusation, as if Billy were at fault.

Stu almost yelled at Mike because he was trying to pin blame on Billy. Stu figured Billy had every right to be sneaky. If he'd been in Billy's shoes, he might have snuck past and he wouldn't have cared at all what the older boys thought of his disappearance. But instead of going ballistic Stu said, "Okay, so if he came through here, do you think he'd go down to Cub Lake? Maybe he went back to town."

"Maybe," Mike said. "But that's the long way. It would be a lot shorter to go to Cub and then hike the Prince Creek trail to Lake Chelan. If he started early this morning he'd be able to get down in time to catch the afternoon ferry."

Stu pictured Billy hiking nine miles down hill. He remembered what the Butte had done to Billy's feet. But blisters were better than being kidnapped so Stu clung to the hope that Billy had chosen to walk out.

"So we go to Cub first?"

"Yeah," Mike said. "And if he's not there then we take the Prince Creek trail to the lake. And if he's not there then we hike to the head of the lake, all night if we have to, and we get the rangers to come back and look for him. At least they'll have horses."

Stu finally felt the weight lift just a tiny bit. At least there was a plan. But there was one last thing to consider before they left Boiling Lake.

"Shouldn't we hike up the pass first and take a look around?"

Mike thought hard. His answer was grim.

"They would see us coming. They probably have guns."

Stu felt gooseflesh on the back of his neck. If the men had a rifle they could pick he and Mike off real easy. And what good would that do Billy?

"Yeah. You're right," Stu finally conceded.

Mike and Stu stuffed their packs and rolled their sleeping bags. They started down the trail to Cub Lake. A mile after the Y where they had turned the previous day the trail began to track alongside a rushing creek that tumbled in from a branch canyon. The creek held boulders the size of cars, with broad pools spreading below as the water rushed past. Stu imagined how Billy would have wanted to stop and try his luck fishing. With every twist in the trail Stu hoped to see Billy standing on a boulder above a large pool contentedly casting for trout. But each turn brought only disappointment. Stu began to wonder if they had made a mistake. Perhaps they should have climbed the pass and searched before starting down, even if it meant confronting men with guns.

By the time they sighted Cub Lake they had dropped nearly two thousand feet. The temperature had warmed into the sixties. They came around a sharp bend and the far side of the lake was just visible through the old forest, a third of a mile long and three hundred yards wide, rimmed on the far side by rockslides. Along the far shore were strewn weathered logs and boulders. At the far end of the lake the exit stream had drawn together a driftwood jam. In the crystalline water they could see the silted brown silhouettes of waterlogged tree trunks haphazardly strewn across the bottom.

But there was no sign of Billy.

"Let's go," Stu said, striding off without waiting for an answer.

The lake was deceptively close from where they first spotted it. The trail cut back into the forest and now they only glimpsed the lake from time to time. Twenty minutes later they finally arrived at where the creek spilled across a flat expanse of worn bedrock and rippled out into the shallow calm surface that reflected sky and mountains.

Stu stopped abruptly and Mike nearly ran into him from behind. Mike was about to say something when Stu pointed. Halfway down the shoreline, just beyond a stand of fir that had hidden him from view, stood Billy, wearing his Akubra, calmly casting a fly line out onto the pristine waters and oblivious to everything except fishing.

"Jeez," was all Stu could manage to say, but there was a world of relief in that single word.

Mike almost said something about Billy that wasn't very kind, but one look at Stu changed his mind.

Stu spotted the Forest Service campsite. "Over there," he said, and began walking toward the log benches which had been set in a rough square around a large stone fire ring.

"Shouldn't we holler—"

"No," Stu cut Mike off. "Let him be."

Mike started to disagree, but Stu gave him a look that said he'd best not get into it, so Mike shut up and followed Stu to where Billy's backpack was neatly laid against one of the logs. Nothing seemed to have been removed from Billy's pack. They set down their packs and Stu collapsed onto the pine-needle-strewn ground with his back to the log, exhausted, trying to figure out what was the next best step with Billy.

Mike wasn't happy. But neither was he stupid. So he found a distraction, for the moment, in exploring the campsite.

The Forest Service had spent some effort making the place comfortable. A trench-privy had been dug several yards back in the trees, with two rough planks between large rocks to form a seat. But the roll of pink, perfumed toilet paper inside a plastic bag? Mike doubted the USFS that had left *that*. More likely it had been hikers that included at least one female.

A beat-up fish net was hung by its handle from the low limb of a fir. Caught in the net were three cans of Spam, six tins of Vienna Sausages, four cans of Pork 'n Beans, and a partly-used can of Crisco. A note explained that the owner hadn't wanted to pack them out. *If you like Spam and beans and wieners*, the note concluded, *Bon appétit!* Not likely the USFS on this one either!

Several lengths of rope were coiled and hung on a wooden peg pounded into a fir trunk. Atop the rope was hung a large black cast-iron skillet. Recalling the past two days of hiking, Mike couldn't imagine how anyone would have chosen to carry such a huge chunk of iron this far, but it was understandable why they had left it.

Then Mike found the great prize—a double-bladed axe wrapped in oil-cloth. He took an experimental swing at a log, lofting the silvery blade in a high arc, and the steel buried so deep Mike had to muscle it out with both hands. The chopping sound reverberated through the forest. Mike was delighted. He took another swing and then another.

Stu finally came to investigate. Mike was by now halfway through the log. A wedge of fresh white wood flew up as the axe blade buried itself two inches deep.

"What in the heck are you doing?"

Mike looked up but said nothing. He took another high arcing swing and again buried the blade in the wood.

"What does it look like I'm doing? Peeling potatoes?"

"I know what you're doing," Stu retorted. "But *why*? I mean, what's the point."

Mike shrugged. "Nothing better to do, I guess."

"Cripes," Stu grumbled.

"Hey!" Mike said angrily. "Why don't you let up? We found Billy, didn't we?"

"Yeah, we found Billy," Stu agreed. "But *you* owe him an apology."

Mike squared up. "Why? He's the one who took off."

Stu couldn't believe it. After everything that had happened Mike apparently still didn't get it. It was simply too much for Stu to take. Rather than blow up, Stu took a long hard look at Mike and said, "You're hopeless," and then he walked away.

"Hey!" Mike challenged. But Stu just kept walking toward the lakeshore. He might have stopped if Mike had kept hollering. He might have even picked a fist fight even though Mike had him outweighed by forty pounds. But Mike had fallen silent.

Stu took the trail along the lake until he was only a few yards from where Billy stood on a large flat rock, casting out onto the glassine water. Billy had two trout strung on a green willow whip laid in the cold water alongside the rock.

Billy kept casting, ignoring Stu. Finally Stu spoke.

"You okay?"

Billy pulled back on the pole and brought the fly line zipping up off the water. The green line, with six feet of clear leader and a black gnat fly at the end, performed a smooth looping arc behind Billy. The pole tip shot forward and the fly whizzed past Billy's head and sailed out into the lake. When the line was floating in a straight line and the black gnat was perched delicately on the surface of the water Billy answered.

"Sure." But he sounded anything but fine.

"Look," Stu began slowly. "I told Mike he was an idiot for ordering you around last night."

Billy gave no sign he even cared.

"We were really worried this morning. We thought maybe those sheep-herders had kidnapped you."

Billy again drew the line up off of the water. A nonchalant flick of the wrist and a *whoosh* as the pole bowed. The fly sailed out to his right and landed along-side a partly submerged log. Billy concentrated on the fly and ignored Stu.

"We were ready to hike all the way to the head of the lake and get the rangers to look for you if you weren't here." There was an increasingly anxious edge to Stu's voice.

Billy's concentration upon the fly wavered just a little.

"You really called Mike an idiot?"

Stu struggled to keep a calm voice despite the surge of hope at finally getting a response. "Yeah."

Billy turned his head and looked at Stu.

"Really?"

"Yeah, really."

Billy forgot about the fly. "What did he say?"

Stu was about to explain Mike's reaction when a flash of silver appeared on the surface of the water. The fly disappeared in a swirl.

"Billy!" Stu pointed to where the line was arrowing down into the water.

Billy turned and jerked up on the rod. With the hook set it was only a few seconds before Billy had the trout flopping around on the rock. It was ten inches and perfect for the pan. He grabbed the wriggling fish with both hands and held it up like a trophy, pure glory on his face. It was silver underneath with an olive-green back and a peppering of dark spots and a neon-pink blush on its sides.

"It's a cutthroat," Billy said proudly. He pointed to a bright red streak beneath the gills.

Billy extracted the hook with a single twist and then put his index finger down the trout's throat and pulled back. The fish died with a squawk. Billy reached down for his stick and strung it through the cutthroat's gills and laid the three fish back in the water.

"Nice job with the pole," Stu said.

"You ever used a fly rod?"

"Nope."

Billy stepped off the rock and held the rod out to Stu. "It's not that hard."

Stu took the rod gingerly.

"C'mon down this way," Billy said, grabbing his trout stick and then leading Stu along the shoreline toward another flat boulder at the water's edge. "Usually there's just one trout that hangs around a place like that log. And even if there are others they won't bite after all the splashing. You need to move to a new spot." Billy pointed to the rock. "Try from there."

Stu stepped onto the rock. Billy stood on the shore out of the way. "Start with a few yards of line. Make sure you loop the line when you cast. You don't want to crack it like a whip or you'll snap off the fly."

Stu began to clumsily wave the pole back and forth.

"Easy does it," Billy encouraged.

Stu concentrated on being smooth and soon had a regular rhythm established but he still had only five yards of line played out.

Billy said, "Okay, pull more line off the reel with your left hand. And remember to keep your line moving. When you think you have enough line, let it sail out as far into the lake as you can."

As the line got longer Stu was having more and more difficulty getting it to stay in a smooth loop. Just as he was ready to cast, the fly sunk toward the ground on the backstroke and caught in a bush. When Stu's arm came forward the hook ripped off a bunch of leaves. The line fell and slithered in a tangle at Stu's feet.

"Damn!" Stu laid the rod down with its tip in the water. Billy wanted to tell Stu not to put the tip in the lake—it was his favorite rod—but he instead said, "A little practice and you'll be a pro."

Stu began picking bits of leaf from the black gnat. He looked up with embarrassment. "I could have broken your pole. I better stick with the casting pole I brought."

No way was Billy going to let Stu off that easy.

"I saw what you did wrong." Billy insisted. "Let me show you how to do it right." Billy splashed one foot in the water and stepped up beside Stu. He lifted the fly rod out of the water and reeled in the line.

Stu said, "I'll watch from the shore," and began to step off the rock.

"No," Billy insisted. "I want you to get the feel of casting."

Stu stayed. Billy handed him the fly rod. In the same way he had seen coaches teach kids how to swing a bat or handle a tennis racket Billy stood behind Stu and softly grasped his right arm. "Hold the rod straight, like this," Billy made sure Stu's arm was out far enough to give the pole good action. "Okay, bring the tip up and play out the line slowly. Take it easy."

Stu began a gentle back and forth motion with the rod, guided by Billy's encouraging hand, playing out more and more line, and for the first time the line began forming nice flattish loops that whizzed back and forth above their heads. Billy finally said, "Okay, let her go!"

The black gnat sailed out onto the calm water and lit neatly on the surface. The green line pointed to the center of the lake.

"Good one!"

"Yeah," Stu said with pride. "I guess this isn't so hard after all!"

Facing the lake, Stu didn't see Billy's satisfied smile, quickly replaced by happy concentration.

As the leader began to sink Billy said, "Okay, let's try it again. This time I want you to feed out another yard or two before you let it go."

"Right," Stu agreed with growing enthusiasm.

Mike was nowhere to be seen when Billy and Stu arrived back in camp with a string of cutthroat trout. A fresh pile of chopped wood was heaped beside the fire ring. The double-bladed axe was laid against the pile. Stu looked long and hard at the firewood. He almost made a comment about the value of Mike's work, but Billy wasn't going to forgive that easily. For the Butte, for weeks of cold shoulder treatment, for Boiling Lake, there was still plenty of payback due. Stu shifted gears.

"He sure was busy."

"Yeah," Billy agreed. He held up the string of trout, not much caring what Mike had done or where he was. "What should we do with these?"

"Take 'em to the stream and clean 'em for lunch. I'll see if I can find Mike."

Billy gave an indifferent shrug. "You want me to start a fire?"

"That would be great." Stu paused, added, "Thanks for the fishing lesson."

"No problem." Billy smiled and turned for the creek.

"Hey, Billy?"

Billy turned and paused.

"Yeah?"

"Can I ask a favor?"

"Sure," Billy readily agreed. "What?"

"I just want you to, well, I just want you to *try*."

"Try *what*?"

"You know . . . *Try*."

Billy spread his hands in a gesture of surrender. "Okay," he said. "I'll try." But there was no conviction in his voice. He turned for the lake and Stu let him go.

Stu stood for a moment and wondered if Billy would come around. He finally turned for the trail. He knew the direction Mike must have gone. Mike wasn't visible around the shoreline of the lake and since there was no way Mike could have gotten past them without being seen, the only direction he could have gone was back up toward Boiling Lake.

Stu hiked a quarter of a mile before he finally spotted Mike, fifteen yards off the trail, sitting on the edge of a massive boulder. In the lee of the boulder a dark pool spread until the current broke the smooth surface and continued its downhill course. Mike's back was to the trail. Stu pushed through the brush and sidestepped down the eroded bank, sending a shower of dirt and stones clattering into the rocks at the edge of the creek. It was enough to be heard over the rushing water but Mike continued to stare out across the pool.

Stu stepped along the rocks at the edge of the creek bed and came to Mike's towering boulder. He looked up and quietly said, "Hi."

Mike twisted around, looked down, saw Stu.

"Hi," Mike said dully.

Mike's fishing pole was leaned against the boulder. In the water at the pool's edge Stu saw a small trout gill-strung on a length of nylon cord tied to a stick wedged in the rocks.

"Looks like you caught one."

Mike stared back out across the dark pool and said nothing.

"Got room up there for me?"

Mike shifted uncomfortably. "I suppose."

Stu wedged his shoe against a cleft in the stone and pulled himself up. He stood on top for a moment with his hand shielding the sun from his eyes, surveying the creek in both directions. It ran in a series of rapids and pools among granite boulders. It fell out of sight and reappeared three times before it was lost in the forest as it raced on towards Cub Lake. Snatches of vine maple clutched at the eroding soil along the far bank. Beyond the brush a group of old-growth pine towered thick and made the forest dark and mysterious.

Stu sat down cross-legged beside Mike. He waited for a couple minutes and when Mike failed to speak Stu finally said, "Nice job on the wood."

Mike continued staring across the pool and into the forest. "Thanks," he mumbled.

Stu felt trapped. Mike had seen him and Billy out on the lakeshore casting with Billy's fly rod. A whisper of wind crept across the boulder and brought a chill. Stu felt uneasy as the thought came that Mike was doing to him what his own mom had always done to him so well. *The cold shoulder.* Stu finally turned to Mike and demanded, "What's the deal, Mike? Is it something I said? Is it something Billy did? *What?*"

A little shudder went through Mike. He remained silent. But Stu refused to move. He was willing to wait for however long it took.

Mike finally said in a voice that made him sound like a tired old man, "I just thought we'd have more fun, that's all."

But Stu thought he knew what Mike *really* meant. *More fun* meant they would be getting their licks in on Billy. Only Mike hadn't figured all the consequences, had he? What was Billy supposed to do? Run for home? Pick a fight with someone who could easily pound him into the ground? What?

Stu's surge of anger crested. And then it faded. Patience was the only solution, if there *was* going to be a solution. Confronting Mike would only make things worse. It would confirm Stu had changed camps; that he was now on Billy's side. And Stu refused to choose sides. He wanted to be in *both* camps. Stu said, "We caught some fish for lunch. Care to join us?"

Mike stared into the distance.

"*Please*," Stu added.

Mike absentmindedly picked at a loose thread on his sleeve. "I suppose so." He slowly uncrossed his legs, pushed them out, and slid off the rock. His shoes hit the muck between the rocks and sent little brown bombs flying in every direction. Mike sucked his feet up one at a time, gathered up his pole, and grabbed the cord holding the small trout.

When they had scrambled back up to the top of the bank Mike looked back at the boulder and then across the creek, and without warning he hauled back his right arm and slung the trout across the creek. The nylon cord streamed out behind the fish, which landed with a smack against a tree trunk and fell out of sight into the vine maple.

"What'd you do that for?"

Mike returned a level stare. Stu realized that the cutthroats he and Billy had pulled from Cub were all larger than Mike's creek minnow. How could Mike possibly give Billy the satisfaction? Mike turned in silence and started down the trail.

"Sorry," Stu said to Mike's back. Mike just kept going.

"I said I was sorry," Stu insisted.

Mike stumbled to a stop and turned around. "Look," he began with forced patience. "I'm not mad at you. I'm not even sure if I'm mad at Billy. I've just got a lot on my mind. Okay?"

"Like what?" Stu puzzled.

Mike barely managed to keep what little of his patience he still possessed. "Just . . . things."

"Like?" Stu said.

"*Things!*" Mike spun around and started back down the trail.

"Hey Mike?" Stu called hopefully. Mike kept walking. Stu trotted to catch up, wanting a better answer.

Mike finally acknowledged the question with one of his own. "What exactly is it that you want from me, Stu?" His didn't break stride or turn his head.

Stu knew what he wanted. "Would you do one thing for me?" He asked.

Mike slowed and gave Stu a suspicious, defensive look. "What?"

"Just say 'okay', okay?"

"Okay, okay."

Stu laughed. Even Mike smiled.

Stu sobered up. "Please just agree that you'll do one thing for me . . . when I ask."

Mike had already felt hurt enough for one day. He said slowly, "Okay, I'll do *one* thing for you. Are you planning to tell me what it is?"

"Soon," Stu promised.

"Wonderful," Mike muttered. "*Soon*." But he didn't push it.

Stu was grateful. The boys walked in silence the rest of the way back to camp.

By the time they arrived, Billy's fire had burnt neatly down to coals. The trout were floured and peppered. As soon as Billy spied them coming he scooped out a spoonful of Crisco and dropped it into the cast iron skillet and shoved the skillet onto the center of the glowing coals. The Crisco began to sizzle, and into the skillet went the trout; within seconds the delicious scent of frying fish filled the campsite.

Chapter 18

*S*hirley and Janet had removed most of the furniture from the house and arranged the silverware and dishes and other small items on card tables in the front yard. The sale would start at nine the following morning. And the morning after that they would leave for California. Two days after their departure Stu was scheduled to arrive home. The thought of Stu finding a house empty of all but his own little bit of furniture made Shirley uneasy. She kept reminding herself that Stu was planning to enlist; he would be in basic training for the Army. The boy would be okay. He would survive.

At noon Shirley took a break and stood on the front stoop and braced her hands into the small of her back. "Looks like we're getting somewhere," she said to Janet who was busy out on the lawn tearing little pieces of masking tape and writing prices on them with a black marker pen and sticking them to the merchandise.

Janet returned a grin. "Another hour or two and we'll be ready for tomorrow's crowd!"

"I thought I'd run over to Safeway and pick up some sandwich fixings. I've got some other errands to run. I'll be gone for an hour. Want to come along?"

Janet considered this for a moment before she answered, "No, I'll finish up with this so we can knock off early this evening."

"Okay. I'll pick up a six-pack."

"Great!"

Shirley found her purse on the kitchen counter and went out to the station wagon. It was blasting hot inside even with the windows rolled down. Shirley was sweating by the time she arrived at Safeway and was grateful for the cold wash of air that hit her when the supermarket's automatic doors swung open.

She grabbed a metal basket and pushed it to the bread rack and pulled a loaf of white bread whose plastic bag was decorated with little red and yellow and blue balloons. She continued down the aisle and nearly turned the corner, intent upon the shelves filled with canned meats, when Shirley saw the one person she didn't want to talk to: Colleen Ward. Colleen was mid-way up the aisle, reaching for a can on the highest shelf.

"Oh shit," Shirley muttered under her breath. She blew past the aisle and pushed her cart until she reached the fruit and vegetable coolers at the far side of the store. She stalled for several minutes and finally picked out two oranges, a head of iceberg lettuce and a bunch of bananas before she decided to risk the checkout counter, hoping Colleen would have finished and left.

At the front of the aisle she nudged the cart around the corner and peeked out and saw no one she knew. She was about to head for the nearest checkout clerk when a voice from behind startled her.

"Excuse me!"

Shirley whirled around and was confronted by an elderly woman with white hair done up fancier than a vanilla-frosted three layer cake, wearing batwing glasses with rhinestones set in the black frames. She wore blue slacks and a white blouse with a frilled collar. The flesh of her ankles had swollen around the edges of her low-heel pumps. Shirley recognized the woman. It was Eloise Parker, who had skipped paying for her paper delivery. Shirley stared dumbly at the woman.

"Well!" Eloise Parker growled.

"Well what?" Shirley replied indignantly.

"You're the paperboy's mother aren't you?"

Shirley's first thought was to deny being Stuart's mother. But this old biddy might chase after her, and the last thing Shirley wanted was a scene. It might cause the manager to take them both up front. And if Colleen Ward were still in the store she'd spot Shirley for certain. So Shirley finally admitted, "Yes, Stuart is my son and he has a paper route."

"He stopped delivering my newspapers," Eloise protested. "I've called the Wenatchee World and had him put on report."

Shirley glared at the woman in disgust. How dare she! But Eloise Parker stood her ground.

Shirley's anger rose like a dust devil. "Stuart said you haven't paid for several weeks and that's why he stopped delivering your paper. And if you have a complaint you should talk to Stuart, not me. It's *his* paper route, not mine."

"That's a lie!" Eloise Parker screamed. "I put regular envelopes in the box with full payment in cash. *Someone* takes them from the box. It must be your boy who takes my money! I'll have to report this to the police!" Eloise's face flushed and a bit of spittle clung to her lower lip. "Yes," she continued roughly. "That's what I'm going to do. I'm going to go down to the police station right after I get my groceries home and tell them the Johnson kid has been stealing my money and not giving me my newspapers! I know what he does with my papers. He takes them down to the resorts and he hawks them to tourists. The little cheat. He should go to jail!"

Shirley was ready to tell Eloise Parker where to shove it when a voice from behind interrupted.

"I know Stuart."

Shirley turned and there stood Colleen Ward.

Colleen was staring at Eloise Parker and Colleen was not happy.

"Stuart is a good boy. He would never do something like that."

Eloise bristled defensively, but Colleen ploughed on leaving no chance for Eloise to get a word in edgewise.

"Furthermore, I've known about you, *Mrs. Parker*, for a good many years. You're a mean old bitch. Everyone knows it. You remember last year when you came to our station and drove off without paying for your gas? When Hank caught up with you after chasing you in his pickup for nearly half a mile, you told him you had left a five-dollar bill on the pump and it must have blown off in a wind gust. But that was a lie. Hank told you to never come back to the station ever again. Do you remember *that* Mrs. Parker?"

Eloise Parker's scarlet flush of anger blanched until her face was white with peachy splotches.

"Well!" Colleen demanded.

"I never heard of such a thing," Eloise fumbled with the purse hung on her shoulder and her face contorted with panic. She grabbed the handle of her shopping cart and swung it around and pushed away at full speed.

"Whew!" Colleen said. "That woman is more trouble than a rabid rat."

Shirley was relieved to see Eloise storm away, but wasn't sure if she was better off now, facing Colleen. She smiled weakly and said, "Thanks for getting her off of my back."

Colleen looked at Shirley as if she had something more important to say. But the tentative look vanished in one of Colleen's irrepressibly happy smiles. "Have a nice day, Shirley," Colleen said. She pushed her cart past Shirley's and turned down the next aisle.

Shirley desperately wanted a cigarette, but had to wait until she reached her car in the parking lot.

This wasn't the last shock of her day. After she finished her shopping and errands and returned home she saw Stu's desk and bed and dresser sitting out in the yard. She carried in the groceries and found Janet cleaning up the kitchen.

"Why did you put Stuart's furniture out?"

"I thought you were selling everything. Isn't that right?" Janet sounded innocent.

Shirley searched her memory, certain she had told Janet that Stuart's belongings were to be left in his room. But she couldn't exactly remember when she had said this and finally decided she must not have mentioned it.

"I was going to leave his stuff," Shirley said as she placed the beer in the refrigerator.

"Why?"

"It's his. He bought most of it with his own earnings."

"Couldn't we leave him the money we get for it?"

Shirley felt an edge of irritation as she turned to face her sister.

"It's just that it's *his* stuff."

Janet looked unconvinced and unconcerned. "Well," she countered slowly, "How are you going to get your cleaning deposit back if you don't have everything out of the house?"

Shirley hadn't told Janet that she didn't expect to get the fifty dollar cleaning deposit back from Jack Handerton. He owned several rental houses around town and had the reputation of being a slumlord. *Jack the Hook* never refunded cleaning deposits.

Janet didn't wait for Shirley's response.

"You told me the boy was enlisting. This stuff won't be of any use to him in the Army. He'd have to sell it before he left. And what kind of a yard sale is he going to have with just that little bit?"

Janet rolled on with her cruel logic.

"We're doing your boy a favor. I've packed up his clothes and the junk from his desk. They're in boxes in his room."

Shirley considered Janet's reasoning and it made sense. What good was furniture to Stuart if he was in the Army? And Janet was right about having a yard sale with the tiny bit that was Stu's. He'd never get people to come. This way he'd at least get a few bucks.

Shirley finally relented. "Well, okay," she said. After all, Janet *was* hauling her back to California. And she *was* putting up Shirley for as long as it took to find work. "You're right. Of course you're right." She switched from the uneasy subject. "Want a sandwich before we get back to work?"

"Great! I'll make them. You look beat."

"I am. Thanks."

Shirley sat down on a chair at the kitchen counter and watched her sister mix tuna with mayo and spread it onto bread. They each ate a sandwich and drained longneck bottles of beer before returning to yard sale preparations.

The final disaster of the day came as they were carrying an orange couch, the last piece of furniture to be moved out into the yard, when Shirley caught her toe on the door mat and rolled her ankle. She dropped her end of the couch and went down.

Janet let go of her end and the couch fell heavily. Shirley lay on the floor, grasping at her right ankle.

"Hon?"

"Ow!" Shirley screamed. "I think I broke it!"

"Oh Lord! Are you sure?"

Tears painted Shirley's cheeks with dark streaks of mascara. "I don't know," she sobbed. "But it hurts. Oh, Janet, it hurts!"

Janet bent down and gently pulled Shirley's hands away so she could look. The ankle was swelling and a bruise was already spreading.

"We better get you to a doctor. Can you walk?"

"I don't know."

"Should I call for an ambulance?"

"No!" Shirley knuckled her fist to her mouth against the pain. "I got no insurance, Janet. I can't afford an ambulance."

Janet looked around and saw the cushions on the couch. "Maybe you could sit on one of those and I could pull you out to the car." She thought a moment. "No. Wait a minute while I think of something else." She looked around the nearly empty room and found no inspiration. Finally she said, "Have you got a wheelbarrow?"

Shirley looked up. "Out back."

Janet went around the house and found a metal wheelbarrow with most of the paint worn off and rust in the pan. She gave it an experimental kick and it seemed solid. She sat down in the pan and the wheelbarrow creaked but held her weight. Janet wheeled it back to the front of the house and with a lot of effort finally got Shirley seated inside. She lifted the two handles and pushed Shirley down the narrow walk, nearly dumping her twice but finally arriving at the street sidewalk. Shirley wound up lying across the back seat of the station wagon.

"Do you have a doctor?" Janet asked as the engine rumbled to life.

Shirley said, "Take me up to the hospital. Welfare will pay if it's an emergency room visit."

"Right." Janet glanced in the rearview mirror at the receding yard littered with floor lamps, pots and pans, clothing, a few framed pictures, books, some ratty old rugs, a metal bed frame and mattress, a painted wood dresser, an assortment of other junk. *She's not going to get much for that bunch of crap.* And now Janet would be stuck with the balance of chores for getting ready for tomorrow's sale. How had her sister sunk so low? And for Janet, the answer came easy. *The boy. Stuart. A walking anchor.* But Janet's take was no longer just a few miserable bucks! She allowed herself a secret smile as she pulled into the emergency entrance in back of the hospital.

Chapter 19

"We'll need more trout," Stu announced as he picked the last morsel of pink meat from the bony cutthroat. He tossed the skeleton onto the glowing coals and watched the tiny bones blacken and curl.

"Yeah," Billy agreed, throwing his fish bones on top of Stu's. They formed a spiny cross, but soon just bits of black ash remained.

Mike was still prizing the last few bits of meat from his fish. He nodded in agreement as he fingered the soft flakes between his lips.

Stu looked at Mike and Billy and figured it was time to launch what he had been planning. "You guys should try casting off the logs at the end of the lake. I'll walk down to the other end and explore the logjam. Maybe there's something flat we could use for a raft. I'll bet there's some real monster fish out in the middle of the lake."

Billy was ready to argue his way out of anything to do with Mike. "Can I come with you?" He said. Didn't Stu understand anything? Fishing with his brother? He'd rather dig a latrine!

"Nope," Stu replied firmly. "I want to do a little exploring on my own. Besides, you guys are the fisherman, I'm just a beginner."

Mike looked disgusted. But when he stared across the campfire, Stu nodded at him silently, eyebrows raised. Mike realized this was the moment Stu had made him promise about. Boys the same age know exactly what another is thinking as certain as radar can spot an airplane and tables can tell the tides. This was *the favor*. Mike knew he could object and even get his way if he really wanted to argue. But it also occurred to Mike that once he had done this one favor for Stu he was *evens*. He wouldn't have to take any more crap about how he had treated Billy up at Boiling Lake!

Billy continued to look betrayed. He searched for some compromise to keep Stu close. "I don't see why we can't all fish together. I could teach you more about casting."

Mike gave a small and hurtful chuckle. "What's the matter? Afraid I'll out-fish you?"

Billy snorted, "No chance."

"C'mon then," Mike challenged, standing up and walking to where his pole was leaned against a tree.

Billy looked to Stu for one last chance to avoid this. But Stu just nodded and said very softly, "You made a promise."

Billy nearly balked, but Stu's eyes were fixed. Billy looked skyward with resignation and got up to fetch his own pole.

"Get a leg on," Mike hollered over his shoulder as he skipped across the creek and cut through the scattering of young firs on the far side. He was striding along the rocky shoreline by the time Billy had his gear in hand. Billy shot one last quizzical look at Stu.

"It'll be okay," Stu promised. "You've got to meet him halfway or the two of you will be at war forever." Stu smiled. "Trust me."

"Okay." Billy resigned himself to the effort. *But only because Stu wants it.* He grimly followed Mike, hopping on stones across the creek, through the trees and out into the golden slant of afternoon sunlight along the shoreline.

Mike headed toward the far end of the logjam. Billy considered stopping at the near end, a hundred yards from Mike, but Stu would be watching, expecting him to join up with his brother. Billy canted his Akubra at a firm angle to the sun and kept moving behind the line of logs crowded along the shore.

Stu watched the brothers pick their way along the tangle of weathered drift that had been pushed up by mountain winds. He sat patiently until they joined up on the far side of the lake and began casting, standing several yards apart, at least not arguing. It was a start. He stood and dusted the pine needles and dirt from his jeans. He wanted just one tiny bit of adventure that didn't involve playing the peacemaker. The large log jam at the far end of the lake beckoned.

Billy and Mike worked their lines across the mirrored water, laying the green filament in great looping casts. Billy caught the first fish but it was only five inches and he had to throw it back. He felt Mike's eyes watching as he tossed the young fish back into the lake, but Billy refused to return the stare. He shifted a few yards to his right and resumed casting. Within seconds Mike had hooked a fighter.

"Whoooweee!" Mike hollered as he pulled the flopping cutthroat onto the safety of the gravel behind the logs. He quickly had its neck broken. He slipped it onto a green stick through the gills. By the time he was done Billy had a fish bending his own pole.

Mike walked behind him, ready to switch to a new spot of undisturbed water. He paused as Billy brought the trout ashore. As the trout flopped down behind the logs Mike moved forward.

"Here," Mike said reaching for the fish. "I'll string it up for you." For a moment Billy considered telling Mike to mind his own business, Billy would cut his own stick and snap the neck of his own trout. But then he remembered Stu's admonition to meet his brother halfway, and so he let Mike twist the hook from the fish's mouth and kill and string it onto the willow whip atop his own.

"Thanks," Billy mumbled as Mike walked on to his next casting spot.

"No problem," Mike replied generously. Mike's superior tone of voice rankled but Billy let it slide. Two could play the *I'm bigger about it than you* game.

The brothers went back to making perfect casts in the afternoon sun. And then something magic happened. What every fly fisherman hopes for, dreams of, and might never see even *once* in a lifetime. In the shafting sunlight far up in the air, a mayfly hatch began. Suddenly the air was full of fat-bodied mayflies falling gently to earth as their mating dances ended.

The trout started to go crazy all across the lake, rising, jumping, insanely intent upon this manna from heaven.

Mike bent to pick up one of the insects that had fallen at his feet. He studied it for a moment. "Looks like a Red Quill spinner," he concluded. He dropped the mayfly and took off his yellow felt hat. He searched for a moment and finally selected a dry fly. "I got me a couple of those!" Mike said joyfully. He pulled out a jackknife and cut off the fly he currently had tied at the end of his leader—a Coachman—and knotted on a small reddish-brown fly with a thin yellow tail.

Billy watched out of the corner of his eye while trying not to look at all interested. But there was deep concern on his part. For if Mike were right, Billy was going to lose this contest. Billy's fly selection was limited to Black Gnats and Royal Coachmans and a few Duns and Hackles. He had nothing even close to a Red Quill Spinner. As Mike tied on the new fly Billy continued to cast intently. Fish were now rising all around his fly. But it lay completely ignored by the trout in the midst of the mayflies that now littered the water's surface.

Mike finished his triple knot, pulled the fly taut to test the strength, was satisfied it would hold, and began casting. Within seconds had a strike.

"Gotcha!" He hollered with glee, pulling a fat cutthroat over the logs and onto the shore. He removed the hook and, as if taunting Billy with this success, he stepped back onto the logs and cast again into the very same spot, and *Blam!* Another trout rose and snatched up the hook.

"Hoooeee!" Mike hollered, as he pulled the second fish ashore.

After Mike had removed the hook and had the trout safely on the willow whip, he paused for a moment to watch Billy cast. Billy was having no success despite the dozens of trout rings that radiated out from where the fish were continuously breaking the surface to gobble up the mayflies.

Finally Mike offered, "I've got an extra if you want one." He reached up and took off his hat, pointed out the second Red Quill Spinner hooked into the yellow felt, and held the hat out to Billy.

Billy studied Mike's hat in one hand and then glanced out to where his line lay on the lake's surface. Billy hesitated.

"C'mon, Billy. No way are you going to get them to go for that Black Gnat when there's mayflies on the water."

Billy knew Mike was right. At this point, with the red mayflies falling practically thick as snow in a blizzard, he could cast forever and get zip, nada, zilch. And it wasn't even like it was Mike's fault. The mayflies had simply *come*.

You've got to meet him halfway. Stu's words echoed in his mind.

"Okay," Billy agreed, reeling in his line.

Mike walked over to Billy's log. As he approached he detached the Red Quill spinner from the yellow felt and handed it to his brother. "This'll do the trick," Mike assured as he stepped back and watched Billy flip open his jackknife and slice the Black Gnat off the end of his leader. He tied on the Spinner in record time.

Billy cast the new fly out onto the lake's surface. And *blammo!* What had to be the biggest cutthroat in the whole lake nailed the Spinner. Billy's rod whipped in a bow and his reel screamed as the line zipped out.

Mike saw what Billy had hooked. He pulled his own line up out of the water and watched as the battle developed, mesmerized. The fish was running hard and Billy's line was screaming as the reel spun. Billy braked the line and it drew taught.

"Don't break it!" Mike shouted.

"I know!" Billy hollered back, concentrating on the monster cutthroat. He eased up on the line brake and more green line shot off the reel.

Just when Billy was certain he would lose the fish, the trout broke the surface and shot into the air, flashing rainbow colors in the sun, and then splashed back through the surface.

"Cripes!" Mike yelled. "It's a whale!"

"Yeah!" Billy hollered back. Mike was right. It *was* a whale. The tension on the pole increased and Billy let a few more feet of fly line zip off the reel with a frantic *zzzzzzz*. He looked down and saw he was coming to the knot that tied the end of the line to the core. He locked the line brake and reigned up on the pole tip and there was a moment when he thought the trout would refuse to turn and simply keep going and break the leader. But the fish turned and now made a mad dash for the safety of the water beneath the logs. Billy spun the reel's handle until his fingers ached from going around, taking up line slack.

"Get your pole up!" Mike screamed, now standing just a few feet away, peering intently down into eight feet of icy water, ready to grab the cutthroat if the chance came.

"I know!" Billy screamed back. But he wasn't screaming at Mike, he was screaming *with* him.

The fish shot beneath the jam and for a moment Billy thought he'd lost it in the tangle of waterlogged wood. But miraculously the fish shot back out. Its dark back darted past them just underneath the water's surface, moving like an insanely fast submarine. Back out into the lake the trout sped. The line again zipped from Billy's reel until there was barely any left.

"Turn him," Mike screamed.

"I'm trying," Billy screamed back. But even as he spoke Billy felt the fish turn again. And this time there was less fight. The fish was finally tiring and the real drama was over.

"Gotcha," Billy said with certainty as he squeezed the drag lever with his thumb. The fish bucked twice, and then turned toward shore, exhausted.

Billy guided the fish carefully along the front of the log and Mike got down on his hands and knees and reached slowly into the water and cautiously slid his fingers beneath the fish. When he was certain, Mike pulled up and his hands closed around the trout. It came out of the water with a little burst of protest and almost wriggled free but Mike managed to toss it behind the logs. Billy and Mike stood over the cutthroat as it lay flopping among the rocks. It had to be sixteen inches.

"Cripes!" Mike said with pure awe. "I didn't think they grew this big up here."

"Yeah," Billy agreed. And a chill raced down his spine. Not for the fish, even though it was magnificent. As he looked down at the fish, Billy saw none of what lay before him. What he saw in his mind's eye was that picture on his desk—of he and Mike in their baseball uniforms, Mike's arm draped around his shoulder. Mike now sounded just like he had when he'd shouted Billy around the bases after Billy had hit the dinger over the center field fence.

Mike knelt before the trout and then paused. Before he touched it he looked up at Billy and asked, "Okay if I put him on the stick?"

"Yeah," Billy said through a grin so wide it was almost painful.

Mike twisted the hook from the fish's mouth and hesitated just a moment before he broke its spine, wondering if they should return this one to the lake. But no way was he going to suggest this to Billy. Because he'd had the same kind of chill as Billy. And if you had asked Mike at that moment if he remembered that late spring day when Billy had hit the towering home run, well, he would have said, "Sure, like it was yesterday."

The fish safely on the willow stick and cooling in the water with the rest of the catch, which now numbered nine, the brothers went back to fishing.

As they pulled trout after trout from the mayfly-strewn mirror of the water's surface, Billy decided to ask Mike something he'd been curious about for some time.

"Hey Mike," he said as he cast his line. "How come Stu never talks about his dad?"

Mike looked down the length of the lake, a distance of perhaps a third of a mile, to where Stu—now a tiny figure—was using a drift limb to pry at something in the jam.

"Cause his dad abandoned them when Stu was a baby."

Billy wanted to find Stu's dad and tell him just how rotten he had treated a really great son. And he wanted to know more; maybe there was something he could do for Stu if he only knew exactly how and why it had happened.

"Abandoned?"

"Yeah. He just left. Stu's mom came home one day, and his dad had packed his clothes and split."

"Why'd he go?"

"Stu's never said. But that's not all. Stu's dad never sent money to help Stu's mom out."

"Ouch!"

"Yeah."

"How do you know all this?"

"Cause Stu told me."

"How did he know?"

Mike gave Billy a pained look. "Cause his mom told him, Dummy." There was instant regret on Mike's face. "Hey, I didn't mean *Dummy*."

"I know," Billy said. His line had sunk below the water's surface. He pulled it up, whipping it back and forth in great figure-eight loops to get it dry, cast it out again. But his curiosity was not yet satisfied. "Has Stu ever met his dad?"

"Haven't a clue. Maybe. He's never talked about seeing his dad. I don't think he'd want to see his dad."

"Why not?"

Mike was getting a bit uneasy. He had asked himself these same questions and never found easy answers. Hashing them over—even with Billy, at this wonderful moment—still brought pain. "What is this?" Mike said. "Twenty questions? Why don't you ask Stu if you're so curious?"

"I'm sorry Mike. I just wanted to know. I didn't think Stu would like me asking."

Mike's voice caught a sad note. "Yeah. It's a sore spot with him. He never talks about it. It's probably better not to ask."

Billy reflected upon what Mike had said for a moment and then his mind turned to a new thought. He turned to his brother. "Hey, Mike."

"Yeah?"

"Thanks."

"For telling you about Stu?"

"No. Thanks for letting me come. I know Dad said you had to take me and all . . . but you could have, well, you know, refused. He probably wouldn't have made you do it, if you really insisted on me not coming."

Mike turned to his brother and there was a soft happiness in his face. "You earned it." He said it with dead certainty.

Billy felt like the king of the world.

"Well, thanks anyway," Billy added. "This is really great!" There were other words that came to mind. Riskier words. Words that said too much. But *great* covered it well enough. For brothers.

Mike thought about what Billy had said for a second. "Yeah. It is great, isn't it?"

They fished on in silence, content to be with each other and to enjoy the sun as it warmed the valley. They were now releasing the fish, having each caught their limit of eight. Neither Mike nor Billy really wanted to stop. An hour passed and the fish finally stopped rising as the mayflies ceased to fall and those on the surface had been eaten.

When Billy had no more strikes at his fly for five minutes, he looked down lake to see what Stu was up to.

"Hey Mike," Billy said after scanning the far end of the lake.

"Yeah," Mike said, intently watching a big trout that was slowly rising towards his fly.

"Have you seen Stu in the last few minutes?"

Mike glanced towards the distant logs, then back to the now circling trout. "Nah," he said. "You?"

"No. And I don't see him anywhere."

"Where do you think he went?" Mike said, trying to maintain his concentration upon the trout.

"I don't know. Did he say anything to you about going somewhere after he went to look for a rafting log?"

"Nope."

"Did you see him walk away from the log jam?"

Mike suddenly lost interest in the trout and began to reel in his line. "No," he said, his voice full of concern. "I think he just wanted to pry out a log and paddle it back down to this end of the lake."

Billy scanned the shoreline. Other than rocks and trees and bushes, there was nothing. He felt a great and sudden emptiness. "We should go look for him," he said. "Maybe he's stuck in the logs—"

"Right." Mike voice held an edge of fear.

Mike finished reeling in his line and hooked the fly into the cork of his pole's handle.

As they were about to run back to the camp, Stu came charging out from the trees near the stream, buck-naked. He sprinted onto the smooth rock where the creek emptied into the lake. Where the ledge dropped sharply into the water he planted his feet hard and jumped high up into the air, his hands arrowed forward in the prayer position. He cleaved the water's surface with a huge splash. He came up immediately and gave a violent shake of water from his hair.

"*Shit!*" he yelled. "It's *cooooooold!*" He began to flail his way back to the shore.

"Oh, jeez." Mike said.

The fear drained out of Billy like molten lead.

Stu climbed up onto the rock and began swiping water from his body, shaking his head so that his brown hair flew out like a dog's. He paused and looked over at Mike and Billy, who were standing at the edge of the log jam.

"What are you bozos staring at?" Stu hollered accusingly. But his big smile betrayed pleasure at being the center of attention.

"Ape man!" Mike yelled back.

Stu bent over, curled his fingers, and began to cavort around the rock shelf. He threw his head skyward. "Ooo! Ooo! Ooo! Oooooh! Eee! Eee! Eeeeeee!" he screamed.

Mike began to laugh.

"Oo Oo Oo Oo Oo Oooooeeeeeeaaaaa!" Stu screamed louder.

Mike was now laughing so hard he was bent over clutching his stomach. And that was when Mike slipped. His arms flailed in big circles for a couple of seconds, but it wasn't enough to regain his balance. His feet stumbled and there was no more log to provide a footing. He fell face first into the lake.

He came up coughing and spitting up water gone down the wrong hole. "Shit!" he yelled after the danger of drowning had passed. "Piss!"

Now it was Stu's turn, naked, bent double, howls of laughter booming across the water and echoing off the valley cliff-walls.

Mike pulled himself inch by cold inch, back onto the log, stubbornly waving off Billy's offer of a hand. "Don't get wet," he said.

"Hey," Stu yelled, mocking. "You're supposed to take your clothes off *before* you go swimming."

"Eat dirt," Mike mumbled. He stood drenched atop the log. As Mike began to strip off his soggy shirt he looked around in a panic. "Oh, shit!" He was staring, furious, down into the water. "Just fricking rat shit!"

"Mike?" Billy puzzled.

"My rod," Mike groaned. Billy followed his brother's stare down through crystal clear water to where Mike's amber-colored fly rod now lay on the lake's bottom atop a little collection of waterlogged branches and silted-covered rocks.

"Maybe we can hook it or something. We can get a branch and pull it up—"

"No," Mike cut him off, cold anger clipping each word. "I dropped it and I'm gonna get it back." He finished stripping off his shirt and unbuckled his belt.

"Mike—"

"Billy," Mike said with cold determination. "I'm doin' it." He pulled down his jeans and realized he needed to take off his tennis shoes first. So he squatted down on the log. "Just . . . just don't say nothing, okay?"

"Okay." Billy knew that tone. He stood back and let Mike do what he had set his mind on. Mike had decided there was just one way and Billy knew trying to talk him out of it was a waste of time.

Mike continued to swear under his breath as he peeled off his dripping tennis shoes and soggy socks and finally the clinging denim jeans. He stood in his boxer shorts and dove without hesitation, frog-stroking to the bottom and groping around blindly for the pole. Afterwards, he told Billy that he had tried opening his eyes for a second but it felt as if nails were being driven straight into his brain. When he surfaced his head barely missed the log and his skin was white.

Mike handed up the reel end of the pole. "Here," he said, teeth chattering.

Billy grabbed the pole and carried it to safety before he came back to make sure his brother was able to crawl back up onto the log. He didn't offer a hand because Mike was not looking up at him and clearly didn't want help. Mike finally stood up with his arms clenched to his shivering body.

"Shit," he said, with all of the force gone from his voice. "A guy wouldn't last very long in there."

By the time they made it back to camp Stu had redressed and had stoked the campfire to a blaze. Mike was still in his skivvies as he huddled close to the leaping flames. In a few minutes he dressed in his second pair of jeans and a brown-checked flannel shirt that Billy had brought from his pack and held patiently until Mike was ready.

"That was *not* fun," Mike said mostly to himself. His eardrums ached from the ice cold water. He looked at Stu, who returned a ridiculous smile.

"Eat me," Mike said.

Stu's grin turned defensive. "I didn't push you."

Mike didn't bother to reply.

"Okay," Stu said, trying to change the subject as he realized that Mike's impromptu swim was no longer funny to anyone. "What do you guys want to do now?"

"Clean the fish?" Billy offered.

"Yeah," Mike said. "I'm starved."

Billy said, "I can gut them if you guys want."

"Thanks Billy," Mike said. "I'll mix up some cornbread. Stu, you want to make up some powdered milk?"

"Sure thing," Stu agreed. And in his heart Stu felt wonderful because they had somehow become a team, three turned into one, all brothers together on an adventure that had had a slow and frustrating start but now finally showed promise.

It wasn't until after Billy had finished cleaning the trout, and Mike's clothes had dried before the roaring fire, that Mike's good humor began to return. A slight breeze had come up and the sun was angling sun diamonds off the lake's surface. They finished their dinner preparations but the fire was still burning too high to put pans over. So while the blaze worked its way towards manageable cooking coals, Mike went exploring for branches to build mattresses to sleep on. He found bunches of them in several old-growth firs fifty yards back into the forest. Billy and Stu came when he hollered, to help carry armloads of the boughs back to camp and to arrange them into flat piles where they would sleep. Nothing was said about Mike's extra effort, but all three knew this was part compensation for Billy's deflated air mattress from the first night, and payback for Mike's earlier anger towards Billy.

They brought in a final load and stepped back to admire their work. "Gonna sleep like kings tonight," Mike said with pride.

"No better living to be had," Stu confirmed.

Billy just beamed inside and tried not to let it show too much. Grandpa had always said, "The best reward is the deed itself." If Billy now said something, Mike would be obliged to play it down. And Billy didn't want it played down. Mike was being downright nice to him for the first time in a long while. All three boys knew exactly what was happening. There was no need for extra words.

Mike picked at a bit of black pitch stuck to his hand. "I'm going to go scrub up in the creek." They had a bar of soap with pumice that would take practically anything off your hands. "After that, let's get dinner on. I'm starved."

"Me too," Stu agreed.

"Totally," Billy added.

"Great. Stu, let's get those fish in the pan!"

"Let's do it!" Stu said.

Before long they were all busy near the fire. The trout, which had been dusted with flour and lightly peppered, were now slid into the big cast iron skillet to be fried in Crisco. The other fixings were readied. And finally the boys sat with tired contentment before the fire, mess kits perched on their laps, devouring cornbread, reconstituted mashed potatoes, trout, beans and cherry Kool-Aid.

"Hey Mike," Stu said as Mike prepared to throw his first trout skeleton into the fire. "Do you ever eat the tails?"

Mike gave a look of disgust. "Are you serious?"

"You bet!" And to prove his point Stu broke the crispy tail from the fish on his plate, put it in his mouth, and crunched down. "Mmm Mmm, good," he mimicked the Campbell's soup jingle, licking his lips with exaggeration.

"You are one gross cowpoke," Mike said. He tossed one of his fish skeletons onto the fire where it blackened and smoked and curled and shriveled down into the deep orange crevices between the coals. He began picking the meat off his next trout and ignored Stu, considering what Stu had done to be purely silly and ridiculous.

"Pure waste," Stu teased, shaking his head sadly.

Mike continued to ignore him and to eat the meat from his new trout.

"Hey Stu?" Billy asked. "Is eating the fish tail really safe?"

Stu threw Billy a look. "Do I look like I'm choking?"

"Well—"

"Am I dying here in front of your very eyes?"

"Uh . . ."

Stu's voice took on a haughty English accent. "They're fantabulous. Little known fact is that all the vitamins in fish are in the fins. Quite tasty actually. Delightfully crunchy. Just like potato chips."

Billy reached for a tail that lay on his plate.

"I wouldn't," Mike dared.

His brother's challenge was all Billy needed. He pulled off the tail and popped it into his mouth and began to chew. He finished with exaggerated gusto. "Stu's right, Mike. It's mighty good!" He reached for another tail as if no other food on Earth could quite compare. Truth was, it took a lot more chewing and it was greasier than he'd expected. But even if it had tasted like fried frog feet, Billy would have gobbled up a second helping just to show how manly he was, and to take Stu's side for the moment.

"Well," Stu said with a grin blossoming. "Now you can say you've had your first piece of tail."

Billy had been set up! And all three boys knew it.

Mike practically fell forward into the fire as he doubled up in laughter, dropping his mess plate holding the last of his cornbread and beans.

Stu began to howl and point at Billy. *Gotcha! Didn't I!*

Billy reddened. The idea of sex was something he still knew very little about, except what the guys said in gym class when they were watching the girls shoot hoops, or from little clutches of conversation with his buddies in front of the school lockers during school lunch break. He managed a nervous laugh. "Funny," he said. "Real funny."

"I thought so," Stu said, as he again burst into laughter.

It was a long while before Mike and Stu quieted down, but even then if one looked at the other it was impossible to keep laughter from shattering the evening calm. They finally had to simply not look at each other to maintain control.

"Okay," Mike finally said as he retrieved his plate, minus the beans which lay in a pathetic brown lump on the ground. The cornbread he was able to dust the dirt from. "If you guys can do it, so can I." Mike took the spatula and lifted a new fish from the frying pan and plucked off the fish's tail. He added in a cocky tone, "I ain't had me a piece of tail in way too long. So here goes . . ." Into his mouth went the crispy tail. He crunched awhile and his face puckered. "There's bones," he said with disgust. He reached in and pulled out a partially chewed glob and held it like the dead mouse in Kelly's orchard. "I don't see what the big deal is." He studied the mass for just a few seconds before he pitched it into the fire with a grim look.

"Wussy," Stu said.

Mike stuck his tongue out at Stu.

"Aw, forget it," Stu said. "I agree the tail's not very good. Okay?"

"Okay," Mike grumbled. But the exchange had dulled their earlier excitement. Billy remembered something to distract Mike and Stu from the awkward moment. He stood up and reached into a nearby backpack and pulled out a bag of marshmallows.

"Smore time," Billy declared.

Within seconds each of them was pushing marshmallows onto sticks for toasting and the fish tail awkwardness as forgotten.

"Beautiful!" Stu said approvingly as his first marshmallow caught fire. It acquired a bubbling black skin before he blew out the flames. He pressed the charcoal-covered mass together with Hershey squares between two graham crackers and watched approvingly as creamy white marshmallow with black specks blended with melting chocolate and oozed out the sides.

By the time they had finished that night's ration of Smores the sun had set behind the mountains. Out on the lake's surface a few concentric rings marked where fish were rising. The temperature fell quickly and a gentle wind *shooshed* up the canyon through swaying pines. The boys sat taking pokes at the fire with their marshmallow sticks and occasionally there was a satisfied burp as dinner began to digest.

"Hey Stu," Mike said.

"Yeah?"

"What are you going to do this fall?"

"Oh, I dunno."

Mike pressed on with apprehension and hope.

"Are you going to look for a full-time job?"

"Who would want to hire me?"

"Heck, lots of people would want to hire you. You're a hard worker."

A stolid and grim reply was all Stu could muster. "It's *who* you know that counts," Stu said. "Mom doesn't know anybody. And neither do I. All I've ever done is deliver newspapers and cut people's lawns. Except for the work we did for Old Man Kelly, and I hated that, to be honest. There's no future in any of that."

"What about college?"

"Aw c'mon, Mike," Stu said impatiently. "I already told you I don't have the grades to get in." Whether or not Stu should go to college had become a sore topic during their senior year, as Mike frequently harped at Stu to get serious and pull his grades up so he could go on to college after graduation. Mike had promised Stu how much fun they would have together at Central Washington. But Stu's grades remained in the low C's and that wasn't quite enough. So Mike now chose a new approach.

"You could go to junior college and improve your grades. Then, in a year or two you could apply."

"Look," Stu said crossly. "Even if I wanted to go, I don't have the money. And anyway, it's already too late to enroll, even at the JC."

"Is not! The junior college lets kids register clear up till the time classes start."

"And since when did you become an expert on the JC, mister big time football scholarship?"

That hurt.

Stu realized what he'd said was stupid and mean and Mike was just trying to be nice. "Aw, jeez Mike. I didn't mean it that way."

There was nothing Mike could say, because he *was* on a big time scholarship and that *was* the simple truth. So he sat not looking at anything in particular, hands limp between his legs and his shoulders slumped a little forward and feeling beaten.

During the uneasy silence that now fell, Billy felt badly for both of the older boys. He knew that Mike had bugged Stu about going to college for a long time, and Mike could be relentless when he set his mind to something. Stu had defended with a number of excuses: he didn't have the money; he didn't know what major he'd like; he wasn't smart enough; and (most bogus of all, according to Mike) that his mom needed him around to help her out. It was the one topic where Mike and Stu had never seemed to find any agreement.

Now Mike had again hurt their backpacking adventure, this time by raising the old quarrel. Billy wondered if his brother was permanently brain-damaged. He almost said that very thing, *Mike, you must be brain damaged*, but thought better of it. Taking sides wasn't going to help.

Stu picked up a small stone and tossed it into the fire and watched a column of sparks tornado upwards. Then he said something that seemed to come from outer space.

"I was thinking of enlisting."

Mike's mouth dropped open and hung in slack horror for a couple of seconds. "You mean Vietnam? Are you crazy? Your draft number was three hundred and twelve! You're safe. You'll never be drafted. Do you want to get shot?"

Stu was ready with answers.

"Not infantry, Mike. Something better than that. I talked to that recruiter downtown. He says I could get specialist training. Then after a couple of years I could come back home and get a real job."

"Training?" Mike shook his head, bewildered. "What does the Army train you for? Loading guns? Stacking shells? Digging foxholes?"

Billy could see Stu's patience was wearing thin. But Stu persisted with his reasoning.

"They've got training for things like radar operators and electronics and aircraft maintenance and diesel mechanics." But when he looked at Mike there was no hint of agreement on his best friend's face. So Stu got defensive and said, "Who made you an expert, anyway? What do you know about the Army?"

Mike's mouth firmed up and his shoulders bunched and that was a bad sign. Billy had heard and seen enough to know the direction this was headed. "Hey Mike," he interrupted. "It's not that bad of an idea. Besides, as a volunteer Stu would get his pick of jobs, wouldn't he? He wouldn't have to go out and shoot people."

"The recruiter would tell him that," Mike replied. "But there's no guarantee once they get him over there. They got you by the jewels, buddy, and that's no joke."

"Life ain't perfect," Stu said quietly.

"Yeah," Mike countered. "But at least it's *life*." Mike stared hard at Stu.

Stu's eyes lingered on Mike's face for a brief moment and then glanced away to stare into the glowing coals of the campfire.

Mike looked down at his boot tops.

Billy was relieved when Mike finally shut up. His brother shouldn't have brought it up. It had been too good of a day to spoil it in this way. They sat, somber and quiet for several minutes. No one wanted to leave the conversation where it had ended, but it was hard to figure out how to backtrack. It was Billy who finally spoke.

"Uh, what are we going to do tomorrow?"

Stu continued to stare into the fire.

Mike tried to sound upbeat as he said to Billy, "I figure we stay here one more night, maybe two. We do some exploring, catch some fish, hang out. What do you think, Stu?"

Stu sounded utterly defeated as he said, "Okay with me."

Mike looked hopefully to his brother. "Billy? You got anything special you want to do?"

Billy did have something in mind. During the first days of the hike he'd kept a lookout for huckleberries. He'd seen bushes along the trail but all of them had been picked clean. Billy figured other hikers had taken advantage of the easy fruit. And maybe the bears had been around. But there had to be better pickings somewhere.

"I want to find some huckleberries for pancakes."

"Okay," Mike agreed. "You're on the huckleberry patrol. Only don't go too far. We want your feet in good shape when we hike on to Surprise Lake."

"I promise," Billy said. But his thoughts were of Vietnam and of Stu whose life was now lurching in that horrible direction. The war was a sore subject with high school boys. Both his brother and Stu had gotten lucky with numbers in the 300's. No way they'd be called up or have to depend upon a college defer-ment. But three kids in this year's senior class were already in boot camp and soon they would be on a jet headed for Southeast Asia. Billy wondered if there would still be a war going on when he reached 18. That was four years away, and it seemed impossible that the war could last until 1973, especially with all the protesting that was taking place. But it scared him just the same to imagine his number coming up a single digit and an Army car pulling up front of the house to cart him away.

Stu continued to stare blankly into the coals. Mike almost said something to Stu and then thought better of it. "Well," he said mostly to himself, yawn-ing. "It's bed time for Bonzo." He picked up the stick he'd used to roast his marshmallows and took one final poke at the glowing orange coals to send up a delicate swarm of sparks. "We better put this out. With all those fir needles we're sleeping on we sure as heck don't want to catch the forest on fire."

"I'll do it," Billy volunteered. "I'm not ready to go to sleep yet."

"Okay," Mike said. "Just make sure the ashes are cold."

Mike got up and walked to the far side of the campsite and began to unroll his sleeping bag. Stu stood slowly and walked over to his own bag and untied the cords that held it in a tight bundle and began to unroll it across one side of the fir bough mattress they had built, on the side opposite where Mike was unrolling his own sleeping bag. Neither boy looked at each other.

Billy didn't immediately move to put out the fire. Instead he sat in front of the dying coals and stared at the gray ashes as they floated up one by one into the slipstream of heated air. He kept replaying the words the older boys had exchanged, wondering why it had happened this way and if there weren't some way to save Stu from the fate of war. Stu going to Vietnam? Would he really enlist?

After a while Stu came back from brushing his teeth down by the creek and he passed by Billy and said softly, "Hey Billy, you okay?"

"I'm fine," Billy said. "I'll be over in a while."

Stu walked to his sleeping bag and stripped down to his shorts and crawled inside.

Billy now remembered Stu's mother walking away from the station wagon, declaring to the whole world that she had to pee. Stu had been humiliated. Any kid would've been. And Billy remembered what Mike had said about Stu being required to pay his own way with money from the paper route. What else had Stu had suffered at home? *No wonder he's thinking about going to Vietnam.*

It was half an hour before Billy doused the last glowing embers of the fire, scooped on a layer of dirt for good measure, and walked over to where Mike and Stu were snuggled in for the night. He unrolled his bag in the wide space between the two older boys, undressed, and crawled inside where the soft fabric that lay against his face smelled of sweat and smoke. After three days in the mountains it felt softer and more comfortable than any regular bed he'd ever slept in.

The surrounding forest was quiet except for one pinecone that came clattering down through the branches, a couple of persistent crickets, and the whining of mosquitoes that couldn't find a way inside Billy's sleeping bag.

Then, Billy heard what sounded like a trout jumping out in the lake and it snapped him full awake. He had a premonition something awful was going to happen. He lay for a long while in the darkness before drifting into an uneasy sleep.

Chapter 20

"The X-ray shows it's just a bad sprain." The heavyset nurse smiled as she delivered the news to Shirley and Janet in the examination room. In her left hand she held the X-ray in a protective folder. "Doctor's got an emergency so he can't come right now. Some kid playing with a pipe bomb blew up his hand." She shook her head in disbelief, and went to the white-painted cabinet above the stainless sink in the corner and opened the door and pulled out a role of Ace Bandage. She laid the X-ray on the countertop. "I'll wrap it so you won't have to wait."

Shirley watched the nurse unroll the elastic. Her leg was propped up between two foam rolls on the extension board between the stirrups. She lay tiredly against a pillow on the elevated table back. Her foot had turned black-and-blue from the ankle to the middle of the arch and there were blue tracers running down to her toes. The swollen foot hurt and the wrapping caused further agony as the bandage began to compress the tissue.

"I need something for the pain. Can I get a prescription?"

The nurse looked up from her wrapping. "The doctor will have to do that. But he may be a while getting out of surgery."

"Haven't you've got something for me now? A sample or something? It hurts awful!"

"Yeah," Janet added. She stood impatiently beside the exam table and held her sister's hand while the nurse worked. She knew a dodge when she saw one. She laid into the nurse, "The drug company reps always leave samples. For Lord's sake give her a couple Valium at least."

The nurse apologized, "I'm sorry, girls, but I've got to follow the rules. I can't give out prescription drugs without a prescription." She thought for a second. "I could give you a couple of extra strength aspirin."

"It figures," Janet said in a mean voice. "I'll bet you wouldn't have no trouble giving my sister a real pain killer if she had insurance."

The nurse fought to keep from reacting. Shirley had been cooperative. But the sister, Janet, had a mean streak. The nurse had seen plenty of her type. Being mean had nothing to do with money or insurance. Mean people could be rich or poor, smart or dumb, either sex. It didn't matter what station in life you occupied when it came to having a good or a bad attitude. She turned on the sister and spoke in a firm voice.

"Makes no difference what kind of medical insurance a patient has. We treat everyone the same. Now," she turned back to Shirley, "If you want that aspirin I've got some down at the nurses' station."

Shirley looked at Janet who crossed her arms and looked off to an empty corner of the room. Shirley forced a smile for the nurse. "Aspirin will have to do," she conceded.

The nurse finished her wrapping and secured the end by tucking it in. "I'll be right back," she said in voice that struggled to sound cheery.

As she walked past the curtain around the bed Janet called out after her, "Check and see when that doctor will be out of surgery and can write up my sister a proper prescription!" No reply came from the direction of the brisk footsteps receding down the hallway.

No prescription came during the next few minutes. And no strong painkiller from hospital supplies, either. Just two aspirin. The doctor was still in surgery when Shirley decided she couldn't wait any longer. The nurse promised to make sure the doctor phoned the drug store for an order of codeine first chance, and also for a pair of crutches. "Well at least it's going to be something strong," Janet told Shirley as the nurse helped Shirley into a rickety stainless steel wheelchair and then pushed her out to the station wagon. The nurse had by now given up any attempt at pleasing Janet. Once Shirley was safely transferred into the back seat of the wagon the nurse clattered the wheelchair up the ramp and through the automatic doors of the emergency entrance.

Halfway back to the house Janet swore briefly, "Shit! We should have asked to take that wheelchair. Getting you back into the house is going to be a royal bitch!"

Shirley groaned. The aspirin had only taken the edge off the pain and her foot now throbbed with a fury that made it seem to have a life of its own. But going back to the hospital with its antiseptic smells and the stubborn nurse seemed like a torture. "Do we have to?" she pleaded.

Janet adjusted the rearview mirror so she could see Shirley. Her eyes softened when she saw the scrunched concentration furrowing her sister's face. "No," Janet said. "I can use that damned wheelbarrow I guess."

"Thanks, Hon." Shirley settled back and tried to keep her bandaged foot as still as possible. All she had to do was survive a few more hours, and then there would be Codeine. Until then she would just have to make do with aspirin and liquor.

The transfer at the house proved easier than expected. Shirley made it inside with just an arm around Janet's shoulder and by hopping on her good foot. There was no furniture except for a mattress thrown on the bedroom floor. "I want to lie down and get some sleep," Shirley said.

"Anything you want."

After Shirley had drunk a hefty shot of Jack Daniels, Janet helped her into the bedroom and down onto the mattress. It was nearly 8 PM. Shirley lay on her back. Janet elevated her injured foot using pillows and then pulled a sheet from a pile of linen in the corner and laid it across her sister. "There," she said.

"Thanks, Janet. I don't know what I'd do without you."

Janet patted Shirley's wrist. "You're a survivor. You would have figured something out. But just the same I'm glad to be here for you."

"You don't have to stay around the house if you don't want to. Why don't you go down to Dale's for a beer? I'll catch some rest. I'm beat."

"You sure you don't want me to stick around? I could pull the TV back inside and we could watch it for a while."

"No. You go out have some fun. You've earned it. I only want to get some sleep."

"Well, okay." Janet stood and got her makeup kit from her hard-shell Samsonite in the corner and closed the top and latched it shut. "I'll do a little repair work and then I'll be off. You sure you don't need me around?"

"Go!" Shirley ordered.

"Okay!" Janet matched her insistence. In a minute Shirley heard the bathroom sink run briefly and after that the front door open and shut.

The only window in the room had a pull-down shade that blocked light and it was almost dark with the overhead bulb turned off. Shirley tried to relax, to find something to keep her mind off the steady throbbing pain; it radiated from her foot up through her knee and thigh and into her pelvis.

Searching for anything to distract her mind from the pain, she began to wonder what her son was doing up in the mountains. Was he having a good time? Was the hike fun? She hoped so. Because when he got back and entered the Army he was in for an eye-opener. Yesiree. He'd find out what the real world was like. *No more easy street for you, kiddo! You'll appreciate just how good you had it with dear old Mom.*

The throbbing intensified and time seemed to grind on with increasing slowness. Shirley's resentment against the hospital nurse increased. *She should have given me something stronger. Or at least more aspirin.* There had only been two tablets. No more had been offered. Ordinarily, she would have had a bottle of aspirin in the house. But most of what had been in the medicine cabinet had been dumped in the garbage can. The effort to get out to the alley and then to dig through the garbage to find the small glass bottle was beyond consideration.

Shirley gave up on retrieving the aspirin and shifted her thoughts to the bedroom. It was too warm. The air was stale. She imagined how nice it would be to have the window open to let in a little breeze. And how good a glass of cold water would be. Why hadn't she asked Janet to bring her a glass of water? She should have also asked Janet to go to the store and get that codeine prescription! If only she had even a few aspirin she could make it through till morning! And then she remembered that Janet always traveled with her own over-the-counter medicines. Shirley turned her head and looked at the large blue suitcase in the corner. Janet might have a supply of aspirin stashed inside. Shirley rolled her head in the opposite direction and eyed the closed door. It was just a few feet down the hallway to the bathroom. She could hop that far, couldn't she? And then she would have a nice cold glass of water to swallow the aspirin with!

The sun had set and it was getting dark. Soon the room would be pitch black. If she were going for aspirin and water, and not waiting until Janet's return, it had to be now.

Shirley rolled onto her side and instead of trying to stand she slid on her thigh with her injured foot held off the floor until she was lying next to the suitcase. She laid the case flat and thumbed the chrome latches and the lid popped. Shirley pushed it up so the top flopped back against the wall. Inside was a neat pile of slacks and another pile of hose and socks and a spare pair of dressy high heels. But nothing that looked like a medicine kit.

Shirley lifted the three pair of dark slacks one at a time and set them on the floor. Underneath she discovered a box that looked vaguely familiar. It was a Roi-Tan cigar box, worn at the corners, rubber banded shut. *Janet doesn't smoke cigars.* And besides, it wasn't her sister's style to be using an old cigar box to carry things in her suitcase. *It's more the kind of thing a kid would use—!* Shirley realized where she'd seen the box. When Stuart was 10 he'd talked a downtown merchant out of an empty cigar box. He had kept his marbles and other kid treasures in it for a long time. Shirley hadn't seen the box in years and couldn't place when it had disappeared from Stuart's desktop.

Shirley eased the bands off the end and pulled up the lid. Inside were rubber-banded packets of paper money and a bunch of coins. And a folded set of papers in an envelope. Shirley pulled the papers out of the envelope and slowly unfolded them, squinting in the half light to make out the print. At the top of the first page in bold letters it read: **U.S. Army Enlistment Form.**

Shirley unfolded the form and squinted in the dim light. The blanks were all filled in handwritten ink and Stu's signature was at the bottom.

Shirley dropped the enlistment form onto the pile of blouses and now traced her fingertips across the packets of wrinkled bills. She picked up the first, then the second, and finally the third banded stack. All three together felt weighty in her hand. She couldn't ever remember holding so much paper money that it felt *weighty*! She peeled through the bills in each packet, counting one by one with her index finger.

Almost a thousand dollars! And there were still a rattle of quarters and dimes and nickels in the bottom of the box.

Shirley dropped the cash and laid her head against the floor. She fought the ugly realization, but the knowing came like a cold wind under a doorsill. The money was Stu's. He'd managed to amass this small fortune and Shirley couldn't imagine how. But he had. And when Janet had cleaned out his room she had discovered the trove and stolen it and put it into her suitcase.

Without telling me!

Warm tears traced across the bridge of her nose and down her cheek and splattered against her ear.

Without telling me!

Shirley began to sob. The pain in her ankle was temporarily forgotten. The hitching of her chest went on for a long while. When she was finally able to choke back the tears she gathered up the cash and put it back into the Roi-Tan box along with the enlistment form and wedged the box firmly under her arm. It took her three attempts to stand. And a good while longer to hop down the hallway and into the kitchen.

Shirley picked up the phone and started to dial and her heart felt like lead and fire.

Chapter 21

Following a breakfast of flapjacks and scrambled eggs Billy was anxious to get off on his huckleberry quest. They had seen very few huckleberry bushes along the trail into Cub Lake. And on those scarce bushes there had been so few ripe berries as to not be worth the effort of picking.

After his raft hunt Stu told Billy he had seen what might be huckleberry bushes at the far end of the lake, so Billy now struck off in that direction. Both older boys offered to come along, but Billy replied that he could do it on his own. "I'm not going very far," he said defensively.

"Well," Stu said, as Billy walked out of camp holding a hopeful, quart-sized plastic Tupperware container. "If you need help just holler."

"See you guys in a couple hours," he said, glancing back over his shoulder to make certain they weren't following.

When Billy reached the far end of the lake he found several huckleberry bushes just as Stu had reported, near the stream mouth and beneath the grand firs and western white pines at the edge of the forest. But there were no ripe berries. Only a very few tiny bitter red bee-bees.

He walked a couple hundred yards down the trail to where it dropped into the canyon, but the trail got steep and the picking prospects down-slope looked poor. Billy was headed back to camp when he spotted a ledge fifty yards up a rockslide with what appeared to be huckleberry bushes around the fringe. It was hard to tell how much flat space there was or how many bushes it might support but it seemed worth investigating. Billy started to pick his way up the loose rock. As he climbed his imagination told him there might even be something more than huckleberries up there, possibly an old mine shaft.

When Billy finally reached the top he discovered the ledge ran about twenty feet deep and supported a small huckleberry thicket. Blue pea-sized berries polka-dotted nearly two dozen waist-high bushes. In a few minutes Billy had collected nearly a quart of fruit, despite having gobbled down several handfuls. The bushes were now stripped, but Billy had plenty for pancakes the next morning and even for the morning after that.

He spied a different route down the rockslide that looked a little easier and was heading in that direction when a buzzing erupted at his feet. The rattlesnake's gray-brown diamond-patterned skin had blended perfectly with the lichen-spotted granite and the snake had remained invisible to Billy. But the snake had seen Billy coming and it was coiled and preparing to strike. Billy froze and dropped the container of berries.

The snake waivered toward the motion of the plastic jug and in that instant Billy scrambled back from where the snake was coiled on the rock slab where it had been sunning. The snake eyed Billy and remained coiled and ready to attack.

Billy saw his precious berries scattered everywhere, and in anger he snatched up a sharp fractured piece of granite and threw it as hard as he could at the snake. It missed and caromed off and went skipping across the slide. Billy grabbed another rock but the snake was now moving fast. Billy's next missile clipped its tail as it slid down into a dark crevice and disappeared.

The adrenaline roared through Billy's body.

He hurled five more rocks in rapid succession toward the place where the snake had disappeared and they ricocheted wildly and left white fractures, but no warning rattle came from within the labyrinth of the slide. Billy edged cautiously up to where the berries lay scattered in cracks and crevices and on the rock surfaces. He cautiously picked up the container and gathered up the berries one by one until he had collected half of what he'd dropped, while on constant lookout for the rattlesnake. He didn't dare to reach into hidden spots or to pry back rocks to uncover more fruit, so he retreated down the slide to the safely of the trail.

As he walked back along the lakeshore Billy reached up and took off the Akubra. With newfound awe he stared at the snakeskin band. What had Gramps felt when he had killed his snake? Had his heart jumped up in his throat? Had he nearly wet his pants? Of course not! Gramps would have remained cool and calm. After all, Gramps had killed his snake, hadn't he? And Billy had let his escape.

When he reached camp he still had the adrenaline shakes and his knees were weak, but he was thinking straight. If he reported that he'd almost stepped on a rattler, the older boys might veto any further independent adventures. And more important was the embarrassment factor. Billy's first rock should have nailed the snake dead to rights. But he'd panicked and thrown wild. *Darn!* It would have been so incredibly cool to bring back a dead rattler.

Stu was seated on a log before the gently smoking remnants of their morning campfire, whittling on a chunk of pine. Mike was nowhere to be seen.

"Hi, Billy," Stu said as he expertly shaved a thin slice from the stick. "How'd it go?"

Billy set the half-full container down on the log bench. Stu whistled in appreciation. "Where'd you find 'em?"

"Secret," Billy replied, now certain that not reporting the rattlesnake was the smart choice.

"Aw, c'mon. Give."

"Nope," Billy said with finality.

"Weenie."

"Dick weed."

"Lizard breath."

"Pig fart."

"Bet your kids will be born with six toes!"

"Only if I marry one of your cousins!"

Stu laughed and relented. "Okay, that was a good one."

Billy looked around. "Where's Mike?"

Stu returned to whittling, inspecting the grain he had exposed with a deep slice of the blade. "Said he was going exploring."

"Where?"

"Back up the trail."

"Did he take his pole?"

Stu pointed to their backpacks where Mike's pole was leaned against a tree. "Nope."

This was the opportunity Billy had been hoping for. The puzzle of his brother's behavior contained pieces he still didn't understand. Stu might know more since the two boys were the same age. And Mike might also have said something to Stu.

"Hey, Stu?"

"Yeah?"

"What's wrong with Mike?"

"What do you mean?" Stu laid down the chunk of wood and folded his jackknife and slipped it into his pants pocket. He adjusted his Yankees cap where the band had begun to itch his forehead.

"Well," Billy began slowly. "Last summer Mike was the best brother in the world. We did all sorts of stuff together. Remember?"

"Sure."

"So what changed from then to now?"

"I don't think there's anything wrong with him. It's just that things are changing fast for us right now, what with graduation and all." Stu paused and Billy saw concern cross Stu's face. Stu seemed to turn some thought over in his mind for a few seconds. "Last year really was a great summer, wasn't it?"

Billy wanted to keep on the subject of Mike. But something told him to let it go for the moment. So he instead said, "Yeah." And he meant it, Because the summer of '68 had seemed truly magical.

Stu said, "We sure saw some great movies at the Ruby. You saw Planet of the Apes twice didn't you?"

"Twice," Billy agreed. "And I saw *2001: A Space Odyssey* four times."

"Four? Really?"

"Yep. And Bullitt and Planet of the Apes, and Night of the Living Dead!"

"Night of the Living Dead was the bitchin' best movie ever made!"

Billy didn't bother to disagree. His own favorite had been, *2001, A Space Odyssey*. Director Stanley Kubrick's story suggested how primitive mankind truly was, but at the same time it held out hope that man might someday move out into the stars. The possibilities were infinite. Stu and Mike had thought the movie was too slow and too confusing. "Needs a couple of chicks," Mike had sagely observed. "Sex in space!" Stu had agreed, "Finest kind."

Last summer Billy had also discovered Kurt Vonnegut. He had gone to the library looking for something on monkeys, interested in evolution after watching the Kubrick film. He had checked out *Welcome to the Monkey House* thinking it was about monkeys and discovered instead an entire new and wonderful world of speculative fiction.

Stu had a far away dreamy look on his face. "What about the music?"

"Hey Jude," Billy offered.

"Lady Madonna," Stu countered.

"The Doors."

"Zeppelin."

"Dylan."

"Donovan."

"The Mamas and the Papas."

"The Bee Gees."

"Cripes!"

"Ditto!"

Billy realized what Stu was really trying to say. Even if things were changing fast for Stu and Mike, they would always have those memories. No one could ever take that away. Billy looked over at Stu. He wanted to ask Stu more about Mike. But Stu didn't seem to want to talk about it, only to relive the glory of what had happened. So Billy set aside his need, at least for the moment. "It doesn't get any better, does it?"

"Nope. It sure doesn't."

"Think we'll ever have it that good again?"

Stu thought a long time before answering. "Probably not. How could you top '68? I mean, really!"

Billy thought there might be something to top that glorious year. Many things, in fact. For instance, this moment, sitting beside Stu, high up in the mountains and with adventures still ahead, this wasn't too far off from the best of what had happened the previous summer. Was it?

After a minute Billy got up and stretched, announced, "We need some trout for dinner. Want to join me in some fishing?"

"Nah," Stu replied. "I'm gonna catch a nap."

"Okay." Billy picked up his pole and headed for the spot he and Stu had first fished.

He took his time along the shore and caught some fair-sized cutthroats, but none compared with the monster he'd caught while fishing with Mike the day before. As the sun arced low toward the mountaintops Billy saw Mike coming back down the trail. He reeled in his line and retrieved the willow stick that now held six fish. He walked up the shoreline with his fishing pole in his left hand and the string of trout swinging gently in his right.

"Heya, Mike," Billy greeted his brother as he entered camp.

"Hey, Billy."

"Where'd you go?"

"I climbed back up to Boiling Lake. I wanted to check and see if those sheepherders were still around."

Stu perked up at this. He had been busy piling wood on the lingering coals in the fire pit. "Did you see them?"

"Nope. Their tent's gone. They must've cleared out."

"Good," Stu said.

"Yeah," Billy added with relief. He'd never spoken of the terror he had felt being alone that night. And he never would.

Mike looked at Billy's fish. "Good catch."

Billy smiled and turned for the creek. "I'll clean them. When do we eat?"

Mike glanced at his watch. "It's nearly six. As soon as you get those gutted we can start."

Billy walked down to the creek.

Later, after the trout were floured and peppered and ready for the pan, the boys opened two more cans of beans. They made biscuits and fried the trout as the beans bubbled in a pot. Afterwards, they finished off the last of the chocolate and marshmallows and graham crackers.

The beans caught up with all three of them as they were sitting around the campfire, and Stu was the first to let off a big one.

"Wheeeeeew!" Mike said, dramatically holding his nose between thumb and forefinger. "That was ripe!"

"It was a *man's* fart," Stu replied solemnly.

Now that Stu had broken powerful wind, it wasn't long before they were contesting who could *cut the biggest*.

In the end, Stu was awarded the honors for an amazing screamer that actually changed tone, twice.

"We got us a regular Mozart," Mike observed.

Later, as they were getting ready to crawl into their sleeping bags, Mike called out to Stu who was down at the creek washing up, "Hey Mozart! Don't forget to wash behind your ears." All three of them howled laughter. Years later, Billy would sometimes say, "Don't be such a Mozart!" to someone who had annoyed him. But he would never explain. There are jokes which by their very nature are private and situational and can never be the same in a different place and time and with different people. But that night at Cub Lake all three boys thought it was just about the funniest thing they had ever heard.

They were exhausted and fell asleep quickly, with the occasional flatulence quickly lost in the smells of smoke and pine.

At 3 AM. Billy awoke in a cold sweat. He had been running, running, running, from something that was chasing him along a twisting mountain trail. At every bend he would almost fall off a cliff, regaining his balance only at the last instant. He could feel the heat of the pursuing monster like hot grease against his back. And he knew that he could never escape the certain death that was coming closer by the second.

Returning to sleep was impossible. So Billy lay quiet in the dark, clammy hands grasping at the liner of his bag as if to keep it from being suddenly ripped from his body. He studied the night sounds for clues. An occasional gust of wind whispered through the pines. The gentle lapping of tiny waves which beat against the gravelly lakeshore. The distant gurgle of the creek over sleek stone.

It was the kind of night a kid never forgets.

Chapter 22

Shirley dialed the first six numbers, paused to listen to the pounding of her heart, and slammed down the handset. She stared hatefully at the telephone. Then she lifted the handset again and dialed again, but at the last number she again lost her nerve. She slammed the handset back into the cradle and leaned over the kitchen counter and lay her head down on her arms and bawled.

When the tears finally stopped she washed her face in the kitchen sink, glared one last time at the phone, and hopped in defeat back to her bedroom. She collapsed onto the mattress; her sprained foot was throbbing like a diesel engine.

She buried her face in the pillow and tried to forget her ugly discovery, but the questions came pounding like breakers against a reef. Had Janet intended to keep the money for herself? Or had she merely forgotten to mention it? How could her sister do this to her?

When sleep finally came it was a welcome relief.

Shirley awoke around 10 PM and it was completely dark. The air smelled of cardboard and dust and an ancient hint of grease lodged in the carpet. She called in a voice that broke with nervous energy, "Janet!" But the only answer was the stillness of an empty house. A new ugly thought intruded. Had some violence happened to her sister? But it was hard to imagine anything like that happening in a small town like Chelan. Something even uglier now occurred. Had Janet left and gone back to California? But within seconds Shirley convinced herself that made no sense. Her luggage was still here. And the money was still in the suitcase. *She's just having a good time.* Shirley repeated this soothing thought over and over until the words became believable from repetition. And sleep eventually came again. Disturbed and restless, but still sleep.

The next morning Shirley washed her hair in the tub under the faucet and wiped her arm pits with a wash cloth. She was dressed and sitting on her mattress, resting from the effort of the spitz-bath, collecting energy to hop back out to the kitchen to call the police and make a missing person report, or maybe turn her sister in for the theft, Shirley still hadn't decided, when she heard the front door open. There were two voices: a man's and her sister's. And then the door shut and only one set of footsteps came down the hallway. They turned in the direction of the kitchen, and Shirley remembered that she had left the Roi-Tan box on the kitchen counter. There was a long pause before the footsteps retraced down the hallway and a knock came on the bedroom door.

"Sis?"

Shirley sat on the mattress and cringed at the unnatural sweetness in Janet's voice. The window blind was rolled up and a shaft of sunlight flooded the room. She made certain her emotions were under control before answering. The lapse was also calculated as a signal to her sister. *I know that you know that I know.* Her gut churned and her head ached as she finally replied.

"I'm up."

Tiny dust motes danced and swirled in the yellow light as the door opened. Janet left it standing wide as she entered. For a few seconds the two women, both on the verge of middle age, both ripe with negotiation and bottled up by uncertainty, looked in each other's direction but not directly at each other. The seconds stretched out for an eternity before Janet finally spoke.

"I was going to tell you."

Shirley heard the lie. She knew her sister too well to deny the greed and disappointment that tempered Janet's words. And with this realization came a feeling of relief. The actions of her sister weren't nice or good, and they surely weren't something you would want to become regular gossip in this churchy little town. Shirley realized with cold comfort that what Janet had done was predictable. And knowing this was how things were with her sister brought a sense of certainty and control. Shirley's next words came naturally and with a twisted kindness born of a white trash mentality.

"I know."

The decision had been made, and both sisters knew it. Everything was salvaged in that instant. The air in the room suddenly seemed lighter and easier to breathe. Things would move forward, as they always had.

Janet said, "Well, we better get outside before people start arriving for the sale."

"Yes. We better."

But before they started greeting people for the yard sale, there was one important thing to do. Shirley had Janet bring her the Roi-Tan box and she reached in and took out the enlistment envelope, licked the gum, and sealed the flap. Later that day, after they had sold off most of what lay out on the lawn, Janet drove Shirley to the alleyway behind the post office, where she reached out the passenger window and slid the envelope into the blue metal drop box.

Chapter 23

The next morning the boys drew straws to see who would catch fish for breakfast. Mike lost. He stalked off along the shore with pole in hand and his hat a blaze of yellow in the morning sun, leaving Billy and Stu to clean up the campsite and finish packing for the next segment of the hike, to Surprise Lake.

"Hey Billy," Stu said as he rolled his sleeping bag into a tight bundle.

"Yeah?"

"You're the best." There was complete sincerity in Stu's words. And a twinkle in his eyes and a grin.

The compliment made Billy happy. "Thanks, Stu," Billy finally answered, trying to downplay the moment. "You're cool, too."

Stu was having none of this downplay crap. With a certainty that left no room for any doubt whatsoever Stu said, "No, I really mean it." Stu braced a knee on top of the tightly coiled red nylon bag and drew the cinch cord tight. "If I could pick a brother, it would be you." He spoke without looking over at Billy. There was both sincerity and a distant sadness in his voice. And not looking at Billy as he spoke seemed to add an even greater weight, as if he might not be able to look into Billy's eyes and make this confession.

What Billy now wanted to do was give Stu a hug. Just wrap his arms around Stu and tell him that he loved him as if he *were* his brother. But Billy was afraid he'd get teary-eyed. So when Stu finally had his bag tied and stood up, instead of attempting a hug Billy took a couple of steps and he reached out his right hand and Stu took it and they shook, firmly, and then Stu tousled Billy's hair and Billy threw a soft punch to Stu's left shoulder, and they went back to cleaning up the campsite and stoking the campfire to cook breakfast, happy as two clams on an endless stretch of empty beach.

Half an hour later they had barely spoken—hadn't really needed to speak. Mike came striding back into camp, casually swinging a string of five cleaned trout.

"Bwanna return!" Stu observed, as Mike laid the fish on the log. "Bring heap good fish."

"Bwanna," Mike said dryly, "not go for unexpected swim. Get more fishing done that way."

"Bwanna getting smarter!"

They all chuckled.

Mike seasoned the fish, spooned a lump of Crisco into the cast-iron skillet, waited till it melted and started to smoke, and placed the fish side by side to sizzle in the oil.

On the opposite side of the campfire Billy began making huckleberry pancakes one at a time in the steel skillet. Once he had poured a layer of batter onto the flat-bottomed pan he would reach into the Tupperware container for a handful of huckleberries to sprinkle across the bubbling batter. The berries would sink into the creamy white surface. Soon the aromas of huckleberries, frying batter, browning trout and pine wood smoke filled the air with the bouquet of trail life.

"Hey Billy," Mike said. "You got enough to make extra pancakes."

"Sure," Billy said.

"Why?" Stu asked.

"For lunch on the trail."

"Really?"

"Got the idea from our grandmother," Mike explained. "She used to cook up a bunch of pancakes at her summer cabin. When Billy and I went hiking or fishing for the day she'd pack them up in tin foil for us to take."

A wistful look came to Stu's face. "I'd rather have a hamburger."

"Well, Einstein," Mike countered sarcastically. "You figure out where to get us some hamburgers—make mine a double-deluxe with cheese and onions, heavy on the mayo thank you—and I'll be happy to chuck the pancakes over the nearest cliff!"

"Yeah, well . . . you got a point there," Stu said. But he retained the wistful look as he contemplated a burger-and-fries combo from Lucky's Drive-in.

They left Cub Lake when the sun was well up and the morning chill was gone. For Billy, leaving the lake was hard. He would have been satisfied to stay for the remaining days of their adventure, then walk down Prince Creek Trail to Lake Chelan and catch the ferry home.

But Mike and Stu had again caught the hiking bug. To Mike's credit, he asked Billy if his feet felt okay, and Billy said, "Yes, they're fine," and both older boys smiled. "Then let's nail some trail!" Stu said, and Mike added, "Yowsa, Boss!" And they left the camp at a happy pace along the shore trail.

As they passed below the ledge where Billy had confronted the rattlesnake, he looked up, finding at least one reason to be glad for leaving. He gave the hidden huckleberry/rattlesnake sanctuary a last glance, reached up to tilt his Akubra at just the right angle to shade the sun from the back of his neck, and settled upon watching Stu's boots beat prints into the trail dirt as they lost sight of the lake and started down.

They spent two hours hiking what seemed more like stairs than trail, constantly stepping across roots and over rocks the Forest Service had left as natural bulwarks against erosion. By the time they passed below three thousand feet in elevation the temperature had crept up into the low eighties. The sweatband inside the Akubra was soaked and so was the back of Billy's shirt.

Near noontime they came to where the Cub Lake fork of Prince Creek Trail split from the main Prince Creek Trail. The branch that headed back up a narrow valley to their right would ultimately lead them to Surprise Lake. Mike was in front when Billy heard him call back, quietly, "Scouts at twelve o'clock."

Stu was too much of a maverick to like scouting, or to have the Boy Scouts interested in him. Neither of the Ward boys had chosen to go into scouting.

Mike had been invited to a meeting when he was fourteen. He'd come home dejected. When Dad asked what was wrong, Mike had said, "When I got there half of them were out in back of the Civic Center smoking cigarettes. The Scoutmaster was late, and after he showed up all we ever seemed to talk about was how everyone should earn merit badges so that when they went to the jamboree the Scoutmaster would be *proud of his troop.*"

Hank had countered that all Scouts weren't like that. He'd been a Scout, and had enjoyed it. Scouting taught good values. And friendships created in those early years might open doors of opportunity later in life.

But Mike had gotten it into his head that the local chapter was a bunch of hoodlums and not the kind of kids he wanted to hang around with. And once Mike made up his mind . . .

So when the three boys came upon a dozen fourteen-year-olds in green Scout uniforms resting at the trail junction, Mike's warning was understood and accepted. There was no inclination to stop.

"Blast on past?" Stu whispered.

"Yeah," Mike replied.

"Right," Billy agreed.

Mike added, "We say 'Hi' and head on up the trail."

The strategy worked fine until they had just passed the last Scout. Then, that last boy, a red-haired kid with a face full of freckles, said, "Watch out for the bears."

Mike stumbled to a halt and he and Stu and Billy turned around. They stared at the kid who had spoken.

"Are you serious?" Mike said. The kid's face was now flushed with embarrassment, and he was catching ugly glances from other troop members. Fidgeting under the pressure from both sides, he continued quickly.

"We spooked two cubs back up the trail. They climbed up a tree. We didn't see the mother, but our Scoutmaster got us out real quick. They're probably gone by now, but I'd be careful if I were you."

The Scoutmaster heard the exchange and paused in his conversation with another boy. Billy stared at the scouts. *They weren't even going to tell us!* He turned to face Mike.

"Bears?"

"Aw, heck," Stu cut in confidently. "I'll bet he's just joking. You know, pulling our leg."

Mike fixed the kid with a hard look. "Were you joking?"

"No," the kid replied earnestly.

Mike unshouldered the straps of his pack and laid it down in the middle of the trail. "Wait here," he told Billy and Stu. He walked back and had a few words with the Scoutmaster.

When he returned he looked disgusted. "They treed some cubs, alright. Fearless leader reckons it was about a mile up the trail. He didn't think it'd be a problem, or so he says, 'cause the bears would be long gone by now.' That's why he didn't say anything, or at least that's his story."

"Bears?" Billy repeated slowly. "I don't want to run into bears, Mike." The rattlesnake scare had been enough danger for the entire hike. But at least you had a chance with a snake. You could kill it with a rock, or just back off. But bears . . .

Mike studied Billy for a few seconds. He looked at Stu. "So what do you think we should do?"

Stu looked at Mike and tried to read his face for the answer Mike wanted. But as far as he could tell Mike really was interested in his opinion. Stu thought about it and finally said, "We've come this far. I don't want to go back the way we came. And those Scouts are below us. We'd look like a bunch of wussies if we went down the trail after them."

Billy said, "I don't mind looking like a wussy if the alternative is being mauled by a bear."

Mike and Stu gave Billy a funny look but that was all.

Mike reassumed his leadership role. "Okay, here's the way I see it. We won't go back up to Cub Lake because we've already been there and where's the adventure in going someplace you've already been? We could head down to Lake Chelan, but we don't want to end the hike, especially if it means following the Scouts back down. I say we head up the trail to Surprise. The bears should be long gone by now."

"But what if they aren't?" Billy persisted.

"Tell you what," Mike said. "I'll take the lead." He reached down and unsnapped the leather sheath holding his hatchet and withdrew the shiny blade. "If the mother charges at me I'll get at least one good swing in. And while I'm keeping her busy you two guys drop your packs and run like hell." Mike smiled as he replayed the heroic image in his mind.

Billy looked at his brother in disbelief. "Are you serious? Mike, there's no way you're going to take out a bear with a hatchet!"

"Correctamundo," Mike confirmed. "But it's the least-wussy thing I can come up with, and at least you guys will get away."

Billy continued to stare at his brother in disbelief. But not Stu. Mike was completely serious. And totally nuts. He intended to face a bear with a hatchet. But for Stu this was the charm of it. It was the completely stud thing to do. Even though a corner of his mind reassured him it was also the most absolutely crazy thing to do.

But for Billy, this was his *brother* who was going to become bear food. "Mike," he said with cold certainty. "I don't want to lose you to a bear."

Mike heard the love in Billy's words. And it almost stopped him. Almost. But he had already convinced himself there was no danger. He resisted the anger that threatened to seep in, and instead said in a very even and brotherly voice, "The bears are bound to be gone by now. And if we spot them we can always back off. I read that bears don't want to see you anymore than you want to see them. And even if I do get attacked I'll just curl up and play dead and things will be okay. Billy . . . I'm certain that things are going to be okay. Okay?"

Stu listened patiently, willing to go with whichever brother won the argument.

Billy nervously adjusted his hat. Not wanting to agree. Realizing he truly had only two choices: go along with Mike, or follow the Scouts back down to Lake Chelan, alone, no longer a part of the older boys' adventure. He finally relented. "Okay."

"Good." Mike reached down for his pack. "If you want to follow a ways back that's okay. There's nothing wrong with taking precautions." He looked at Stu. "That goes for you, too, Stu. Hang back a ways if you want."

"No way," Stu said. "If there's a bear up ahead and we flush it out I'm not turning tail and leaving you to fight it alone."

To Billy this was nonsense. How could Mike and Stu be so stupid? Fight bears! But Billy realized something more important was at stake. They were now a team, finally, and maybe if all three of them stood up to a bear it would be more likely to back down. And beyond any measure of the possibility of success was the fact that Billy knew he'd never forgive himself if he ran while the other two boys stood their ground.

Mike swung his pack onto his shoulders and started up the trail, hollering back, "You guys coming, or what?"

"On it, Boss," Stu said as he shouldered his own backpack.

Billy gave one last look back at the Scouts, who were now studiously ignoring them. Stu and Mike were well up the trail. Mike turned again, "You coming, Billy?"

"Yeah, yeah. I'm coming," he said reluctantly, lifting the pack onto his shoulders. It suddenly seemed very heavy. He trudged up the trail and lagged several yards behind for a few minutes, but finally picked up his pace and caught up despite being certain that at any moment a black bear with rippling muscles, snarling muzzle, and long, sharp, yellow fangs, would come charging at them from the thick brush. But he was one of the guys, *darn it*! His brother had finally accepted him—completely—into the adventure. And back at Cub Lake, Stu had said he'd want him more than anyone else as a brother. *Better to die with my brothers than to turn chicken*!

So Billy fell in behind the older boys and began to study every tree, every bush, even the soft soil alongside the trail for bear sign. And it wasn't long before he saw the first blackish droppings embedded with bits of undigested berry and seed. The first three piles were dried hard. But the fourth was fresh and covered with a swarm of flies.

Billy thought hard about turning around, but only for a moment. He looked at the backs of the two older boys as they marched on ahead. Took a deep breath. And continued on the lookout for more bear sign.

The trail now cut into the sharp slope of the hill. In the thirty or forty yards that formed the width of the valley floor there were massive thickets of brush, even where the trail paralleled Prince Creek as it carved a course through tumbling boulders and deep banks. This creek was smaller than the one that flowed into Cub Lake, but the drop was steep and the cascading water made plenty of noise. A bear could easily be hiding in the brush, or over the bank, maybe taking a drink out of the creek. Billy's head panned back and forth like radar, straining to hear above the rush of water

Because the trail twisted and turned with the violent contour of the narrow canyon Billy could never see more than a stone's throw ahead. Perfect ambush conditions for an angry bear. Up ahead Mike was intent with his head down making steady progress and seeming unconcerned about a bear attack. Billy couldn't figure it out. Was he truly unconcerned? Or was he trying to prove something? Maybe he was too concerned with being cool to be afraid? Billy didn't think his brother was so dumb that he didn't appreciate the risk of encountering a bear. Billy finally had to admit that Mike was behaving in a strange way, one he couldn't puzzle out. Just thinking about Mike's strangeness helped a little to take Billy's mind off bears.

Time passed and they made fine progress. To Billy's great relief, there came no crack of branches, no growl, no sounds but the rush of water and the sound of their boots on the trail.

They came to a spot where the trail flattened for a short run. A great tree trunk encrusted with graybeard moss and brown lichen had rolled down the hill and lay alongside the trail. The limbs had splintered off as it rolled and several seasons had weathered the bark to fudge brown; the pitch which had flowed from the injuries it had suffered when it had come down was now solidly crystallized in hard little nodules.

"Take five," Mike called out. He took off his pack and leaned it against the log and sank down beside it with his legs tiredly splayed out into the trail.

Stu dumped his pack and sat down beside Mike.

Billy took one last look around, saw no sign of bears, and joined them.

Stu took a long swig of water from his canteen. "Jeez, I was starting to hope a bear would jump out of the woods just so we'd have something to do other than climb this darned canyon!"

"Not me," Billy said.

"Ease up, Billy," Mike said gently. "Stu's joking. Aren't you Stu?"

"Sure, just joking." But Stu didn't smile.

Do you think we've gone past the place where they treed the cubs?" Billy felt dumb even as he spoke. He'd been scrutinizing the bark of every large fir and pine, looking for fresh claw marks. He hadn't seen anything that suggested bears, except for the poop he'd spotted, but that was easily a mile behind them. He wasn't sure what else to look for.

Stu said confidently, "We've gone way past the place the Scouts described."

Mike nodded. "From what the scoutmaster said it sounded like they treed those cubs less than half a mile up the trail. I think I saw the place he described. I'm sure we're way past it, wherever it was."

Billy finally chose to believe they were past the bears. At least *those* bears. It didn't mean they wouldn't run into *other* bears. Heck, the woods could be seething with them. A grizzly was probably watching them at this very moment!

He said nothing. *Just suck it up. Grow up.* But he found himself wishing they were back at Cub Lake, catching fish, finding that flat log Stu had wanted for a raft, taking it easy and enjoying the high country rather than challenging it.

"How are your feet, Billy?" Stu asked.

Billy felt a small stab of pride. His feet had held up exceptionally well; they seemed to have adjusted; his boots had felt comfortable since they left Cub Lake. "Fine," he replied confidently.

"Good," Mike said.

Billy looked at Stu. "How much longer are we going to be hiking uphill? Sooner or later we have to come to the top, don't we?"

Stu dug out the map from his pack and scrutinized it briefly. "Look here," he said, pointing to a curving dotted line. "That's the trail we're on. It circles around to the northern side of Surprise Lake."

Billy looked at the trail line. It performed a three-quarter circle before it joined with the oval marked *Surprise Lake*. "Why doesn't it just go straight into the lake?" he asked, puzzled.

Mike pointed west, up through the trees. "See for yourself."

The answer was obvious. Across the valley and tearing a line against the blue sky was a massive jagged mountain wall. No trail could have been built over it.

"Oh."

"So," Mike continued, "I figure we've got another two or three miles before we're on top. You okay with that much more hiking?"

"Of course," Billy replied, happy that Mike was asking. I'm getting better at hiking, he thought confidently. And . . . his brother was now asking for his input. But he still wished they were already at the top or at least that the trail they were on wasn't so steep.

"Well, then," Mike said. "Let's get the show on the road." He stood and reached for his backpack and Stu and Billy followed suit.

It seemed like forever, but they finally came to the end of the narrow valley and crested one last ridge and broke into high meadow country where countless clumps of Indian Paintbrush made the vast rolling meadow resemble a green quilt with orange polka dots. There were also a few purple lupines, yellow glacier lilies and buttercups scattered about. Tiny blue-winged butterflies flitted among the blossoms and crowded together wherever there was a damp patch. Not as nice as Horse Thief Basin. But nice.

They came to a small creek running quick and clear amongst a tumble of smooth rocks. Clean yellow sand had collected in small bars between the rocks and formed a center ridge down the middle of the creek. The Forest Service had placed a twenty-inch-wide log, split in half, as a bridge. They stopped for lunch, taking off their boots and socks and dangling their bare feet to let the icy water wash away the trail heat; sitting like pigeons on a split-rail fence; eating syrup-soaked rolled-up blueberry pancakes.

"This is great!" Mike said, digging his toes into the bottom to dislodge a few small stones and send sand swirling in the current. "How far do you reckon we've come, Stu?"

"Maybe five, six miles."

"How far to Surprise?"

"Another five."

"Are you really are going enlist in the Army?"

The question caught Stu off guard and there was a long and awkward pause before he answered. His face settled into a rueful look of acceptance. He looked at Mike, practically nose to nose. "Yeah, I guess so," he said quietly.

"You'll be careful over in 'Nam won't you?"

Stu gave Mike a hopeless look. "No, I plan to jump on the first land mine I see. Whadda ya think? Of course I'm going to be careful."

Billy had been mulling over Stu's plan to enlist ever since it had been revealed at the campfire. He knew Mom might have told him not to *get into a dither* about it, because it was Stu's decision and Stu had a right to make the choice. But Billy figured it was something worth *dithering* about. As he'd turned the problem over and over in his mind, an idea had come. But he'd wanted to sort out all the ramifications before he spoke up. Now seemed like a good time.

"Our Uncle Charlie's got a job with the PUD," he said.

The Public Utility District, or *PUD*, operated three dams on the Columbia River, plus two generators at Chelan Falls. Uncle Charlie had been with the PUD since before the Ward brothers had been born.

Mike looked at Billy as if he'd just reported spotting a pink rhinoceros. "What?" Mike said. "Earth to Billy!"

Billy ignored the jab and ploughed ahead with the reasoning he'd spent a lot of time working out every angle on.

"The PUD hires a college kid to work summers at the Chelan Falls Power Plant."

Stu guessed where Billy might be headed and cut in defensively. "So what? I'm not going to college, and besides, summer's almost over."

"I know," Billy said. "But Uncle Charlie's a manager, and he's the one who hires the summer help. He might be able to find you a job at the PUD even if it's not summertime. Maybe there's other work at the Falls. Maybe there's some kind of work in Wenatchee or at one of the other dams. If you could find even some temporary kind of position you'd have time to, well, you know, see how things go and look at all your options."

Mike was about to respond but as his lips parted his face turned thoughtful and he softly licked and then closed his lips. Billy had never seen his brother change direction so quickly. Mike gazed out across the meadow and said, as if speaking to no one but himself, "It might actually work."

Panic came to Stu's face. "Now wait a minute! Who said I wanted a job with the Power Company? Anyway, they probably wouldn't hire me. I don't know anything about electricity or dams or that kind of stuff. I'd probably end up getting myself electrocuted!"

Something in Stu's voice told Billy there was more to his enlistment than Stu had revealed. *Stu was scared of rejection!* And why not? Everything his mom had put him through must have made him think he was practically worthless. Joining the military was a sure thing for Stu. All he would have to do is follow the rules, and the Army certainly had rules that were easy to understand. There would be no shifting emotional sand in the Army!

Mike was oblivious, and he warmed up fast to Billy's new way of organizing Stu's future.

"They've got apprenticeships," Mike said with growing excitement. "They train you on the job, and they can even send you to technical school for workshops and training. Uncle Charlie got on when he was practically a kid. He started right out of high school. Now he's in management. He's made enough dough over the years to buy a ski boat, and he takes a vacation to Palm Springs for two weeks every winter. And—"

"Whoa!" Stu's hand came up as if to ward off an attack. "I thought this was supposed to be a hike, not a career-planning session."

Mike stopped.

Billy was embarrassed. It had seemed an innocent enough idea and he'd thought Stu would be interested. There was a long, awkward pause in the conversation. Stu finally volunteered one more reason why Vietnam might be preferable.

Stu said reluctantly, "I don't know where I'd live even if I did get on."

"With your mom?" Mike said innocently.

Stu's face reddened as he made the confession he'd hoped to avoid until after the hike. "She's giving up the lease on the house and is moving down to California to live with her sister."

"Giving up the house?" Mike was dazed. "What's the deal, Stu? How come you didn't tell me about this earlier?"

For Billy it was one of those weird moments, when things that had been a puzzle about Mike and why he had been acting strangely suddenly made sense. Mike wanted to come home on school breaks and long weekends and spend time with Stu. Go to the Ruby Theater for a movie; walk the beach out at Wapato Point looking for arrowheads; ski up at Echo Valley; bowl a line at Chelan Lanes; or play the pinball machines at the pizza parlor. Just like they'd always done. Billy had heard people say, "You can never go home again," but until that moment he'd never really understood it. Yet here it was. Mike's best friend simply wasn't going to be there when he came home from college. Things weren't ever going to be the same. And the thought of this was going to tear Mike's picture of his world just a little bit apart.

Billy now also saw one more big piece in understanding Stu. Shirley was about to dump him and move to California. After all he'd done for her, helping her out with money from the route, she was going to stick it to him.

They all sat quietly, not knowing what to say. And then Billy saw Mike's composure brighten, like someone had flipped a switch and a hundred-watt bulb came on.

"Hey," Mike said. "How about if you stay at our place for a while? My bedroom will be empty. I'll bet we could talk Mom and Dad into it. What do you think?"

Billy was stunned. Mike's room was hallowed ground. Everything in there might as well have been made from rubies and diamonds. On the walls were his prized movie posters, particularly the one of Raquel Welch in *One Million Years B.C.*, for which he had traded hours of scraping gum from under the seats at the Ruby Theater. There were also *M'A'S'H, Patton,* and *Alice's Restaurant.* Along one wall stood a pine bookcase he'd made in wood shop that held his collection of paperback science fiction. There was his bird's-eye maple desk that served as a storehouse for treasure: crystals, magnets, knives, comic books, a can of cat's-eye marbles. Mess with anything in Mike's room and you were dead meat.

"Yeah," Mike continued, completely unaware of the impact his offer had had upon his brother. Or for that matter upon Stu, who sat slack-jawed listening to what Mike had come up with. "I can bunk up on the sofa when I come home on breaks. And it'd just be for a while, till you get enough dough saved out of your salary to get an apartment. What do you think, Billy?"

"Sure," he said meekly, suddenly proud of his brother.

"What do you think, Stu?" Mike asked eagerly.

"I don't know," Stu said slowly. But there was finally an edge of uncertainty, of hope.

"Well," Mike concluded as if it were already a done deal. "You give it some thought. We can talk about it more after we take the boat down lake."

"I'll think about it," Stu slowly agreed. Maybe he would take up the offer. Maybe he'd opt for the military. Stu was too confused at the moment to know what to do.

All Billy knew for certain was that he felt a lot better for having brought it up in the first place. And he thought Mike maybe deserved some kind of medal for being willing to give up his room to make it happen.

"How 'bout we get back on the trail?" Mike reached down into the cold clear water to wash his hands of the last bit of sticky syrup from the blueberry pancakes.

"Sure," Stu replied from some distant universe.

Billy thought of a million things he wanted to say. Mostly he wanted to encourage Stu to take the offer. But everything that counted had already been said. If he accidentally said the wrong thing he could jinx the whole deal. So he dried his feet, rolled down the cuffs of his jeans, pulled on his socks and boots, and kept his mouth shut.

The three of them stood and walked over the bridge to where their backpacks lay. And just before Billy reached his pack he brushed close to Stu, and that was the second time that he felt like giving Stu a brotherly hug. But for the second time, he didn't.

Chapter 24

They hiked the remainder of the great lazy circle, skirting rockslides and crossing meadows and patches of light forest. The going wasn't difficult, but it seemed endless. Around six, they came to an open reach of hillside, and Stu, who was in the lead, pulled up.

"At last!" He said with relief. The Ward boys caught up and then looked . . . down.

Surprise Lake had lived up to its name.

"Jeez," Mike said with exasperation. "It sank!" Surprise Lake lay hundreds of feet below in a crater ringed by rockslides. Reeds and cattails had formed a marsh swamp along its shore.

The trail split, one branch switch-backing down to the lake, the other continuing on towards Stehekin at the northern end of Lake Chelan.

It'll take twenty minutes to hike down there," Stu said.

"Maybe we should camp up here," Billy said.

Mike shrugged. "We can't catch fish up here. Besides, there's a campsite down on the lake." He pointed to where the trail ended at a clear patch of ground with a stone fire ring and a log bench. "So what's the problem?"

"Mosquitoes," Billy said flatly. He got two blank stares. "See all that swamp? I'll bet there are a billion mosquitoes in the mud."

"Okay," Mike said, but there was no agreement in his voice. "But where are we going to get water?" It had been some time since they had passed even a trickle of a brook. "And up here is a rotten place to camp." The soil was rocky. There were few trees, so wood was a problem. It was going to be a long, cold, dreary night up on the ridge.

Stu said, "Maybe it gets cold enough at night to kill the mosquitoes, or maybe the trout eat them all?" He gave Billy the briefest of glances. Billy understood.

Mike's high mood from the footbridge had slowly disintegrated as the afternoon had worn on. Billy thought it was because Stu hadn't come out and agreed to the offer of Mike's room.

Mike gave Billy and Stu a tired glance.

"Okay," Billy said to Mike, and he set off down the trail. Stu followed wordlessly. In a few seconds Mike fell in behind.

Mike's mood got worse when it turned out that Billy was right about the mosquitoes. Despite double latherings of mosquito repellant and a roaring campfire, the boys were continually swatting at the pesky insects. Even the good-sized trout Mike caught in the slack water did little to make things better.

"I'm hitting the sack," Stu announced as soon as the pans and utensils from dinner had been scrubbed clean.

"Me too," Billy agreed.

Mike had remained glumly silent throughout dinner, and now said, "I'll be there in a couple of minutes. I've gotta do my business." He walked off into the darkness.

As soon as he was gone Stu turned to Billy, "What's bothering your brother?"

"I don't know. After what he said on the bridge I thought he'd have a great day. I can't figure it out."

"I hope it's not me," Stu said. "Maybe he's having second thoughts about letting me use his room. Maybe if I told him I'd rather—"

"No way!" Billy said. Mike might be having second thoughts, but if that was what was upsetting him, then he should have thought it through better before he'd opened his big mouth and offered Stu his room. "No way," Billy repeated stubbornly. "Mike meant what he said about you using his room. I don't know what's bugging him, but I'm going to get it straightened out." He stood up.

"Hey, Billy," Stu said. "I really appreciate it, but I don't want to make trouble."

"You aren't making trouble," Billy said flatly, walking away from the campfire. There was a half moon which, together with the band of the Milky Way, gave enough light to see by.

It didn't take long to find his brother, who was standing about fifty yards down the shoreline, staring up at the stars.

"Mike?"

"Yeah?"

"What's up?" Even as he said it he wondered if Mike would snap back at him about it being none of his business. But there was only silence as Mike continued to stare up at the night sky.

"You okay?" There was a long moment before his brother replied.

"Yeah, sure." But he sounded anything but okay.

"You've got Stu thinking he isn't welcome to use your room." But now he was wondering if he had entirely missed something that was happening to Mike. There was a long silence, and Billy began to wonder if it were true that Mike was reconsidering his offer.

"That's not it," his brother finally said in a gloomy voice. "It's just that talking about Stu being in my room got me to thinking."

"About what?"

"About going away to school. I guess it never really hit me till now that I'm leaving home."

"Seattle's only a couple hundred miles away. You can come home weekends if you want. Besides, I thought you were excited about meeting girls and all the neat things you'll get to study. And the football program and all of that kind of stuff." Billy waited for his brother to reply, but when none came, he continued hopefully.

"There must be lots of neat stuff to do in Seattle. You could go to concerts and plays." He was running out of ideas when he heard Mike pull back a sniffle and his breathing hitched, and then hitched again. Mike was crying. Not bawling out loud, but the type of crying you try to hide because it hurts so much. Billy had never heard his brother cry like this. Without thinking about what he was doing he walked over and put his arms around Mike, and he found Mike hugging him back. For a minute heavy sobs racked Mike's body, as they stood, embracing, under the stars.

"Jeez, I'm going to miss you, Billy," Mike finally got out, and then sobbed even harder. Billy held on and he finally understood. Mike had to go out and face the real world. And he was scared. A part of Mike still wanted to be a kid. And that just wasn't going to happen.

After a while Mike's sobs eased, and slowly, the two brothers separated.

"Thanks, Billy," Mike said. "You're the best brother anyone could ever have."

Billy's insides turned to jelly. "Hey," he finally said. "Thanks. You are too, Mike."

Mike put his arm around Billy's shoulder and Billy put his arm around Mike's waist and they walked slowly back towards the orange glimmer of the campfire. When they arrived, Stu had already disappeared inside his sleeping bag.

"Thought I'd have to send the rangers out to look for you guys," came Stu's muffled voice from deep inside the warmth of his bag. "You okay, Mike?"

"Yeah," Mike replied, giving Billy a smile. "I'm fine."

The Ward brothers brushed their teeth and stripped down to their shorts and climbed into their bags. Billy pulled down the flap so that he was sealed inside, safe from the pestering mosquitoes. He thought about Mike and what had happened between them. It was still hard to imagine Mike being upset. College was the most exciting thing Billy could think of, well, except for girls. He tried to imagine what it must be like, really like, to leave your high school friends, your room, your brother and your folks. And he began to see it wasn't as simple as it seemed. *Out there* was a vast and uncertain world. It could eat you alive.

As he drifted towards sleep and that time when the mind unbends and becomes fluid, he saw the world as he imagined his brother must now see it: filled with overwhelming ideas and so many different kinds of people. A place where how well you carried a football, who hired you for a summer job, or where your father worked, didn't amount to a drop in a rainstorm. His invincible and courageous brother was on the verge of losing the safety and security of home. After eighteen years of hometown predictability, he was starting over. There was no guarantee it would be fun. He might not make the cut.

His last thought before sleep was wondering whether he, too, would be afraid when his time to leave came. Billy thought he would be okay with leaving. But he was suddenly glad it was four years away. He could be a kid for a while longer and that felt really wonderful and safe.

As he fell into a deep, peaceful sleep, he could not have guessed how dramatically the next two days would change that comfortable view of his life.

Chapter 25

*I*t was near freezing the next morning and even the mosquitoes were hunkered down waiting for warmth from the sun. Billy hoped Mike or Stu would get up first. But after half an hour of waiting on the hard ground, unable to return to sleep, Billy reluctantly peeled back the flap of his bag, hurried on his jeans and sneakers and a sweatshirt, and kindled a fire. It was crackling and snapping before any sound came from the closed bags of the older boys.

Stu surfaced first. He coughed roughly as he peeked out. "When's breakfast?" He asked sourly.

"We serve breakfast here at the Alpine Hilton at seven," Billy replied solemnly. "Will the young sir be having hot chocolate with his Eggs Benedict?"

"Very funny," Stu groaned and coughed again. "I think I'm coming down with something. I've got a scratchy throat."

Great thought Billy. *That's all we need.* Still, it was just a day's hike to Stehekin, and Moore's Point was even closer. Stu would make it out with no trouble.

"I take it by the gentleman's reply that he will be skipping the Benedict and cocoa this morning. Having the usual then? Powdered eggs and flapjacks?"

Stu finally warmed to Billy's humor. "Cakes 'n eggs it is," he agreed as he crawled from his bag. "But I sure wish we still had some of those huckleberries." He quickly pulled on his jeans and a shirt and finally socks and shoes and stood to warm his hands against the fire, his breath fogging in the crisp air.

"Me too," Billy said, remembering how much better the pancakes had tasted when you bit into the tart-sweet burst of a warm huckleberry. *If it hadn't been for that darned snake!*

Mike was up a few minutes later. After breakfast they packed up their gear, and were off before the sun was a hand's width above the steep eastern wall of the lake crater.

As they trudged up the switchbacks, Billy noticed that Stu's cough had improved to a throat-clearing *Ahhhmmmm*. By the end of the day they'd be in camp at Moore's Point, where the boat would pick them up the following afternoon. And they were supposed to be rugged, weren't they?

When they cleared the lip of the Surprise Lake crater Mike was in the lead, Stu second, Billy brought up the rear, spaced about ten feet apart.

"You guys tell me if I go too fast," Mike called back, but it was a decent pace he set and the boys were soon warmed up by a sun that beat down direct.

Billy's attention began to wander. There was no particular reason to concentrate because the trail was on a mild downhill slope and his feet seemed to glide forward. Within the first hour they entered a zone of light forest. It was now turning into a warm day at the lower altitude and the trees were a welcome shade.

Billy wished his grandfather could see him now. Maybe Gramps had even walked this same trail! WWI would have just ended. The young Gramps would have had his Akubra pitched at a jaunty angle, no doubt whistling a French ditty he'd learned during the war, cutting a dashing figure as he stalked a bear with his 30-06 Winchester held casually in the crook of his arm. Billy reached up and tilted his hat so that it shielded the sun better from the side of his face. Thoughts of his grandfather were so strong he could almost feel his presence.

Somewhere far off a jaybird was scolding. Pine scent was heavy on a light breeze wafting up the canyon. Billy would, at that instant, have pronounced it the most perfect day of his life. Then, Mike's cry of shock and alarm brought him out of his reverie.

"*Oh Shit! Oh Shit!*" Mike screamed. Mike was tearing at his pack-belt. When he had it unbuckled he lifted his pack from his back and slammed the pack down on the trail at his feet. Then he stumbled away from it, swearing nearly every cuss word Billy had ever heard his brother use.

Stu was as puzzled as Billy; he dropped his pack and grabbed Mike by his shoulders and tried to stop his raving. "Mike!" he shouted. But Mike just turned into Stu's arms and began to sob violently.

"What's wrong?" Stu asked.

Mike pointed at his pack with a shaking arm and one accusing finger straight out. As Stu and Billy watched, the pack moved by itself, just a little, and now, crawling out from the edge of the canvas, they saw what was the matter.

A timber rattler, as thick as Billy's forearm, was desperately squirming beneath the aluminum and canvas. As it emerged a dark red streak was smeared across the gray-brown-tan, diamond-patterned scales. Its forked tongue was flicking rapidly in and out, testing for the scent of this new enemy that had tromped up as it innocently sunned itself.

Mike, having recovered from the shock just a little bit, looked around and spotted a baseball-sized rock. He picked it up and hurled it at the snake. It struck the mid-section of the snake and that provided just enough extra *oomph* to drive its tail out from under the pack. Finally free, it wriggled in wild pain for a few seconds and found its bearings enough to assess the human foe.

Billy now saw why no one had heard a rattle. The snake was molting – shedding its old skin. Several inches of cellophane hide were bunched up on its rattle, forming an effective muffler. There was no way it could have buzzed a warning.

Mike continued to hurl every rock he could put his hands on, and the snake began slithering away from the bombardment as quickly as its damaged body could manage. Most of the hastily thrown rocks skipped harmlessly off the dusty ground, sending up little *poofs* before rocketing into the bushes.

The snake reached a thicket and abruptly slid out of sight. Mike hurled two more stones, which crashed through the dense brush where the snake had vanished. Then he collapsed onto his knees in the middle of the trail.

He whimpered in a dazed, hurt voice, "It bit me. I can't believe it. The bastard bit me."

Billy dropped his pack. He and Stu were standing beside Mike. There wasn't anything obvious to show that Mike had been bitten; his blue jeans looked the same dusty, trail-worn way they had all during the hike; his ankle-high leather boots seemed intact.

"Mike?" Stu asked shakily. "What do you mean it bit you?"

Mike didn't seem to hear. He just kept repeating, "I don't believe it. I just don't believe it."

Stu reached out and touched Mike's shoulder, which finally got Mike's attention. "Are you okay?" Stu said slowly, looking directly into Mike's eyes.

There was finally comprehension in Mike's face although he still looked completely bewildered by what had happened. "I don't know," he said matter-of-factly. "I don't know."

"What did you mean 'the snake bit you?" Stu asked. "I didn't see the snake strike. Billy, did you see the snake strike at Mike?"

"No," Billy said nervously. He hadn't seen anything like that. But he really hadn't been watching, and this wasn't like Mike. He didn't make up stuff like this. "Where did it bite you, Mike?"

In answer, Mike carefully sat down in the trail, favoring his right leg. He extended both legs. He reached down and slowly rolled up his right pant leg. When he had it up to his knee, having pushed the white cotton sock down, he turned his leg sideways. Midway between his ankle and knee were two small welts, an inch apart. Redness had begun to spread out from the marks. In the center of each welt was a droplet of blood.

"Oh, shit!" Stu said.

"The little bastard bit me," Mike said in soft surprise, as if it could not have been a possibility and yet it had some happened to him despite it being a complete, total, absolute impossibility.

"That wasn't no little bastard," Stu said, shaken. "That was not a *little* bastard! That was the *biggest frickin' snake I ever saw*!"

This observation did not help Mike. "Oh shit," he moaned, grabbing his right leg as the pain began to blossom.

For a few seconds Billy struggled against a crushing wave of fear. Then he pushed it back. This was no time to panic. Without speaking, he turned and began rummaging furiously through his pack, ripping open the zippers on all four outside pockets and strewing their contents onto the ground. He finally found the snakebite kit he had purchased at Sav-Mart.

He twisted the gray rubber capsule and dumped the contents into his hand, fumbling with the tightly folded instruction sheet, tearing it twice before he got it spread open. The words were in tiny print and difficult to read. *Hurry*, he kept telling himself. *Hurry*. But it took precious seconds to learn what he thought he needed to know before he went to work on his brother.

"We've got to cut where the snake bit," he finally said. He tore open the tiny package containing the sterile razor blade. "Stu," he said as he crouched beside his brother with the blade grasped between his thumb and forefinger. "Swab the bite with the iodine."

He handed the foil packet containing the iodine to Stu, who tore it open and nervously swabbed the area around the bite.

Mike was already going into shock and had only vaguely followed what was happening. Now, he realized that his little brother held a blade.

"Hey," Mike said. "Billy——"

"Hold still, Mike," Billy said crisply. "The instructions say we've got to get out as much venom as we can and we need to do it *now!*"

Billy set the edge of the blade to the skin next to one of the puncture wounds. The instructions said to lance as deep as the fangs had sunk. Billy had no idea how deep that was, but it had been a big snake and he guessed its fangs were awfully long. He began to cut and let the blade slice deep across the first puncture.

"Shit! That hurts!" Mike screamed, but he kept his leg still, his eyes riveted to what was happening. Tears were now running freely down his cheeks.

A small amount of blood flowed from the incision. Billy made a cut across the other puncture and it too bled only a little. Billy worried that it might start to bleed more. "Stu," he said, turning to Stu who stood watching all of this with a stunned look on his face. "I need a T-shirt."

Stu grabbed his pack and pulled out a grimy shirt. By now, all their clothing was filthy. "Here," he said. Billy took it and didn't think twice about it not being clean.

"Thanks."

He triple folded and pressed it against the incisions. Where slow rivulets of blood had been dripping into tiny puddles on the dirt the shirt now soaked up any blood from the wounds.

Mike had had enough of watching himself be operated upon. He collapsed back onto the trail dirt and closed his eyes. "Oh shit," he moaned. "*Oh shit, shit, shit!*"

"Don't worry Mike," Billy said as he pressed on the shirt, hoping the blood would clot. And finally it seemed like the blood must have stopped flowing. He peeled back the shirt and just a little fresh blood appeared, but he now saw that around the wounds the flesh was beginning to swell. "Stu," Billy said. "I need more antiseptic."

Stu tore open the second iodine wipe. "Here," he said, holding out the small orange pad.

Billy tore off a corner of shirt and placed the iodine pad on the wounds, folded the cloth into a three-inch square, and pressed down hoping to force some of the iodine into the incisions he had made. It worked a little too well for Mike.

"*Shit!*" Mike screamed. "*That burns, Billy! It burns!*"

"Sorry," Billy said. "We need to do this to prevent infection." The tiny page of instructions said you could survive most rattlesnake bites. But it would be hours before they could get a horse or a helicopter or a motorbike up the trail to take Mike out. Something he had learned in school about gangrene had come swimming up out of his memory. In eighth grade biology he had read that if gangrene set in, you sometimes had to amputate. He pushed that thought away. Being scared was for later. At the moment, his brother needed him rational.

As soon as Billy had taped the makeshift bandage firmly, they unrolled one of the sleeping bags and together helped Mike move off the trail and under the shade of a large pine.

Stu motioned him away from Mike. They moved several yards to where Mike couldn't easily hear.

"I'll go for help," Stu said quietly. "It's only fifteen miles to Stehekin. In tennis shoes, I can cover that distance in less than three hours. Help should be able to get back up here before it gets dark." He paused, and in a voice filled with admiration said, "You really acted fast."

"I guess," Billy said hesitantly. It *had* happened quickly. And what he had done had seemed right at the time. But now that it was over, something felt wrong. He wanted to go back over the instructions.

"I'm glad . . . you did that . . . with the blade," Stu said nervously. "I'm terrible when it comes to blood."

Billy said with complete sincerity, "If I would have thought about it, I would have freaked out." He wasn't just being nice to Stu. Billy now had the shakes and he couldn't picture doing again what he had just done to his brother. It had been almost pure reflex.

Stu said, "I'm bad when it comes to blood." He looked embarrassed as he admitted a dark secret. "When I was ten, my mom came home from the bar late one night and she'd got cut by a broken bottle. Her hand was wrapped up. She was too drunk to know she was hurt bad. Some guy dropped her off at the front door. She came in and I woke up and went out, and she was taking off the wrap. All of a sudden the blood came gushing and went everywhere. I wet my pants I was so scared." Stu looked down at the ground. "I thought she was going to die right there in the living room. I called for an ambulance and then she got mad at me but I didn't care. I just didn't want her to die." Stu was crying a little. Billy reached out and touched him on the arm and it seemed to calm Stu a bit.

"Hey, it's okay, Stu. We're going to get out of this just fine. I know it."

Stu looked up. "We sure were wrong to ever doubt you, Billy. I'm so sorry for that. Can you forgive me? Ever?"

Billy finally overcame his earlier reluctance for physical closeness and gave Stu a big hug. Then he said, "There's nothing to forgive." And after the briefest of pauses, "You need to get started for Stehekin."

Stu smiled and wiped away his tears and walked back to his pack, got his sneakers, and started unlacing his hiking boots. Mike saw what was happening from where he lay beneath the tree.

"Hey," Mike called out. "What are you doing?"

"Going for help," Stu replied.

Mike hoisted himself up onto his elbows. *"And leave me here? Like hell! I'm walking out of here with you guys. Right now!"*

"Billy's staying with you," Stu said patiently, ignoring Mike's panic, double-knotting the laces of his black-and-white, high-top tennis shoes. "I'll be back soon."

Mike hitched up further on his elbows, wincing from the pain in his leg. "I've got to get to a hospital." He tried to stand up, but fell back onto the dirt beside the bag. Now visible on the wound compress were two spreading red spots.

Billy helped his brother back onto the bag. "You started it bleeding again," he said. "You wouldn't get half a mile, Mike." He glanced at the bandage and saw that the leg around the wounds had swollen quite a bit more. He felt his heart begin to pound. "We've got to do it this way, Mike." He turned to Stu. "Hey Stu, you better get going," and he gave Stu a glance that said: *Get it in gear because we're going to have a big problem real soon!*

"Gotcha," Stu said. "Mike, you hang tough. And don't try walking out of here. You're in no shape for it. I promise I'll have someone back here pronto." Stu looked at Billy. "Hang in there, Billy. Be back as soon as I can."

"Be careful, Stu," Billy said. "Don't—"

"Hey," Stu cut him off, confidently touching the brim of his Yankees cap. "No problem."

Billy considered completing the sentence, and telling Stu not to run too fast. But he knew that kind of warning would be pointless. Stu was going to run as fast as he could. Billy would do the same if he were the one going for help.

Stu turned towards where the trail went down through the trees, looked back briefly at his two friends. "You do what your brother says," he admonished Mike. Then he was jogging down the trail. Within seconds he reached a bend and passed beyond a clump of small pines. Billy caught one more glimpse of Stu's yellow shirt and the bobbing Yankees cap, and then Stu was gone.

Billy turned back to Mike and pointed to a flat area where it would be easier to build a fire. "Mike, do you think I could move you over there?"

"Sure," Mike said glumly. "I should have tried walking out," he continued. "I wanted to walk out."

"Well, it's too late now. So let's get you comfortable and wait for help. Stu said he could make Stehekin in two hours." This was over-optimistic, but Mike needed reassurance. From the look on his face, Billy saw Mike was calculating how quickly Stu could get down to where help could be sent back.

"They'll be here before dark," Billy continued. "Besides, I got most of the venom out. In fact, I'll bet I got all the venom out." He tried to sound more confident than he felt.

By the time he had Mike moved, the area around the wound had swollen more and the skin was red several inches up and down the leg. Mike glanced at the wounded area and quickly looked away with a quiet, "Oh, boy . . ."

Just don't think about it big brother. It's going to be okay, so don't panic.

Billy gathered everything that had been hastily pulled from his and Stu's packs and moved it to where Mike now lay silently staring up through the pines at the blue sky.

"How do you feel?" Billy asked as he laid their gear down.

"It hurts," Mike said absentmindedly. "It hurts, and it tingles, and I'm thirsty." Mike's voice trailed off in a scary way, and Billy remembered something he had read in school. A poem. And the bit of poetry he now remembered had read: *wee and far*. It was a place he didn't want his brother to go.

"Is there anything I can do to make you more comfortable while we wait for help?" Billy focused upon that last thought, imagining the sound of horses or motorbikes coming up the trail.

"Water," Mike said.

"I'll go right now." Billy reached for a canteen. They hadn't filled their canteens that morning because they had expected to cross several small streams on the way down, like the creek they had crossed half a mile back. Why carry the extra weight? Billy wanted to go down the trail to look for water, with the hope of meeting up with the rescue party, but Stu had been gone way than half an hour. It would be at least two or three more hours before Stu could possibly be back with help. And Billy had no idea how far downhill the next stream might be. Best to go back to the stream he knew was there.

"Billy?" Mike asked softly.

Billy had pulled his tennis shoes out of his pack and was changing into them. He looked over at Mike.

"Yeah?"

"Was I running before I got bit?"

The question made no sense. Mike had been walking along just like he and Stu had been walking along, at an easy pace in that nice warm morning sunshine. "No," Billy replied cautiously. "Why?"

Mike said in a spacey voice that seemed lost and confused, "I just can't seem to catch my breath."

Billy hadn't read anything in the kit's instructions about not being able to breathe. He reached into his pocket, pulled out the instructions, and found the *symptoms* section. There wasn't a lot, but what there was frightened him.

The instructions described several possible effects of the neurotoxin in rattlesnake venom. People who were bitten might have difficulty breathing. In the worst case, respiratory failure could cause death. Swelling around the wound was common. It was important to keep the victim (How could he associate that word with his brother? *Victims* were people killed in car accidents, drowned, or burned in fires!) warm, and to immobilize the wound to keep the venom from spreading. Fluid loss from swelling around the wound should be countered by drinking plenty of water.

Then Billy saw what he'd missed earlier. When he'd first read the instructions, he'd just read the part about how to lance the bite. That was what he remembered about snakebites: you lanced them. Billy had assumed that the bleeding would clean out the poison. Now, he discovered the instructions said that it was necessary to use suction. The rubber capsule halves should be squeezed and placed against the skin to suck the poison out. If you didn't do that, the poison stayed in the tissue where the snake had injected it.

He looked up from the instructions. Mike was slowly clenching and unclenching his hands, concentrating upon taking long, slow, deep breaths. And looking bewildered.

How could I have missed something so important!

"Mike," he said, as calmly as he could manage. "Are you okay?"

Billy thought Mike hadn't heard him, but Mike did finally turn his head a little and look up.

"I think so. But I have to think about each breath." Mike took slow experimental breaths, as if to demonstrate. "I'm real thirsty Billy. Could you get me that water?"

Billy fought to hold back panic. How could he leave his brother now? But then he realized he had no idea how to save Mike if he did stop breathing. What was he supposed to do? Mouth-to-mouth resuscitation for hours while waiting for the rescue team? *Impossible.* The only thing he could do was go get water and hope Mike's condition wouldn't worsen.

"Mike," he said gently, kneeling and grasping his brother's hand; it was cold and clammy. "I'm going for water now. There's a stream a little ways back up the trail. Try to relax. Keep breathing. I'll be right back."

"Right," Mike said. "Keep breathing . . . be right back . . . relax." Mike stared up at the sky. "Relax. Keep breathing. Going for water."

Billy gave his brother's hand a final squeeze and felt a weak squeeze in return.

"I'll be okay, Billy," Mike said unconvincingly. "Just please get me some water. I'm awful thirsty." Mike *never* said please, except when adults were around. Billy stood and turned away from his brother before the tears flooded his eyes.

He started to sprint up the trail but after a couple hundred yards he got a side ache and had to stop for a few seconds until the spasm eased. When he started up the trail again he held an even pace so the stitch wouldn't return to his ribcage.

As he ran he thought about the suction cups. *How could I have missed it? How could I have skipped over that part of the instructions?* He wanted to scream. After he decided that screaming would do no good he suddenly wanted Mom to hold him and tell him that everything was *okay* and that it was all going to work out *just fine.*

By the time he reached the little brook he had begun to focus upon what needed to be done. *I should have brought all three canteens. We'll need more water to drink and maybe to clean Mike's wounds.* But he hadn't brought all three canteens; he'd just brought one. So he'd need to make another trip.

Why am I missing so many things?

As he ran back down the trail the skin under the ball of his big right toe began to feel loose and stingy, just like it had after the Butte hike. It didn't seem a big deal. He'd only need to make one more water trip. And the rescue team would certainly carry him down on horseback or motorbike and he wouldn't be carrying a pack. But it bothered him just the same. One more thing had gone wrong.

When he reached his brother, Billy's biggest fear eased. Mike was sitting up, alert.

"What took you so long," Mike demanded. He was still in obvious pain; he held the injured leg motionless; but he smiled as he spoke.

"Here." Billy handed the canteen to Mike and crouched beside his brother to catch his breath.

Mike drank half the contents and handed the canteen back to Billy. "Looks like you need this as much as I do." Billy took a few sips and checked his watch. It was half past one. Stu had been gone almost two hours. With any luck, he'd already be in Stehekin and the rescue party would make it back before dark. Things were looking up.

Chapter 26

*M*ike seemed okay for a couple more hours. Billy began to feel optimistic. He made another water run, this time with all three canteens. As he jogged back down the trail and approached the temporary campsite he half-expected to meet the rescue party. No such luck.

He had only been gone half an hour, but in that time Mike's condition had worsened. His breathing was rough, and there was a rattle in his chest. Mike's eyelids kept fluttering, and he complained that it felt like they were made of lead. Then, there was Mike's leg.

The leg continued to swell. It now pressed against Mike's jeans like a summer sausage. Billy decided he needed to look closer at the leg to see exactly what was happening. Maybe there was something he could do. He couldn't think of what that might be. But there had to be something!

Billy sat down beside Mike and began to peel back the denim.

"*Owww!*" Mike screamed. "*Shit, Billy, stop that!*" Mike gritted his teeth, took a deep breath, and looked stoically at Billy. "They better get here soon," he said.

Billy gave up on peeling off Mike's pants. He sat beside his brother and wondered just long it took to get back from Stehekin. It was now four p.m. Stu would certainly have gotten there by now and someone was bound to have started back for a rescue. Maybe they were waiting for anti-venom to be flown up the lake? Maybe it was further to Stehekin than Stu had thought? Billy decided to be positive. What good was negative thinking? Help was coming. It had to be. Stu had made it, and help was coming. He repeated it over and over until he began to believe it.

Time stretched out like cooling taffy as the sun sank towards the mountains, but the only sounds drifting up the trail were of birds and the afternoon breeze. Mike was half asleep and conserving the little energy he had left. Whenever he moaned, Billy took a deep breath and reminded himself to be patient. Help was coming. There was nothing he could do about the swelling, and he had no way of relieving his brother's pain. He had to be patient. Any moment now, he'd hear voices coming up the trail. He found himself straining, listening. Help was coming. It had to be.

As the sun set and the forest grew dark, Billy's panic found a new level. What if nobody came?

Mike had fallen into an uneasy sleep punctuated by nightmares. He lay mumbling a few words. Mike said "Mama" several times and that began to scare Billy more than Mike's swollen leg. But at least Mike was asleep and missing the agony in his leg. Billy resolved to wake him only after the rescue party arrived. Surely they were coming, even now in the dark.

After listening and staring down the dark trail for what seemed like forever Billy reluctantly lit the campfire he'd laid earlier.

Mike came awake when the flames were licking high and casting a dancing yellow halo into the dark forest. "Where am I?" He sounded confused.

"Mike?" Billy said softly.

"Billy?"

"We're still up the trail."

Mike didn't answer. The campfire crackled and spit out sparks. Billy watched Mike, lying on his back, his eyes open but appearing to see nothing. Billy began to wonder if his brother had fallen into some kind of coma. But Mike finally spoke in a dreamy voice.

"No one's coming," he said calmly. "Something has happened to Stu."

"No," Billy said. That was unthinkable!

Mike slowly turned his head until their eyes met in the flickering light. In a patient voice Mike measured out each word. "Something's . . . happened . . . to . . . Stu."

Billy felt stupid for disagreeing. It had to be true. Otherwise, the rescuers would have arrived. Even if they didn't have anti-venom. Even if they couldn't get Mike out till morning. Someone would have come to help get Mike through the night. They would have used flashlights or lanterns if necessary. They would have brought blankets and food. Stu would have made at least that much happen.

Billy felt lost, and the weight of it came like a mudslide, relentless and suffocating. "What are we going to do, Mike?"

"As soon as it's light, you have to go for help," Mike said, and then firmly repeated himself. "As soon as it's light."

"What about tonight? What about your leg?" Billy had wild and ugly thoughts about what might happen.

Mike gave Billy a grim smile. "What can we do?" Mike looked away with a dull and fatal acceptance of what was to come. "We just have to wait for morning."

"Mike?" Billy asked cautiously, dreading the answer. "Does your leg hurt much?"

There came a distant crashing sound in the forest, and both boys waited to hear it again, but whatever it was had gone. The tiny hope that it might be people vanished. Mike answered his brother's question.

"It hurts a lot," Mike said, closing his eyes.

Billy watched his brother across the flames. It was only a few feet, but it seemed like infinity. After a while, Mike fell back into the same disturbed sleep as before.

The fire burned down and Billy was finally driven by the cold to unroll his sleeping bag. He removed only his tennis shoes and shirt, leaving his socks and jeans on just in case he had to do something in a hurry. He lay awake in the half-zipped bag. His stomach was grumbling, and he realized that breakfast had been his last meal. It had also been Mike's last meal. *And Stu's!* Suddenly he wasn't hungry. Just scared. And full of sadness for what the following day might bring.

Chapter 27

*I*t came close to frost that night. Autumn was pushing summer out of the high country. The vine maple, huckleberry, dogwood and sumac would soon color the mountains with yellows, orange and reds. In a few weeks, perhaps even just a few days, snow would begin to fall, leaving the evergreens towering above a deep white blanket.

Billy had burrowed into his bag to escape the cold and finally fallen asleep from the sheer weight of exhaustion. He awoke at dawn to the chirping of morning birds. He pushed back the flap of his bag, sore from the lumpy ground.

As his thoughts cleared, he sat bolt upright, then skinnied out of the bag, hurriedly pulling on his sneakers. He kept glancing nervously at the outline of Mike's body inside the other bag. There was no movement, no hint of Mike's condition. When he was dressed Billy went over and squatted next to where his brother lay.

"Mike?" he said softly. There was no answer. Billy pushed slowly against the outline of Mike's shoulder. "Mike?" he said anxiously.

"Mmmmmmmm."

Some of Billy's panic eased with his brother's response, but it still sounded as though Mike's condition had worsened. "You okay, Mike?"

Now there was movement inside the bag. In a few seconds Mike's fingers crawled around the edge of the flap, pulling it down to reveal his ashen face. He gripped the orange nylon as if to hold on to reality, blinking at the sunlight; then his eyes fell upon Billy. "Hey," Mike said groggily. "Stu back yet?"

"No." Billy fought the urge to cry. He pictured Stu's big grin and his brown hair raked back under his Yankees cap, striding confidently up the trail, leading a troop of rescuers. Billy knew that was now only a fantasy.

"Okay," Mike said, slowly digesting the fact that Stu hadn't returned. "You've got to get to Stehekin." He paused, working out a thought. "You know how Stu was always rushing around, Billy? How he sometimes didn't care about the risk, like when he went out on that logjam at Cub Lake? Or the lightning storm in Chelan?"

"Yes."

"You have got to be more careful. Stu probably fell and got hurt. You'll probably find him on the trail with a twisted ankle or something." The way Mike said it, the "or something" was more likely and Billy knew he might find Stu busted up real bad, or even dead.

"You're going to want to run all out," Mike continued, measuring his words slowly, carefully, making sure Billy was listening. "That's what I'd want to do if you were hurt instead of me. But you can't run too fast, because if you fall and get hurt . . ."

Billy nodded in agreement. But he felt anything but agreement. Of course he was going to run!

Mike must have seen this in Billy's face because he looked Billy straight in the eyes, almost angrily.

"You can't run too fast, understand? You can't be in too much of a hurry!"

Billy wanted to argue. He wanted to tell Mike that he had to run, not only because Mike was sinking fast, but also because Stu was out there somewhere and he hadn't had a sleeping bag last night. He hadn't had Billy to get him water, or to build a fire. But Billy also understood what Mike was saying. He couldn't risk twisting an ankle or busting up a knee. Because Billy was now Mike's only hope. And Stu's only hope. If he took a bad tumble and got hurt maybe none of them would make it out of the mountains.

"I'll be careful, Mike," he replied solemnly. "I promise."

"Just a jog."

"I promise." And at the moment Billy said it he truly meant what he said. He'd jog along at a safe pace and he'd keep his eyes open and he'd be careful because he had to be careful.

Mike was satisfied and relaxed his left hand's grip on the orange nylon of the bag. And in that instant, a thought came to Billy as raw and sharp and clear as if it were imbedded in crystal. He might lose Mike. Memories flooded his mind. He and Mike making fun of each others' new haircuts; kicking up freshly raked piles of autumn leaves when they were just four and eight years old; hiding bags of trick-or-treat candy from each other; skipping stones at Lakeside Park; standing lookout for cops while the other jumped from the river bridge on hot July afternoons.

Just as quickly as they had come, the images vanished. Those times were now a million years in the past. His brother lay in an orange sleeping bag with a leg swollen from a rattlesnake bite, and also, somewhere between here and Stehekin, Stu was injured, or . . . Billy pushed that thought away. Stu was okay; he'd just broken something that would heal if Billy could bring help. Mike would be rescued. So would Stu. Billy was going to get help for Mike and Stu and everything would be alright!

"Mike," Billy said, as he made sure the last full canteen of water was within easy reach for his brother. "You rest. I'll be back real quick, I promise."

"Remember," Mike cautioned, his voice now fainter, as if he were using the last of his energy. "Be careful. I'll be okay for at least another day."

But Billy knew Mike was wrong. His brother wouldn't last until dark. He gave Mike's hair a gentle stroke. "You take it easy, Big Brother," he said, and before the tears could flow, he picked up his Akubra and put it tight on his head, and after one brief look at Mike he turned away and began to jog down the trail. When he was out of Mike's sight the promise he'd made lifted like smoke, and Billy began to run the most desperate race of his life.

Chapter 28

$\mathcal{R}$unning felt good at first. There was an end in sight, closer with each patch of forest that flew by and each new turn in the trail that took him lower towards the lake and to Stehekin. It's like cross-country track, he told himself. No sweat. The thought of what might have happened to Stu kept intruding. But it didn't slow him down. Not one little bit.

Then the trail cut down into a new part of the canyon where the angle of descent was nearly doubled. As Billy doggedly kept his pace the pounding began to hurt his knees and back. His feet began to burn, and he knew the blisters were returning. This time it might rip the skin from his feet. He banished the thought. Mike's pain was greater; his own suffering was unimportant.

But as the pain blossomed Billy realized he needed to reach Stehekin, and if he kept this pace his feet wouldn't hold up. Finally, reluctantly, he cut back to a jog. And by this strange twist of fate, the blisters actually saved his life.

The trail was now a twisting chute along a steep bank and it was coated with gravelly dust. The day was getting hot. With the pain blossoming in his feet where blisters were forming and then breaking, his rate of descent was now at best a scrambling, sliding jog.

He had just entered a stretch of trail that cut across a precipitous hillside. Billy never saw the pine root beneath the powdery dirt. All he remembered of the fall was that he put his foot down in what seemed like a safe place, and the next instant his toe had caught on something and he was airborne.

He came down hard on his right shoulder and rolled, which kept bones from breaking.

When he finally came to a stop he was sitting on his rump, feet pointed downhill, and by some miracle he was in the middle of the trail. A bloody scrape ran half the length of his right forearm, the skin peeled away like old varnish, the blood beading up on his raw flesh. His Akubra had gone flying during the tumble and was now perched precariously on the edge of the trail three yards downhill.

"*Shit!*" Billy cried out, but the epithet was filled with gratitude and spoken with not even the tiniest bit of anger. He had survived. Nothing seemed broken. And despite the pain that seared his right arm, he knew he could stand back up and continue on to Stehekin.

He crawled onto his knees, pounded the dust from his pants and shirt, and was about to retrieve the Akubra when a sudden, sharp gust of wind came sweeping up the canyon, caught the hat's brim, and lifted it like a leaf. It held the edge of the trail for a second before it tipped and went cart wheeling down the almost vertical rocky bank. He watched its progress with dismay until his eyes froze on something the Akubra had passed directly over.

It was Stu's baseball cap.

The Akubra continued until it lodged in the low brush twenty yards beyond the cap. It might as well have been shot onto the surface of the moon. But it wasn't the Akubra's loss that held Billy's attention. Billy was looking for Stu.

He cupped his hands to his mouth. "Stu!" he yelled. Echoes reverberated through the narrow canyon. "*STU!*" he screamed at the top of his lungs, and still there was no reply.

He looked at the baseball cap; thought about the root. Stu had been running. Had he been hiking at a normal pace, even jogging, it might have presented no problem. But Stu would have been running *hard*. Had Stu been caught off guard like Billy? Had he tumbled down the slide? Was he down in the ravine? Had he crashed through the brush and landed in some hidden place where he now lay unconscious or dead? Or, would Billy find him further down the trail, injured, waiting?

Billy considered his options. He might be able to climb into the ravine further down the trail, but then he'd have to fight back through the brush and that might take hours. One final look at the steep bank convinced Billy there was no way he could climb down from here and hope to climb back up.

Billy pulled off his shirt, found a chunk of rock, wrapped his shirt around the rock, and set it in the middle of the trail.

As Billy resumed his painful jog he prayed to God that he would see Stu at each new bend in the trail. But as he put mile after mile behind him, his hope died. In his heart he knew Stu was back at the bottom of the ravine. Maybe Stu had been asleep? Maybe he was out of earshot? The maybes haunted him with every stride he took.

It was only after he had jogged for an hour that the trail finally flattened out and he could again dare a faster pace. It jarred his body and it hurt his feet to run flat out, but he no longer cared.

Chapter 29

The final miles of that forced retreat from the mountains would forever remain a blur of pain and sadness. But he would always clearly remember the instant when he first saw the lake and burst into tears and still continued to run as fast as his searing feet would carry him. It wouldn't be long now before he could send help back to his brother and Stu; he nearly sprinted the last three miles on the lake trail. When he finally came out onto the Stehekin Landing, he fell to his knees, grinding gravel and dirt into the skin. Then he started yelling as loud as he could.

"Help! My brother. Stu. They're hurt. A rattlesnake bit Mike. Stu's fallen. Help! *SOMEBODY PLEASE HELP ME!*"

One of the boys whose family rented pack horses to tourists went to find a ranger. In two minutes a man in his fifties, wearing the khaki of the USFS, came running, followed by two younger men who were working Stehekin on their summer college breaks.

"All right, Son," the ranger tried to reassure the exhausted boy as he squatted down, putting an arm around his shoulders to settle him down. "Just take it easy. Let's start with where your brother is—"

"And Stu. *You gotta help Stu!*"

"And Stu," the ranger continued calmly. "We'll help them both, Son. But you've got to slow down and tell us where they are."

Billy paused, gathered his thoughts. They had to know exactly where Mike and Stu were. Billy started again, more slowly; beginning with the rattlesnake; then how Stu had gone for help and hadn't returned; how Billy had tripped, and where his Akubra had rolled over Stu's Yankees cap, and Billy's shirt wrapped around the rock in the trail.

As Billy spoke a small crowd of curious tourists gathered. As they heard of the snake-bitten young man and his companion who had fallen down a rock-slide, most of them drifted away.

Three more rangers arrived; one, a young woman, who stepped forward as soon as Billy finished explaining where the boys were. She held a metal box with a red cross on the lid. She had seen what none of the others had noticed: just above the tops of Billy's sneakers his white socks were blotted a dull red.

The head ranger now ordered one of the young men to get on the radio and get Doc Manley to fly some anti-venom to Moore's Point, where the rescue party would meet the plane. Then he ordered up an army helicopter from the Yakima Proving Grounds.

The brothers who ran the pack string had come out of the hills the day before and had several horses available. They needed no encouragement from the ranger to volunteer and within minutes were galloping up the lake trail in the direction Billy had just come from.

Two men carried Billy—he now found he couldn't walk because of the pain exploding in his feet and shooting up his legs—to the tiny general store that sat on the bank above the landing. A cot was brought from the ranger station and the young woman cut off his shoes with blunt shears from the medical kit. Billy didn't have the courage to look down but he heard one of the young men say to the others outside, "Good Lord! Did you see that kid's feet? How did he even manage to stand up, much less run?"

When the lady ranger had his feet disinfected and bandaged and had his arm cleaned up she looked at him with eyes that held all the sympathy and admiration in the world. "No one could have done more," she said.

It was as if someone had lifted the weight of the universe from his shoulders and Billy broke down. She held him while he cried.

Chapter 30

*A*fter repeated assurances that both Mike and Stu would be flown out by helicopter direct to the hospital in Wenatchee, Billy allowed the rangers to carry him down to the seaplane.

The flight seemed unfairly easy. The boys had taken days to traverse the same distance the plane now slid calmly over in just half an hour. The slate blue lake was placid from two thousand feet. The mountains folded and ran like a vast, soft, dark blue-green quilt, broken up pleasantly by gray patches of cliff and rockslide and by the occasional brown patches of brush and yellow grass. It looked like a picture you might hang over the living room sofa.

Hank and Colleen met him at the dock. His mother had been crying, and immediately started crying again when she saw his face inside the plane. Dad was standing, waiting, as the plane tied up. He stood on the pontoon, gathered Billy into his arms, and carried him onto the dock.

Somehow both Dad and Mom managed to hold him at the same time as the floating dock swayed gently. All the while Billy kept thinking of Mike and Stu. They were still up there, waiting for rescue.

They wanted to take him to the Chelan Hospital and have his feet and arm examined but Billy would have none of that. He said, "We have to go to Wenatchee, to the hospital. We have to wait for Mike and Stu."

"Billy," his father said gently. "You've been through a lot. There are some good people out looking for your brother and Stu. They'll be okay." But even as he said it Billy sensed his father's uncertainty. Dad might not care too much about Stu, or maybe he did. But Billy knew that Mike's survival wasn't certain. And the knowledge of this was all over his parents' faces.

"Take me to the hospital in Wenatchee," he insisted and he continued to refuse any compromise. Finally, his father sighed, and when his mother began to protest Dad said, "No, Dear, Billy's right."

They loaded into the station wagon, Billy lying on the back seat with his feet propped up. They drove thirty-five miles to the Deaconess Hospital in Wenatchee, to wait.

Chapter 31

They brought Mike in by Army helicopter five hours later. Billy had been given the use of a wheelchair as he now found it impossible to stand on his damaged feet. Dad wheeled him to the emergency room entry and he was allowed a few seconds with his brother. Mike was on a gurney, being wheeled towards surgery. The doctor told the attendants to hold up for a second.

Mike's lips were peeled and dry and he was having a hard time keeping his eyes focused. They had cut his pants off and placed a white sheet over him; under it, Billy could see his ballooned leg.

"Hey, Billy," Mike whispered. "Good work."

"Mike," was all Billy could manage at first without bursting into tears. He wanted to be strong. He wanted to carry his brother through. And crying just didn't cut it. *Be cool!* He bit down on his tongue and felt the salt of blood in his mouth and he managed to choke back the tears.

"What about Stu?" Mike asked. "What happened to Stu?"

Billy managed to shake his head in the negative and then choked out, "They haven't found him yet." Tears came to Mike's eyes, and the doctor stepped up.

"Okay, Boys. You'll have plenty of time to visit later on." He looked at Billy. "You have to let us help your brother now." Billy found himself searching the doctor's calm face but the man's thoughts were hidden behind the stethoscope and his surgeon's greens.

"Okay," Billy conceded. He watched the gurney slide through the double doors and disappear.

Back in the waiting area, Billy listened for the beating of rotor blades outside that would mean the helicopter was bringing Stu out of the mountains. But in the three hours that the Ward family waited for a doctor to emerge and tell them how the surgery had gone for Mike, there was silence from above.

Chapter 32

*A*nother few hours up in the mountains and Mike would have lost his leg, maybe his life. Flesh around the fang marks had gone necrotic and had to be cut away. There would be months of grafts and physical therapy and Mike would limp for the next year but he would eventually regain full use of his leg. He was young and resilient, but he would never play college football.

No word of Stu came that day.

It was the following morning that a knock came at the Ward's front door. Colleen answered and there were quiet words spoken. When she came back into the living room, followed by one of the young rangers from Stehekin, tears were coursing down her cheeks. The ranger was carrying Billy's Akubra in his right hand, and something else in his left.

"Billy," Colleen said with a sniffle as she wiped the tears first from one cheek and then from the other. "This is John Grunion, with the Park Service. I'm afraid—" Billy now saw his mother do something he had never seen, and would never see again: she sank down onto the sofa and completely dissolved into tears.

Billy looked up at the ranger who stood uncertainly before him. "Stu's dead," Billy said softly, and the emotion seemed to drain out of him until his chest felt like a bottomless well.

"I'm sorry, Son," the ranger began slowly. "He was barely alive when we found him down the ravine nearly half a mile from where you left your shirt. He'd developed pneumonia." The ranger seemed to have something stuck in his throat and took a few seconds for it to clear before he could continue.

"We told him how you found where he was," he said carefully. "Your friend smiled when he heard about your hat. Then he said, 'You make sure Billy gets his hat back. And make sure he gets my Yankees cap. Don't tell my mom you found it. You make sure Billy gets it.'" Now there were tears running freely down the ranger's cheeks. "Here," he said, extending his hand with the cap and the Akubra clutched together.

Billy reached out and took both, laying the Akubra next to his mom on the couch before gently smoothing out the folds in the Yankees cap. He traced the stitched letters with his finger, picturing Stu with a big smile, his brown hair flowing out the sides and back, headed up some trail towards wherever heaven was. Then he looked up at the ranger.

Colleen sat on the couch, ready to hold her son. Billy wanted that: to be held. But first, he extended his hand to the man and said, "Thanks for saving my brother. And thank you for trying to save Stu." The man gave Billy's hand a firm shake and then moved for the front door saying, "I'm sorry Billy, Mrs. Ward. Truly sorry." The door closed quickly behind him.

And then Billy and his mom held each other and both cried for what seemed like forever.

Chapter 33

Billy was quiet and withdrawn through the fall. His parents considered calling in a psychologist, but his mood finally improved just after Christmas. He seemed to have regained his emotional footing.

One day in early January he announced, "I'm going to be a doctor." Happy to have their youngest son fully back in the fold, the Wards encouraged the career choice, though privately they agreed that in a year or two Billy's decision would probably change.

It didn't.

Billy's grades had been a solid "B" average since grade school, but by the end of his sophomore year he was pulling A's and A-minuses. The following year the minuses went away.

He was accepted into Reed College in Oregon and graduated summa cum laude. Several medical schools offered him a place, but he chose the University of Washington because it was more affordable and it let him visit his family in Chelan and particularly his brother who had dropped out of college after his second year and gone to work with their uncle at the PUD in Wenatchee.

Epilogue

*Y*ears later there came a day when Billy arrived home with a medical diploma in hand. He had been invited to a prestigious surgery residency at Boston General that would begin in two weeks' time. But there was something he knew he needed to do first. Hank and Colleen and Mike all tried to talk him out of it but Billy wouldn't be dissuaded.

He lay in his old room, staring at his student desk, thinking about the following day; thinking about the two hats: a battered old Akubra with a rattlesnake hat band, and an equally battered, beloved NY Yankees cap. Hats that hadn't been worn for twelve years. It was June of 1981, and the mountain trail from Moore's point to Surprise Lake had been declared open, finally free of heavy winter snow, just the previous week.

The following morning Billy met the seaplane at sunrise. It was a beautiful day: blue sky without a trace of cloud, a light breeze, and a temperature that would climb into the low 80's by mid-day. It was very much like the day he had held in his mind for the past twelve years. It was very much like a day that it was time to put to rest.

The plane landed on glass-smooth water at Moore's Point and taxied slowly up to the battered dock. "You sure you're going to be alright?" the pilot asked.

Billy turned, smiled, and said, "I'm sure." He set the Akubra on his head and made sure the Yankees cap was tucked securely into his back pocket. He started towards the trees.

At two in the afternoon Billy found the place where he had taken off his T-shirt and wrapped it around a rock. In the intervening years, a large pine tree had fallen across the trail near where his hat had taken its tumble. The part of the trunk that had blocked the trail had been cut away. The two ends had begun to rot and the bark was slabbing off where ants had worked up under and loosened it. The trail seemed wider and better maintained.

He looked out across the slide, down to where Stu had fallen, and pulled the Yankees cap from his back pocket.

"Hey, Stu," he said. "I made it through medical school." He gave the cap a few loving strokes, straightening the creases that had fallen into the fabric, picking off a few pieces of lint that had gathered over the years.

"Mike went to work for our uncle, just like we wanted you to do."

Somewhere in the forest a Stellar's Jay let off a raucous scolding. A gentle breeze eased down through the pines and firs. From the bank above the trail a grasshopper with red and black wings sputtered to life, sounding like the playing cards Billy used to fix to his bike's struts with Mom's clothes pins when he was a kid before riding around the neighborhood pretending he was on a motor bike. The grasshopper buzzed down into the ravine, found some hidden place to land.

"Thanks for the cap, Stu," Billy continued after a moment of reflection. "It got me through some tough times, knowing you were up there looking after me. It kept things in focus real well." Billy smoothed the cap again but there were no longer any creases in the fabric. There were tears now, blurring his vision. He tried to say something, choked it back, swallowed and blinked several times, found his voice again.

"Thanks, Brother. I owe you one . . . big time. And I thought you might be needing this . . . for the trail." Billy took the cap by the brim and pulled his arm all the way back, then let fly. The cap caught the breeze and sailed neat and flat out towards the middle of the ravine, finally sinking out of sight in the brush and small pines at the bottom.

Dr. Bill Ward turned and began to jog down the trail. The sun was setting in the afternoon sky. In just a few hours the shadows would stretch from the tall peaks and the forest would begin to darken. As he jogged, Bill checked his watch. There was plenty of time to get there before dark. He knew just how long it would take to reach the Stehekin Landing at the pace he now set. He'd run it once before.